Existing

<u>Existing</u>
A Present Solution

Story by The Father
Compiled by The Priest

Written by
Philosopher Stephan Pacheco

"Yes, I was consumed by madness. But I never had to be. It just happened. It just took me. My passion to love is strong and it made me force others to believe and to understand, and that warped my meaning."

<u>D</u><u>EDICATION</u>

For the non-believers.
For those that saw nothing in words.
For those that don't read books.
To the knowers and the seers,
that saw nothing in no one,
deeply through the void beyond the mind.
They that faced Darkness and faced Light
and came out clean, unowned, on the Otherside--
Free Floating.
To those with the courage to defy god
and find It.

And to the many ones that told me I was
too smart for my own good,
to attempt to manipulate me
into their sense of safety,
muttered as I walked away.
To their smiles when they were surprised that I did not bring them
the condemnation they would have brought me to defend their
sides, when whence my path wound back to Release them.

WARNING:
There is nothing to be afraid of. If you accept your humanness and
do not think it is your eternity, then unfold these pages.
You are welcome here.

Welcome: to the Journey that is greater than
the consciousness that knows it will die.

WARNING:
Do not read this book. You are not smart enough to understand it.
Everyone I know should not read this book. Everyone will twist
these words through psychotic minds and see it as self-indulgently as
themselves. This book is not for you. Do NOT read it. It will rape your
mind and leave you alone and afraid. You are not strong enough for
this.

If you could read the previous and know no doubt: then read.
But be wary still, you may have not seen through your own idiocy,
or you may be blinded by your own blazing ego that wants to matter.
Either way, hopefully you will plunge into any pain or discomfort you
feel and alleviate it.

Warning:
The new idea will be rejected by the same historically reoccurring
personalities until they are given the thought by enough other
people, like the media, meaning the followers, guessing imitators,
the cowardly, the reactionists, those that will not think, you
probably...and long after those that created it...it will exist...
but warped...the ideas will be used to assume power and make
religions and create things to belong to...and control and use and
feign authority in order to have something not tangible...and
slaves will believe what they are told, because they don't know or
realize the courage to direct them in which direction to think. That
knowledge is denied the greedy mind. And some people will see

and grow upset and grow angry at the assumption of power and control and they will fight and make an idea and they will lose it to the power hungry.

In the great ones, that create without ordainment or permission that die in jail cells, by themselves, or in prisons, have defined the same players, recast in societies, over and over, for thousands of years. Personalities, egos, these are the things that make suffering in the world. Pride is destruction...even if it makes people happy. Happiness tainted by a pride that will damn is worthless and weaker than paper. We move on to a world without salvation, because there is no need for it, because there is no damnation, with cures for inEquality. If you can't see this, then you should overcome your mind so that you can understand it. Afraid to lose your mind? You are already lost. Having the guts to not be afraid if you have a mind or not, and you have the will to be able to shut off the ramble of propulsion that drives you into every next selfish, cruel, beneficial solution, that clings so desperately to life and its fleeted satisfaction...well, then you can be free, and trust those ahead of you that know it is alright to have had all the thoughts. Are you brave enough to be calm and not worry about everything around you, even while you are worrying about it? Too much, I think. This is the mind. Brilliant it is. But, you don't need the mind to understand this. You just need to let yourself stop thinking so you can spend time and listen. It is easier to think when the mind is not so tired by the disease of constant chatter. When your brain gets cancer and the mind is gone, are you still the mind? Is the mind what you are? Be warned. Freedom lies within.

WRITER'S NOTE: I never reference anyone. Everything is from one source and it is possible that you may occur within it.

ARTIST'S NOTE: It is irrelevant what the artist provokes. A person will either be in a negative state or positive state to receive the message. All an Artist does is provoke.

The dragon presented the eagle with a delicate broach.
The dragon said, "Take this to your mother."
The eagle replied, "I can't. I've killed her."

Table of Contents

A true to life story is non-linear. A life is talking and some events. Friendship is listening to the talking and existing through the events.

INTRODUCTION

<u>Uncovering the OverMan</u>
A Ballad in Prose
by Philosopher Stephan Pacheco

The OverMan has overcome all doubt. He acts when he wishes and never when someone wants him to. He acts without fear of persecution and persecutes no one, but those that persecute. His mind does not strive for power. He is 100% complete from the moment of birth. His image is unimportant, he is what he dreams to be and doesn't need to be anything else. He does not think of these things. He is these things and these words are only figurative illusions that the non-OverMan will think he understands, but will not. The OverMan will not read this. And if he does he will laugh at it. Or smile at it. Because happiness is his nature, even in despair. This cannot be understood by one that is not an OverMan. He will not be concerned that he is a she, he is not so insecure. He will not think it is sexist to call it an OverMan and not an OverWoman. He does not need to have pride for anything. He is calm. He is free from all of it. His life is real, fleeting, and constant. If you try to tell him to be something else, he is free to destroy you, or let himself be destroyed. He can choose anything at all times. Want does not control him so he can want anything or not want anything. He is controlled by no psychosis, even if trapped with one. He is free. He is still calm, even if you are charging at him. He is not controlled by fear. He is not controlled by rage, but he can have it, but it is not real. He knows this. That every emotion he has he can let go or manifest further, or forget about. He needs to cling to nothing. He is changing and is free to. Regardless of what anything thinks he should be. He is not controlled by words of power, like duty, or taking orders, or faith or damnation or salvation. He does not need to believe in anything. He is present, that he knows. For every discomfort that may have been programmed into his mind or his genetic code, he has faced it, he has quelled it, he did not run from it or believe it was what he was, and he never felt guilty or bad about it, but he knew he could get rid of it, and sometimes he did. He knows that he is not this mind, this body. Because of this he can be anything. He is unowned, even in shackles. At any time he can fight and die or live. He holds no grudge against circumstance, even if that circumstance is deliberately caused by someone else, for the weak minds of those that surround the OverMan are circumstantial, unlike the ever flowing mind the OverMan uses to think with. He can have a hundred thoughts or no thoughts at all. He defies the reaction to circumstance. He is in control of his mind, because he is not afraid of losing control of his mind. The OverMan realizes he exists with or without his mind. He seeks no power and no control, he has no fear so he does not need the vices of weaker men that fear their own inferiority, but he can enjoy their vices and manage them. He will not coddle or praise; you must already be at peace to truly befriend him. He will not cater to those that need him, he likes what needs nothing, and appreciates it, and still he will give until you have proven your selfishness, and still he can choose to. He can think for all HumanKind, or he can survive, and have no regret to doing either. He can be sad, he can be happy, he can be angry, and he is none of these things. These are only things he is doing, like burping or smelling. He realizes in his wisdom that he must do, but also that he doesn't have to do anything. He has had every thought for something, and every thought against it, and so, when he is confronted with fearful doubt from lesser minds he is free to not be affected by what someone else has pridefully thought had to be right because they thought it. The OverMan sees through the reasons people create to manipulate other people. He does not need to be right. He does not need to be told he is right. He is always neither right nor wrong. He is. It is unimportant what may or may not be, but it will always be greater than what you are. He knows this without pride, building a future he will not touch. It is as circumstantial as the wind or the rain, and just as vital. You can not please him, he does not need to be pleased. You can disappoint him, but he does not need to remember you for it. He will not tolerate hypocrisy unless he knows it's not important to you what you are, but you had to have considered it. He respects only what doesn't need an image. Only the OverMan can understand his glory and his irrelevancy. He sees through every mind at once because he doesn't have to cling to any. He can know you in an instant, hear your thoughts, your fears and your wants from him, because his mind is that open. He can be a part of any group or reject everyone. He does not join, but he can be joined, and still not above belonging. He can believe in himself, always knowing that what he is will never stay the same, but is present as Time moves. And he is free to let himself change. He is free to never need to remember what he was, although he can. And if the OverMan forgets you, he will be happy to know that you are fine with that. He won't please. The OverMan is always free and will always be stronger than everyone that seeks strength. He is immovable and he moves freely, unaffected by the doubts and hopes and fears of those that walk or yell near or at him. He is unimprisonable. He is rarely impressed, but can be by those that have faced what he has. He knows how hard it can be. He is Over and Beyond everything you could hope and dream for. He is everything you really want to be, and the only thing that can be and be and be. He is the permanence that those that seek permanence, that try to hang on, will never achieve. He needs nothing, and will not be corrupted into arrogance by having everything. He is how Freedom defines itself if Freedom wanted an embodiment, which it doesn't. The OverMan will appear to be a contradiction to anyone that needs to be something. He never uses pride, but uses will. He is freed from all sin and any sense or condition of damnation. You can't hurt him, but he can cry. Just as he is free from heaven or any condition or reward of approval. Everything is equal, just as he realizes the true nature of the only real reality is, which just happens to be, his own. He uncovered the truth of what he really is. He uncovered the OverMan that he had always been. Without doubt the OverMan whether alive or dead or dying or killing or ending or beginning himself, he will continue to be that, and it will not matter if he is not. And yet this definition is incomplete just as his unfolding life is. He is finished, but will never stop beginning, and so willing to look the fool again. And he is free to know passion and free to love deeply. Because he is not afraid of his own vulnerability or losing what he has because he knows he can never really own anything. He does not have to appear strong or great, even though he is. He cannot be programmed. He cannot be warped. And the weak will resent him for it, because it means they cannot be strong, and they will doubt their own greatness. He sees the truth beyond manipulation. He sees how the ignorant try to change people to justify their own reasons for greed, for power, to feel good about their crap. Though he can have he has been without, and needs nothing, not even life, that which you manipulate for. He does not need to be justified. He is the cure to suffering, with intentions and his hands. The cure to oppression. It is the duty of all people to cure it in themselves. If happiness is the goal of all human life, this is the way towards it, unaffected by resentment or judgment. He does not reason towards his OverMan ways, he explains what he has become by telling you what he has always been. He is the confidence that others use faith to fake. He will not join you because your cause is the same as all others, and so he may fight against you, and others alongside him, but he chooses for his central self not the mob or the job. The OverMan is individual and unpredictable by any way of defunct science or fake religion. He has overcome the reigns of pattern. He cannot be stopped, and so this is his beauty. As he creates he realizes its naturalness, because it is the spring he has uncovered for anyone to taste. Though few will, all can become him. That is why he came. That is why he gave birth to himself. Unaffected by opinion, his hand is always open, and when you take the fruit and scurry backwards, you will see that his hand is still open and he has not hurt you and fearlessness will lead to his love, though he will tell you not to love him. He expects a positive response and is sad when you give him selfishness, but his forgiveness is instant and not an effort when you just show him true kindness without expectation of gain. The OverMan sees that the general minds of the doubting people will believe in anything that they are told, so long as it is laced with the hope of winning. The OverMan does not need hope. He is hope. Hope moves with the OverMan. He is telling you that no one needs to be saved, so there is no one that you must worship, or follow, or pay, or kill for. The OverMan is constantly at peace, even when his body chooses to survive and prolong his current situation with the release of reflex and adrenaline. He has never been a coward, although he has lost, and he has ran, and he may lose again, and he may choose not to fight. He can love within his striking rage, he is not trapped by the doubts of duality. And as he overcomes, he knows the simple enormity of all that lives and dies and exists and ceases. Everything that may damage you, does not damage him, though it can make him see beyond his own reason and possibly consider something new, this is why the OverMan has sympathy for your weakness, his beloved enemy, instead of malice, and also why he will not tolerate it near him. His time is precious, and short, and usable, and his own and it cannot be had or purchased or taken or apologized for. The OverMan does not think or dream that he will be great like a god, he is beyond such want, and wouldn't waste his mind for something so dying. He *(She)* is himself. And his echoes ring across lifetimes in the trickling impact passed to generations that may know humility and strength without the need for power.

What Nietzsche predicted, what Shaw knew, exists now, dawning by the Knowledge Society. The path has been uncovered and beneath it was the steady truth. And Freedom for all of HumanKind.

www.LibertyCore.org
www.ManifestUtopia.com

This letter arrived three days after He, The Father, was dead:

Father,

I loved the way she called you "Father." And only because it's why I called you it and she picked up so lightly on what was easy labeling. As raw as could be...as simple and pure...as majestic, without illusion. As is a Life of Freedom.
My suicide came quick. It built for weeks before. I just began to let go of more and more things. I left my pistol at a bus stop. Just left it. Unafraid to die. The paranoia fallen away. I hadn't thought of it until now. I became happier and happier. Taking what money I had and eating ribs in the lodge, not concerned about the next step in the war. Not concerned with the next movement of thought to avoid another person believing authority exists. I lingered beside the edge of the Lake for some time. The clouds were grey and turned the whole valley that purple shady hue. The wind came up and rocked away every thought. And it felt Free. But only because I had a little money. To slave or not to slave?
I sat beside the Lake. The color of Topaz. And went in. Into the depths of instant stillness, and then deeper. The stillness crushing my lungs. My heart beating. Beating. Pounding. The only load sound to my drowned ears. I calmed it. But my consciousness was stuck there. Pounding. I was afraid that I might accidentally stop the fear by stopping my own existence. The emotion I keep there. The care I have. I was frightened. But I endured. Knowing that those that had gone had no real loss from it. Meaning, they hadn't lost their souls, they just came back shinier. So I went on. Burning away everything I kept. Losing every thought that I held to define myself to this point. Gaping a chasm between life and death. Wanting to matter, and realizing nothing matters, and realizing it is that which makes Equality real. Then...there I was. Like water it surrounded me. Killed me. I walked out in and I continued to sink. Very much aware that I was still sitting beside the Lake. But I could not feel the senses of my body anymore, but still felt very much like I could return to it instantly. Though I was fully aware that I had not moved; It appears as if all reality and perception is built directly over this non-moving tapestry of matter. Everything that matters. The truth lies beneath every illusion

someone tries to sell to you as real.

And then...suddenly and yet gradually, like time was irrelevant, She was real. And I could hear Her. In that way she tried to inflect into a conversation taken from far out of the mainstream and placed as a comment bewildering her company with what was actual and truly beautiful. She had no ego to break, nothing to speak through or convince, I was Free to just believe Her. And to hear Her transmission was to know the Truth. What I received, what is not translatable to the untouched mind, led me easily to walk calmly into the mountains. Wandering. Without aim. Finding food as I do. Drinking from rivers. Stealing and killing an untended sheep and tanning its hide with its brain, and sleeping softly on it beneath a cool still span of stretched starlight beside a brook that laughs its tiny lapping smile, singing gently the song of the Forest.

I returned to the realm of God, where it could have no name, as after the death came. I was glad to find out you were still alive. I hope we get to see each other again. Babble On dear friend.

      Cordially,
       Zarat

PS: She will come for you if you go.

<u>A Message</u>

The People of your time will likely not believe your quest for Revolution, although it is amongst them that you will gain the arrogance to create your War. The Will in these children was for Freedom. The strength to be used for killing and loss was their virtue and glory of the death they had mangled across their psyches to become what they knew they could be. Their closeness to death taught them that they could redirect themselves, and they did so early, before they came to believe in the most appropriate identity to keep them from being attacked. There was true virtue in the willingness to not seek total satisfaction. It is children that fight wars along the words of old men. It is only them together that have the strength to reject the illusion of authority, wherever it is laid. Penalties and rewards lie only upon the flesh, the spirit cannot be penalized. This world will Remain Free.

BAPTISM

A collection of conversations, writings,
and utopian dreams of a surrendered Hero,
fading out of life, and burning up his heart.

A nation by the seaside,
a drop witnesses,
the sink back to void.

The Alzheimer's is early onset.

The First Communion

The Old Priest had not offered much in describing the man, only that he was a revolutionary, someone angry, like me. Those that knew him, chose to serve under him, and exulted him, and all called him The Father. I'd been growing frustrated with my rounds. How could this prisoner view me with the eyes I want the world to see with? I thought on the Old Priest's fading white eyes and the roll of his reaching voice, wanting to get out of me what I could not get out of others. This Baptism would be by instant drowning.

The cell was warm, but not hot. Ultimately, it was pretty sparse with basic amenities. There were some papers, and poor man had a pencil near down to it's nub, but a sharpener, at least it wasn't a quill and his paper a nude nurse like other estranged Marquises. The barred window faced an elm tree. Several birds sang outside. The Sun's rays were yellowish in their whiteness. A man, with dancing eyes, sat in the corner. He turned slowly as the door to the cell opened. He was not startled. The priest entered the room. Eyes and minds locked in analyzation and assumption. With a blink, the Priest's eyes scanned the small room. The Priest smiled at the sway of the tree, glad that this man could be close to natural life. He looked back to the man who was now standing.

"I have read some of these books," Priest, with careless vulnerability.

"I have never read any of them. I have read parts of most of them, but I have never finished one," Father, "I reread parts of them, mostly randomly. Mainly a few lines of someone else's works are plenty to see where the author is going and to propel me deeper into my own tangents. It sets me in a direction I guess," The Father.

"Hmm. Do you want to philosophize with me?" The Priest.

He doesn't hesitate, "There is no reason to do as we are told. There is no reason to fear penalties for anything you might do. Someone will come after you anyway, probably several times in your life, no matter what you do. The society is a society of Power. The People are corrupt. The people are cruel, and vengeful, and seek a majority over you no matter where they go so that they can rule you and optimize their comfort. This is you. You do this. You oppress a planet. Money separates you from humanity. It places you in charge of it. And you will come for me. Of course you will. To propel your career. To gain power and keep the fear that initiates survival away. I will not serve you. Or anyone. I am not oppressing you. I do not care what you do. Just leave me alone," The Father.

"What's that? Your philosophy is the philosophy of disdain and bitterness?" The Priest.

"Sorry, if I apologized. It is just easier to nab fake philosophers by saying something like that. I have not gotten to have good philosophy in a long time. I gave up on the discussion of it. Besides, what can I really gain from anyone else?" The Father.

"I agree. So far I can pretty well agree with you. I don't think that I can gain anything from you either, but for now I am open to it," The Priest.

"Well..how often does someone actually agree with me? Or that I can agree with their style. Ah, true isolation. The real prison is my futility," The Father.

"I can see that you are all warmed up for it now. But not today. I just wanted to see if I wanted to do this. I do know that I do not have to meet anyone's requests to act. Is tomorrow good?" The Priest.

"I suppose that is your current freedom, to choose time. Can you bring some tea?" The Father.

"Oolong?" The Priest.

"Stimulating," The Father.

"Tomorrow then," The Priest.

Content with the oncoming fantasy of philosophy and expectations that both knew were fake, the two smiled as they thought of any genuine human connection laced with the truth in the personal, sex, and war of inner and outer life set to open and defend the justifications that led and lead to the same basic emotions, the same continual few actions, and the echo in the meaninglessness of every mad poets final thump on a cavernous chest to get out a warrior's last breath.

Many of these conversations are recorded. Some of these conversations have been transferred to a digital format and preserved. Some are re-accounts, others documented that day, some rewrites, some purposefully not rewritten, and some I do not remember being there for, but I swear I just knew. Most of whom he is, is lost to recordless time, but still, his meaningless life and his death that I witnessed gave me meaning and the will to raise the questions that would define me as a sovereign human being.

"I have been in a lot of situations that I have risked hurting other people, where I could have suffered many dire consequences, from death to jail to the destruction of friendship to my emotional or psychological mangling. Always my ultimate fearlessness of these consequences is what pushed me to take on the action, whatever it may have been. And I'll tell you what, I've seen all of those consequences face to face, be them in an angry friend's eyes, or a cop's tone, and I regret no action. My actions were just not advantageous to them, their weak futile fury engulfed them and harmed them when they did not have the will to put their vengeance on me in a way that would harm me, to end me. Thus is the dance of life, especially for the adventurer," The Father.

"I have a fear of sounding like a fool. Blabbering. It is something that rarely arises these days, but sometimes I remember where I came from and what I've become. If we remember who we have been we can remember not to be that again," The No Body.

"I have the genius to create a Reason for anything, like the Prophet Ted Bundy," The Father.

"The perfect job for the writer, or the Actor, or Entertainer, certain he or she is Existing, and willing to effect. Because he can be in anyone's mind," The Priest.

"Words have never been what I am, even if it's all I am known for,"
The Father.

"Why are you a priest?" The Father.

"I knew that I did not want to be a part of a system that the fakest, cruelest, greediest most selfish people succeeded in or fortune birthed them into. I did not want to be a part of a society that was based on the root of all evil, money. It rips down every virtue, it promotes every desire. It breeds envy. It glorifies gluttony. It pushes products with lust. It builds obsessions and insecurities. It worships fear. I could not, and would not contribute to this. So, there were two paths for me. It was my choice to do anything that I had to ta' stop it. I pulled a couple of jobs, they were well thought through. And I slightly compromised my views for it. But I took from people that I saw the disease in more strongly than any other. These people were pretty easy to find. They stand right in front of you and tell you how wonderful and holy they are. It pained me deeply the cruelty that swam in these shallow souls. It pained me that what they had done to people were not crimes so they carried no shame of stigma. So I would always commit the crime to teach them humility. Not to harm them, but to even the field for good people, and offer them vulnerability to realize equality through. To teach them that they were not as glorious as they thought. A little suffering brings people to a point where they can notice God. But when my wife died I found another way. I realized that thinking as hard as I had to ta' commit the crimes to survive was equal or more than the effort I needed if I was working within the system. Never a fool, but I was still selling myself for nothing. Just to get by. I was aiding no power or cruel malice, and I had time to write my sermons, but still, I was pulled from what I truly wanted to be. Just helpful to the people that were wrought by their egos. Anyway... even though there is much corruption in the message of the Church, I found that I could be what I wanted to be here. I first became a monk. I had plenty of time to meditate while in prayer. When I actually had the chance to slow down and silence myself I came to know God in the unspeakable way that taught me where <u>freedom</u> lies. At least this was a system, though still dependent on money, and still a whore for it...in the roots of it, there were people that honestly believed in everything that the capitalist world did not believe in.   It was basically a system without rank, at least within the orders. From the monk hood I only became a priest so that I could give sermons and bring a message that was logically thought out and actually humble to the people. Plus I saw where the biggest problem was. People that were worshiping the Church in this exact country were those that sought power, that were the most desirous and cruel. And they believed that they would be "forgiven" for their ways just by worshipping. It made them think that they were the good guys, living without the shame they used on their own naked children. They are the chosen, to themselves. It built congregations, this tolerance of cruelty and greed. Congregations got rich from it too. So the churches of this country became a haven for hypocrite sinners that wanted salvation from the madness and greed they did not want to be. And for an hour on every Sunday, they felt good, righteous, high like the junkies they are, and even more favored and even more powerful. The churches aided the spread of the <u>darkness</u> more than it deterred it. Unfortunately, the most holy people have to reject this tainted world and become monks, and hermits, and talk to no one. They don't spread the good word, because people hear it wrong. It frustrates them too much. So, tired from shouting into the ears of the deaf...I was sent to you," The Priest.

Without a second to judge the sludge of who I am claiming to be, "Doesn't it bother you to be sent? To be commanded where to live and what to do?" The Father

"I was asked to come to you, actually... An Old Priest I council with said that you carry the calmness and grand expanse of heaven within you, even through war and eventual damnation, he said...I read some of the things you wrote, and then I chose you," The Priest.

The Priest pulled his chair close to the madman that sat against the cool wall. "I am still writing sermons. I have only you as an <u>Audience</u>, so can I speak them with you?" The Priest.

"I wouldn't mind hearing your act Priest," The Father.

The Priest pulled out a mug that was quickly recognized as a pint.

"Let me explain the soul to you as I've witnessed it," the Father smiled as the Preacher spake, "Let us say that this mug is the body. Frosty and cool. This amber beer is the soul. It is easily poured in. It is easily poured out. But while the glass is upright, it holds the beer. The beer warms the mug. It sort of gives it life, as life causes a reaction. It certainly makes it useful. Now, although the beer is in the mug, although it is stored there, does the beer become the mug? Are they part of each other, even though they are together? No, they are separate. The beer is easily removed. If the mug breaks does the beer cease to exist? No, it only spreads out across the floor. And don't worry about being on the floor, there is no health department in the afterlife. There aren't any prisons either. You see, this body isn't what we are and if it stops being useful, we simply move beyond it. We don't have to be so afraid of dying that we do anything to survive. We don't have to sell ourselves for approval or comfort." The Priest.

"Hey, you added that prison part for me," The Father.

"I did," The Priest.

"That's good work Priest," The Father.

"I had a dream about it. It happened and I knew what it meant as I saw it, in the dream, I had the vision of it and the words too," The Priest.

"Did you maybe add that message to a scene that meant nothing?" The Father.

"It is not that I heard it described, it is not that I thought it out, I just instantly understood what it meant. In my experience through prayer, and focusing on being separate from this mug we call a body, I have found that there are other layers to knowing. More than just the brain," The Priest.

"I didn't disagree with you. And I thought you explained your point well, I was just asking," The Father.

"I know, Father, you were listening. I am just here talking to you. Just listening. And you can tell by how I act that I am not trying to be a shrink inside your skull. Hell man, I like talking to you," The Priest.

"I haven't talked to anyone in a long time that I didn't think was trying to tell me what they thought I wanted to hear or what they needed me to be so they felt less responsible for me. I do enjoy our visits, as well," The Father.

Without gates and walls two men walk through the kingdom of the other. The banners, tributes, and stylized paint of the graffitied mind, a settlement within it, where we feel ways about...stuff, and we talk of whom we have never really been, but were only another defiance of another and another generation terrified to lose us.

FORCEFUL FANTASY

Forceful fantasy engulfs the Priest too hard. Sexuality is the root of this man's interactions with other humans. [Able to see himself internally again.] The repression of this sex that is so natural to such a drive that is drawn to pursue entertainment, or politics, or vivid and deliberately bare literature, or, and all the sex in the popping, drives me into my vivid head:

Her touch was so soft like her sprouting breasts, and wanting to be treated and had and held and known as the woman inside this young girl she was conscious of being. Always holding the memory of this man, she loved too deep to ever say, and knew too smartly would never, could never, and should never stay to affect her life beyond the impact of this subtle secret relationship that was made wild and wet and deeply gorged into the sex buffet of offering that existed because this man, this priest, painted into a scenario in a fantasy released by writers a long time ago, forbidden, and offered, as a girl that realized her place in her time and used herself with the safe and loving ride of a spiritual priest that is relieved to have her smile before, after, and during. Her happy want never breaking. Her victory achieved in the climax of the existence of the event. Our event. Alone, with her, a secret in our hearts forever. I secretly, and whisper clearly into her ear that I want her to offer her body like I offered mine to her when she's spun around the sun more times and aged and never changed, but got better at what I willingly and lovingly broke out of her in a very creamy mess.

"Of course you cannot simply tell someone to not ever have sex and not teach them how not to have sex. It is the body's natural function to want to rape with and despite grace. When one's balls are full of cum it is his instincts to empty them. No matter how gently you say it, it is true. A man will find a way to serve his deepest survival programming. He will have sex with boys, with girls, with his mother, with his cousin, or his sister, or anyone's wife or girlfriend, if the female is or sexual attraction is nearby. It does not matter. If a man is owned by desires, as all men can be, he will fuck. This is the root of our problems in the Church," The Priest.

"I see. Yes. It is the same with the power of Existing. When you overcome so much programming, and you have no fear, and you recognize no oppression, it is easy to screw boys, girls, your mother, your cousin, your sister, it is almost as easy to kill them...we know that there is no consequence for these things besides an end to the existence as this one person. We are breeders and killers. But truly this would bring much suffering and much complications. If one is possessed by these basic desires then one cannot truly be free, or know the grace that it takes to walk hand in hand with an audience that has come to trust you to take them there, whichever anywhere that could be," The Father.

"And one can certainly not be Holy," The Priest.

"The only way that I see to overcome such basic programming that brings such basic suffering is to realize that this world is not real. It is a place of dying, recycling itself. Of course this can bring one in the other direction of rational where the person becomes a serial killer, or a police officer, or a politician, or any other number of dark agents of authority and tyranny. But if one is devoted to easing suffering, to caring and to loving, and to not assuming authority, if one chooses this path and won't contribute to the Dark Society that propels it, then truly one could overcome it," The Father.

"One could become a true Holy Man. You're right. It is the knowledge that the Holy Spirit is untouched by these things. By existing, by what matters in the realm of matter, meaning, matter. Since the Spirit is our true identity it makes it possible to overcome the torturing nature of our own basic functional humanity. Knowing the Spirit truly is a means to salvation," The Priest.

"A true Master of Existence. Not controlled by any man, even himself. By no thought, instinct, or desire. We can make a Utopia in our own minds. If we can overcome the weakness that alters us and turns us into what we fear to be, into what we don't want others to be," The Father.

The Father knows the truth in this man's philosophy. It makes it possible to talk to him. They wanted to get out what was in their heads, even though they both knew how to silence it, because they chose actions that led to the same sustenance of life, only their random and NOT unique reasons and intentions led to the moment that is visibly slipping away as they keep finding themselves again and again. The Father's appearance...he just seems skinnier suddenly, not a lot, but I noticed. *Sometimes I am struck by the grandeur of his tone and receive the significance of my placement in a moment in the macro-tapestry of history, and I am drawn to write to the 3rd person, bearing witness. Don't hold me to my tone. You cannot do that to anyone. Doing so makes a bird stop singing. It makes a friend someone you remember knowing, and it makes a relative estranged, "don't" or "shouldn't have" is not a cruelty an actually good person gives to someone at door to something so unremembered it is unknown. (My honor to display the method they used to show my duplicity.)*

"Any young one that asks, I tell. I educate them with what they need not what their parents can't feel instinctually comfortable talking to them about. I teach them about sexual release. We let ourselves get aroused even while it happens. And yet, nothing happens, besides that education and that arousal. Without ever speaking it I taught them something personal about their own kept sexuality. I let them feel that it is theirs. At least 7 out of 10 go and masterstroke after, I'm sure, and it makes me so glad. What a gift toward the pursuit of happiness I gave them. It's too easy to marvel at the impact across a life. And for the others that ask I teach them how to take that <u>sex</u> that <u>makes the events happen</u> and use it toward the accumulation of spiritual power. With the Hero's sex drive there are countless opportunities to direct sexual arousal toward meditation. Funny how we all realize it, all of us on the path. Taking the opportunity in the moments we see coming in the reality and grandeurised humans on the television screens, in books, and throughout cinema," rambled The Savior of Children from the cur of ownership parenting.

The Father, "Presenting a descriptive examination to them on the pluses and the minuses of lives lived one way and what happens when lives are lived the other way. Defensive and damning, or free, happy, and accepting of their very existence. Well, nothing wrong with being a cat, or any other living being, bleeding, scratching, and digesting across minutes."

A Memory

His eyes tear open from a memory too sad to dream. The pretty blue light from the corridor annoys him as he wakes, again, reminding him that he does not possess the relative situation that would let him think the lights were pretty. How many times had his mind awoken him tonight? Too many. Too many to count in between the haze of sleeping and waking. He could smell the cold coming off the concrete floor. A smell that burdened him every night and every day, musty, filthy, and sharp. He wished he had a proper bed to lift him off of it. He'd slept on fine beds and knew the difference like an animal once brought inside. The Dark Society programs people to think that its enemies, its criminals, aren't people, and that they must suffer even more than the natural living of life makes them suffer already.

The dream swept over him again, brushing his mind in flashes of her beauty. Crushed into sadness by the kindness he remembers. Like most heroes before him, The Father was betrayed over and over, by the broken vows of the weak that had failed him. So, it was deeply natural for his mind to remember those that tried so hard to not betray him, but the good ones always think they had. Surprised to find himself in high school, stunned to believe he stayed through the length of it. When it began he fell deeply in love with a woman that would not have him. Those with soft souls he could have loved so gently, never accepted his love, sometimes because their love was too big. They were so blinded by his strength. They could not see his ease. They were too afraid to really know him and to let it come out in the course of an affair. He thinks on the dance he took her to. He thinks on the smell of her hair, knowing he doesn't remember it correctly. He can't remember where they ate that night. But he remembers dancing close to her. He can still manifest the memory of the pressure of their bodies together. He never wanted to let her go. All in this Revolution seem to have the power to feel souls, generally because of a loss that felt great and a sudden need to let this world go, and for hers he would have died twice. He wanted to know it, to hear it form words to speak to him, to feel it make heat to warm him. He smiled as he remembered his adolescent emergency following that dance that stole a part of him and locked it in time. Excusing himself to the bathroom to adjust the pressing passion that was pouring out of him leading to a behavior modifying choice, from that night on he would never wear underwear that loose again and that he would be devoted to briefs for the whole of his passionate life. He laughed a bit, knowing that half the room must have been more than half-cocked during those slow dances. The teachers and their smiles, watching the young boys running, though leaning slightly forward to four-sided stalls and thoughts of sports line-ups. He remembers pressing into her, wanting her to have him. She remembered the hug they shared, equally, at the end of that one night they had together in the beginning of their banging ignorance. He asked her out the next day. She declined. And some darkness, just a little, the sad kind, took his heart that day. Four years later she signed his yearbook, and she told him that that hug that they both remembered was a sign of True Friendship. Even to think of it now, in the cold, and in this cell, made his nose burn with the sting that only comes over you when your eyes mist up. The Father, even then, was isolated and misunderstood by what he was, even though he was accepted and reached out to diverse groups. In those days, as in these for him, no one understood the ego enough to see the great kindness beneath those that know they must make themselves hard to try hard. Oh well, fate will go its way anyway. We only have the gift to perceive fate's circumstances in the way we wish, so long as we break away from the ego as much as possible, but still we are fate's slaves thrust into our lives by the very ego we try to break. In the end we cannot stop most of it. Man's prisons are weak compared to the prisons of ourselves. Later he heard that his friend who she chose to be with in those early years had chosen a different route other than her because he had chosen to not have children or have marriage, wisely to his freedom and may he be free of the Sin of Reminiscence. But surely the Father would have vowed to her for that. In those days. He would have built empires for her, planted trees for her, offered his dreams for her love. And in the days that followed for him, he broke up with the girl that loved him and wanted all of those things with him, because he knew that by that point only war waited for him. A war he chose. Over love. Because his love was that great. And like all of the glorious greats of this revolution, he fought that war completely alone with allies near him. He never vowed to that girl that he left for war that he would be with her and breed inside her. But he would have, to that first girl, at that best dance. Men like The Father take few things deadly seriously, because everything lacks permanence, but their own vows were created in them and spoken by them, writ hard as a scar in their hearts. And when the slaves make them break those vows, like the band of criminals he fought with in the beginning, like loves since then, he never forgets. Those from his past that now dwell within his haunted mind that forced him to destroy vows of loyalty and friendship through the course of their selfish desires...they truly harmed him, and for too long he didn't truly let that go, 'til The Girl manifested herself to him. But if there was no vow, there was no betrayal, and no grudge, no pain. Only the welcome pain of love left behind, that can never die in him, and deepens through time, to love him truly and not harm him it's true jealousy that must be overcome. A holy act must occur to know him, to befriend him, love him, and gain from what he emanates naturally when delighted. Hearts are set free from suffering from holy acts, these acts that something loose and lose a sense of control, as the Father did, to forgive the scars in his heart. He said to me, "Forgiveness is the suggestion for the sinner that has already damned someone. Real holy people don't ever forgive, because they never damn, or they instantly resolve hatred from their instincts if something makes them jump in the dark." For the life of influence The Father chose he found it unfit to go full holy. It was a luxury of freedom he would not afford himself. Transcendence was for the joiners not the participators.

All great men fight alone, love alone, remember alone, and die alone. Partially disconnected. Always detached. There is always too much sadness in the thick groove of their greatness.

Ah, yes. What he would have done for a dance partner. Maybe even joined the Dark Society to fight it from the inside, which he did, until he had enough from it to give up all he gained from it and fight against it deliberately. But then his cause would have been partially lost, hitched in a way that quelled him. If not entirely compromised. Fate keeps the brave honest in their own and its own different way. The Father imagines what she looks like now, so late into their lives, slightly less ignorant. He fancies the thought of her being fat, or at least chubby. At least. Then he would know that her soul and her mind remained pure and good. Not so hindered by the slave mentality of this society's vanity. Then she would have won her victory from this shameful tyranny, in her own natural way. Existing. Happy.

And even now, the Father knows that he would give her anything he had, anything she needed. No matter what the situation was that he was in. Even if he was married for thirty years. So long as love and ease was still the nature of her soul there would be opportunity to love her and care for her. There is always room in the heart of the man that cherishes true kindness and gratitude for not forcing him to betray. Always, but his heart must be free to love those that he might take in. And she would have to trust in the love itself, not the circumstance of her sought after primary glorification in love.
And now...he has been awake for too long. Too long. The Father's mind wanders away from the caring dream that woke him with its longing...it moves to the expectations he holds for people. Knowing that he damns them for their betrayals. Knowing that so many had failed him with their fake pledges of love and honor that it has become a waste of time to trust anyone to be worthy enough to fight for what they truly need. That misunderstood Love. Oh...His mind

swirls with the Darkness that echoes as knowledge. And he is all too aware of it. Tortured by what he hates. Truly...truly...his Love is lost. And truly his war for freedom has failed.

All the mind does is reason. Taking look upon look at ourselves, over and over, defining and redefining, constantly contradicting, always changing, forced into the course for the energy it must burn--like a blood vessel. If one sees through the ego one creates the Reason that benefits it. If one sees through the Spirit one does not need to use the Greed and Fear that seeks benefit. One is content to survive, because he knows only the body dies, it does not need supremacy for itself.

His Girl

This Girl had the gift of gifts. She knew the truest reality to the world. She knew how to set everyone free from pain and suffering, from anger and madness. But no one would believe her. No one would listen. She would tell the truth about what people were. She would show them the straight and quickest path towards peace and the deepest cruelest anger always arose in them as an immediate reaction. Over time she too was consumed by her frustration, and anger and madness took her. To have the most precious gift, to know the path to the deepest, greatest, most free thing, in all the universe, and not know how to teach it. Every time you try people hate you. The ego is a delicate thing. It teeters with electricity on both sides of it. To provoke it can mean your violent death. And to help people you must speak directly to it. The ego is the fierceness of identity. If you were not thrust into the mighty secret of the world and did not know that you did not truly exist in this identity, it would be hard to believe. You would protect it, you would speak from it and defend it, because it is what you thought you were. When dealing with something like this, when dealing with such forceful emotion and belief, you cannot simply tell someone that they are what they are, whether it be true or not, the rage comes quickly from the ego, the ego cannot understand what I am trying to tell it. But...if I can allow the force of identity to realize it on its own...to guide a person towards it and allow this person that I am trying so desperately to help...then through their own realizations and drawn conclusions, they will naturally find the path and the ego will remain unprovoked. Perhaps the ego will arise at times and the student will reject the depths of truth, but even these upheavals will be less rageful because the person will know that they themselves came to a part of realization. If you put the cat on your lap she doesn't stay, but if she moves on her own, possibly with the temptation of treats, she will demand to stay and that you now pet her, a human ego is no different or less wary. Their own movement will be more concrete in them because it was the ego itself that found the salvation and if the ego found it, it must surely be true as it is a movement to destroy itself in order to wield it, or so that is how the person will see it plus a couple steps in Enlightenment.

This is the climax. This is the point that changes everything. This is the point for the holy soul, with the brilliant mind, that knows the deepest truth, learns the solution that will save us all from the madness of not being able to communicate the grace that was presented to us. There is a way to free a person from the shallowness, the insecurities, and the Crusading fear that racks them and takes our physical freedom from us all. I must be here for this man. I must remind him of what he truly wanted to be. There is no doubt he is a good man, though he has killed, though he has stolen, though he has lived as a man surviving on an Earth, but he has been consumed by the Darkness. His frustration, and his will, and his strength, drove him fiercely against and directly into the open arms of the Darkness itself. And it consumed him, making him a Crusader. It is this that I walk along the banks of this river beside.

"All I wanted was to set people free. I knew how to do it in the physical world. And I was not even as wise and as pin pointing as the mighty Zarat, that suffered deeply from his brilliance. And no one would listen. People lashed out at us again and again whenever we would try to offer them freedom in the physical world. They hated it. They refused it. They immediately thought it was a conspiracy. Fear runs deep and into everything," The Father.

Found in writing on the floor of The Father's cell:
I had spent so much time telling other people how to free themselves that I lost so much focus on myself. I had to become what I hate. I became a Crusader for my own cause and I chose to take freedom away from other people. I think the Girl's revolution is happening. It happens slowly. One person at a time. I am the problem with the world. I could not relax my ideals and I made people do for me, to aid me, to become like me, but this is futile. I cannot force them. Their egos merely retaliate. They only build more military, their fears only deepen and their anger swells and spreads to so many others unless they with discrimination grant me value in their mind. The cure is surely a hard one. The disease that steals freedom from all around us is harsh indeed.

"I chose to be what I really am. Not the fake image that people create for the world to see. I tried to live my life as a genuine human, my concern for health and physical safety alone, and that made me professional. I fashioned and graced it as only I desired, by means that only my willingness to be a slave, to give of and up myself, got me the means to do so. And amongst it I retained my utter sovereignty, autonomy, and right to it, as I made my defined contribution on the set. I felt that I owed genuineness to my very life as this very man. It is a choice of raw courage. A choice of a hero. I can see that. So be it. I don't care. It is just my choice. I never wanted to be the renowned child psychologist who's children killed themselves. I wanted to become what I could imagine. We have found the way to become it. The style of thinking that makes us functional and real, and lets us become the happy and free OverPeople, within and among," The Father. "I went to the place that people could understand my argument, and even be on my side. It was always LaLa Land, I was born on the Day of the Entertainer, you know."

The Power of the Adaptive Mind

"Your average ignorant idiot, meaning those that fancy themselves intellectuals, often view the adaptability of our creation into the OverPerson as a split personality. They do not yet understand that whether we are in war or in love or caring or killing or committed to crime or charity we are still reasoning towards the same point. We can prosper in any system, in any situation, in any time, this is the height of our adaptability. And we gain this by reasoning towards nothingness, by accepting malleability. By focusing on nothingness we have no form that we must take to please anyone, even ourselves. We prosper because we have no concern of winning or losing, even though naturally we do strive towards a win for nothingness. We become formless, like water. We are like water, Bruce Lee. All others suffer because they cannot accept change, they cannot accept their own decay. We prosper because we are in our best form, our finest advantage, regardless of what we are thrust into, like prison or a throne," The Father. "This is the power of no mind. We don't have to be anything. Thus, we are free to be anything. Unaffected by others that cannot comprehend our freedom from them."

He'd been writing on the floor with a pencil. We got him a writing desk, and an old electronic typewriter with some memory, but pen and paper suited his generation, and reflexes to get thoughts down, best.

History

It is true that all History dies when we die. Everything we were told to think about all things, all labels, damnations and glorifications created by the arrogant mind of man, in this isolated society, cease. In death, all things become equal. And knowing that History is written by those that have won wars...History and what we think of it was created by Man. Tyrants and Kings have told us who is mad, great, and stupid. We know these things to be true by the direct experiences of death and through the courses of logic, we know we can be anything we want to be without concern of what anyone thinks. This is the nature of this revolution. To overcome the limit of Man's controls upon itself. To free people from things they do not even know imprison them. It does not matter if you are a "criminal," a "hero," a "clown," or a "dog," you are still yourself. Don't fear what anyone tells you you are. You are still what you are no matter what. The fears in others will hold you back. Be: Individual and Free. Give yourself a name, if you need one. But be wary...if you need a name... you are not on the right side of the revolution, or you have chosen to fearlessly survive, ironically with all the others, and get your benefits, and work your days, somewhere your tinkering echoing in the annals of History.

"I lived my life without a net. I knew, and always knew, by how many people I watched die, by how many times I died in career, love, and intestinally...I knew it could end at any moment. Any. Now. The Girl told me. I knew. So, if I was going to try I would try harder than anyone, with no care for what I could gain. So, I gained, from time to time, and like all situations for one to gain, one doth lose. So. I succeeded more greatly in life because I risked the most. It doesn't matter if I rot here. It doesn't matter what a Tribunal says. It doesn't. How does that effect the majesty of the life I have lived. Even now. Listen to the riddle of my babbling triumph. It does not matter what happens. It matters that you lived, and that is all. It is good that you died. Sometimes things work for ya, sometimes against ya, but a Great Man makes up his own reality and swings with it," Thus Is Will. The phenomena is occurring. Quickly to the open and expanding priest. The Priest is beginning to feel the sway of the minds of the participators in the steady wave offered and emanated by the almighty intangible Cause.

"Our greatest power (all equally great, so all equally the greatest) is that we gained the ability to let go of habit. To release any programming we built up along the way. It allowed us to work across many genres of Entertainment, which defied all expectations, and compounded our earnings. The mind is habitual. To free the mind from habit you must overcome the mind. You must be able to see it triggering. Habits force the mind to work in a specific way, over and over again. Not only does it slow the ability to learn, and not only does it take away and go against the whole Philosophy of Freedom, but it warps the mind. It builds a progress slowing gap between the generations because the Generations of Children cannot see the way that their children are thinking, because they will not try what their children are doing, this is why the children reject the parents and flush the parents as they grow older, and never buy a new and improved product leaving marketers targeted on the youth. It is all because of the lack of faith in another person's mind. People learn little from their children. It is all because of the lack of real education, that which turns from Darkness. People do not understand that they can change their minds and have any mind that another person has. Some Actors know. The knowledge that they built might be formed in a completely different way inside someone else's head. Any personality can belong to any soul, and any body can, and any brain can belong to any soul, and, more than one can be inside a vessel at one time, but still come out as one uniform personality," he speaks with full theoretical certainty.

"Sometimes it seemed like it was important where he was talking to. In his mind now, he doesn't even have a name, all he can do is exist. In fact, he can't *do* anything. Though, it seemed like it might talk deeply to me. But, it would only be talking to my mind. A mind I am trying to lose. I can talk to myself more deeply and know or understand whatever he was going to say. If I allowed my mind to be tantalized by it I would be directly pulling myself from the path. I would be distracted by lights and buzzers, current buzzing through my brain. *A holy soul will always guide his right mind deeper and deeper into itself. Imploding in omniscience,"* The Priest. **"The evolution of HumanKind <u>must</u> be forced. Up until this point all evolution has had to be forced. Science. Civilization. Feeding. "Advancing." This rule of the physical world, the idea that it takes work to improve, is true in the spiritual world. It should be accepted as a rule for the course of a perpetual existence. It is factual, we, individually, are our own salvation. No God, No Man, No Whore, can give it to us.**

The Father's Will engulfs by existing. Simply being near it will bear a holy test
for the Priest. Bravery is the only choice for those that wish to endure it. And
how it bends at the mind,
and proves the bounds of Friendship and
the risks of an open heart willing for Enlightenment.
How will you think everything, and make something work out of it?

Nurses Dose Morphine Regularly Now

"There are not many ways to deal with the erraticness of the unstable city mind. Most people use the most common technique of current human perception. They repress all people out. They don't make eye contact. When you stare at them they blink, blink, blink, and some try to push you away with the cocked chin. ***The lonely make it that way.*** And it makes them part of the unstableness. When the mind has a series of blocks in it that make what people think is their true personality than (I just thought of an old girlfriend that spoke down to me simply because she believed her reason was stronger, but no, it was because her brain wasn't as smart as my brain. I wish I still didn't feel I had to justify it. It is hard to let the mind stop fighting. It is supposed to fight to keep us alive. A gift (for no holiday. Holidays are fake days. Made up days.) was the programming, but now we must change it. Blocks. Breaking me from my true work.) **(there was no break in my speech, but the thought had to be given physical space to exist as a text, but actually, that's not true. I zoned out for several minutes and forgot what I was originally thinking. Back tracking through my thoughts is a far greater mystery than you deserve to see.)** Anyway, we..."

Sometimes we hated. Sometimes we loved. It did not matter which we were doing. It mattered that we were able to stop doing either at any time. That is real power.

The Father is asleep. At least he's quieter now.

A NOTE:
Thoughts of his profession:
Do you know what I used to like about TV? When a person would
come forth that came up with a plan and laid it on the line, had
to slightly sacrifice their ideals and know what it is to earn it. To
understand what it is to have nothing. And someone that did it all
because they love it. People see that in sports sometimes. I see it
when Emeril bites into his food.

"First I wanted bravery. I journeyed towards it, changing myself to have it. I was small so I needed to learn to fight. No matter though. I could still feel fear. Anxiety at my impending doom. Fear within unstableness. Stress. I could see that I had to journey towards calmness. It was the only way I could have the strength to fight those that assumed power over us. So, in my pursuit to bravery began my pursuit towards calmness. In my soul I could feel something that had once died within me. I felt some sort of damage, a situation, something in my past emotionally damaged me in a way that I was humbled. A portion of my ego broke away and I could feel its ebb and flow, its sadness, and below that, something real, something non-residual. It felt dead. And I could see that the death I felt was the absence of the ego. And it existed after I was dead. I knew it. I felt it. The Girl's influence forced me far down into it. It led to who I know I am, and took away my ability to name it. Knowing that this shell sheds itself into freedom changed me into something entirely unimagined. My philosophy had taken me there. Within I felt the throbbing pulse of my own true existence. Pounded like a heart, beating this other heart.
It sounds moving because your soul knows it's true. If it is calm it is real, if it is swirling, moving or angry, if it makes you think more, than it is false," KNOW A WAY TO IT. To calmness. To peace. Towards victory. Towards yourself. Toward a life without our constant reoccurring destruction.

Don't you see?...a war...that happened, and never did, that changed many, and kept everything intact. A massive wave liberated perception.

"I saw it in her eyes just before I struck her. I saw her peace, in the absolute certainty of what comes next. I felt the surrender back to the place that she belonged. In her first death she lost all that does not matter in this world. She told me of it. You could feel it from her. Something amazing, something that other people warped by their ignorant perceptions saw as evil, something non-existent. But it wasn't, it was truthful. Why? Why can't they see it?" The Father.

"It was her great advantage, wasn't it? To be able to surpass the ego in an instant. She did not have to deconstruct it. She had a straight ticket to the truth," The Priest.

"She had an ability to surrender. Something I never had the time or opportunity, or even the knowledge, to experience. Surely I knew it, because I had thought myself there, but it was not the same as what she was, or what I face now," The Father.

"Was she more than you are?" The Priest.

"In depth, pure vastness, and so potential, I suppose," The Father.

"If she knows it, don't you think it is possible that you can know it," The Priest.

"I would have to die I think to know I was feeling it for sure, and not just by imagining it, or making the body feeling something that it isn't," The Father.

"If death is the loss of all history, all opinions, all questions, lies and anger...couldn't we bring ourselves to that without dying? Since we can rationalize what it is by what she taught us? She already told us what it is. We just have to go towards it. She could do it because she knew what it is. What death is. She told us; you wrote it. We know too," The Priest.

The Father pulled in a deep breath. A breath of surrender. Knowing that the Priest had spoken him to the point where he had no fight to give. He looked to the floor as he breathed, his mind reaching into a point of vanishing. He could not speak, he had no will to. In a single breath, for a second, he encapsulated it. His love for The Girl, his trust for her, his Faith, would lead him to his salvation.

Faith is valuable; Religion is not. Religions are reasons to damn. Abandon tradition for direct experience; to know others as yourself.

A SINGLE PAGE OF MANY NOTES:
Man is not the god he thinks he is. He is an entirely different kind
of god. One that knows nothing for power. One that is without.

You will not get everything you want. And you should not want
everything you can get.
There is a generation of spoiled hearts. The Silent Generation,
secretly pilfering their parents' finances and dignity. They tainted the
world just before the Baby Boomers.

When I got involved in Entertainment, I knew that eventually I
would lose every fan I could create to support me. I knew that for
everything I said that one person could like and want to belong to,
I would say four things that would deeply offend them. Because
everyone has an ego, and when that veil of fear is touched it bites,
and that was the best method we had to reach them through the
medium. Hate mail was equally as abundant as fan mail when the
show of shows was on and I was the show runner. Everyone wants
to hate and complain and justify themselves over and over.

We have a society where the most prized thing is to become a
manager, where one assumes power over someone else. Except, for
being the owner, so you can control the manager. I see the dark
arrogance, and hear it when people brag about their first jobs that
never last and becomes eleven other jobs along the way. But all
business owners are controlled by the government, so the wealthy
seek more power and more power, in politics, leaving poor families,
oppressed by confidence and momentum.

PAGE OF NOTES CONT'D:

Capitalism has many great benefits, it caters deeply to desires, it forces acceptance of many races and religions because you can make more money off of a wider clientele. Unfortunately, Capitalism just isn't practical. It exploits man's darkest, cruelest, most manipulative impulses. Children are born naturally cruel, and violent, and destructive. Ask a parent, or a brother, or a sister. To be more than this you must force your own evolution, that is what learning really is. Evolution is as rapid as your own life.

People are fools, they are too stupid, too distracted, too lost from hope, to see that everything they think is catered to them. Fed to them. Taught to them. They are manipulated into feeling bad about something, and good about another. It is all right for a policeman or a US soldier to kill someone, but it is a dark and an unforgivable sin if a lone mad man kills someone and you don't benefit from it. You are to worship the empire always and condemn any threat to it. Put the idolatry of a flag all over your car. We will identify the threats, you just hate them. This is the Darkness of a Corrupt unbalanced Empire.

I could argue every side of anything and make it true to some person. Every Philosophy is a lie. Every one can be reasoned. A system is an applied Philosophy of living, if it fails it was not correct, it created inequality and therefore instability as criminals retaliate and become liberators, again. If it succeeds it becomes what all societies and Philosophies become, the destruction of all parts of the world it can touch, to make reality naked, and bare, and comfortable through the tool of discomfort, and acceptance, and tolerance and beyond the need for tolerance to a world without damnation. All societies failed because man sought power out of an idealistic Philosophy. The Devil is anyone that you can hear tell you anything about the way the Universe is. Your god is the silent man you didn't even know died, but wrote the papers that spawned a billion identical opinions.

SERMON OF THE PRIEST
THE CONTROLLERS, THE FEARED, THE RIGHTEOUS, THE COMPLAINERS LOST IN THEIR PARENTHOOD

The Sunday crowd grippe quick to the voice of the sub-Priest:

"There are those that subscribe to the idea that Capitalism is advanced by listening to the complainers. That one can sell more if they make things more general for the aching initially-educated masses. The complainers, the hateful, the Afraid to die, they scream out from society like they are drowning. Like everything around them can kill them. Politicians hear the zealots, and they understand their words because they too are zealots. My works; meaning, the exhaustion of energy needed to form this mind to spring an endless thought; meaning, my sacrifice, my choice of how to burn up this body, has been spilt for those that no one hears. No one hears them because they don't seek power, they do not need to communicate with the vile powerful, it would harm their peacefulness. They are The Other America. I have spent myself for those too beautiful to speak anymore. The fading. The dying. For those that try to make everything they do great for the only good reason...for Love.

(pause for applause)

Whether it's the best job, or the most useful job, or the burn-off: can you hear these words? To see the truth before the end, not of the world, who cares?, the end of you, the world you know, to know what God is, turn, turn towards that which you fear. For people to control you, for you to follow Leaders with prejudice and glorification of yourself, you must be turned away from truth, from peace; or else, why would you do it?

The first step in a path to success is to get away from the family and everything you can't do, and get to the whole world of things and all the rest of the people you can do. Oppression starts at home; moving out, and money, ends it. Remember good charity is giving money."

"I was in north Las Vegas once, trying to score some weed. I drove down the street, in the Dark ghetto, not many lights in the ghetto. I heard the stereotypical black guy voice, with the fake universal accent, call to me from the sidewalk. I drove to the end of the street and turned around. I pulled up along side the guy and he asked me what I wanted. I said, "Weed." He said, "I don't have that," accept like a black person wants to sound to be accepted by his crowd. What an insecure sect of power mongers. Another man, a friendly man, came up to the truck. He talked to someone else. He said he could get it. We waited. Then he approached once more and asked if I wanted to see the guy weigh it out. I asked, "Should I?" He said, "I don't know should you?" I went with him. Through the darkness. Between the cages of the slum apartments. His paranoia peeking around every corner. Looking like a criminal. Fool. He made small talk with me. Asked me what I did. I told him I write novels. He didn't believe me. There was a section that was very dark, an empty lot, a man called to him, they didn't know each other. I later realized that had this man, that this man did not know, not been there, this was the place he had planned to take what he wanted from me. After this area I walked beside him up to another group of dealers. He told me to walk by and he would grab it. But he didn't. He stopped just down the street and told me that I was "trippin'" that I was "fucking up." He said, "This was the place. What was you doing?" he questioned. I handed him the money and told him to go and get it. I waited. A fearful abusive man yelled at me. Told me to walk up the street. I was earlier told that this guy did not like white guys. These men hated authority and wanted nothing more to be it. I felt no fear as their cruelty was displayed. I decided to walk back to the truck and wait for the nice man grabbing my stash. Another guy ran up to me, in the dark, dark lot. And spoke, "Did you get your weed?" "No." "That guy just took off running," he said in earnest, "I have your weed." "Do you know who that guy is," was the first thing I thought and said. "No. Man that guy's a burner. He smokes rocks, man," he said. No one ever knows anyone in the ghetto, but they have all done "business" together. United in ignorance and prejudice against what they have been told whites are, and against themselves. Riddled by hatred and the want of supremacy, forever dividing us all. As I was leaving the shadows and the chosen life of these betrayers, a Rasta approached me, and lied to me about the amount of weed he was trying to sell me. But I gave him $40 dollar for a gram and a half of the best weed I ever smoked. One tiny hit and I was in a type of mellow, peaceful heaven-esque intangible place that gave me natural access to my spirit which felt so peaceful. It was for this that I took the risk of walking into the cave without light. I never once felt anger for what the nice man had done. I never once regretted the observation and fascination of the absolutely human lifestyle I was allowed to witness. To do anything for money. To crave power, and having, above all else. Well, what did I care...It was stolen money anyway. Why would I waste my time running down the man that stole from me, running him down with the strength of my rage. I didn't have the rage to use anyway. I did not hate him. I did not crave that money like these dealers did. I do not do anything for money, just what I can rationalize, and never without compassion even or especially in war. I forgave him when it happened because I know that I too am, and you are, capable of surviving, even though my style is far different. I know that I am human, exactly like those participators near my life that night. And I know that his life has no honor or depth in its hope. His avarice for supremacy has already damned him to the curse of wanting, a trap people don't realize until they look into the moment of their dying. To me, the hundred and twenty dollars he ran off with was a fair trade to know the darkness in the thoughts of these men trapped in the circumstance of fearful poverty. To know what fear makes us. To see the choice of desiring as a lifestyle," Priest, but sounds like the same rebel voice of The Father.

"Often times it seems that it is not the actions that we commit, but the reasons for why we commit them. But that too is wrong. It is easy to think it. It seems it is all just a way to feel justified. Just a way to try and pretend that we are all just gods over everything else. Truly, I have never seen any right or wrong in this world. I have only seen want and the desire to be what we are not. We will all suffer so long as people want to keep the illusion of their own greatness and enforce the illusions of their own greatness into the minds of others, and mass murderers; in politics, on playgrounds, or in movie theatres; and serial killers often try to prove that illusion of safety is fake and the Universe is unpredictable and power is fake," Father.

"You and I have drive to fight. Drives to be heard. But it is without gain. It is a work of goodness. It harms us to be heard because the Dark Society won't let itself be criticized," The Priest.

"Oh yes, the Dark Society...The dark criticizers are part of the disease whose cynicism furthers their own comfort. But we do not seek power or control with our criticism, we seek independence. We seek a stop to the drive for power. We don't seek a majority to rule a democracy. This is the difference in our side. It has no loyalties, only truths based on observations, an individual's wars set to join and make the wars and peace of the time" Father.

"A psychic once told me to be wary of two men. Both dark, with dark hair. One short and one tall. I think that that night with those men, in those allies, was the situation I was supposed to be careful in. The whole situation felt like a vision. It was slow and calm, even though I was obviously in danger. I believe that moving passed this situation led me to this moment, and to any other moment after that moment. There are absolutely people that somehow feel their way into the time stream and can see futures and pasts, and it will remain unproveable. Most people imagine they can have visions of the future with the illusions of the mind, people can make themselves believe anything, but to actually do it is far different. A wise person can tell someone with real knowledge. The person with the real knowledge generally does not see an advantage to it. I know that through my own spiritual advances that I have gained nothing useful, nothing that would give me a real advantage over anyone. I think it's uselessness how we can know that something is real in the spiritual world. The advantage is only to ourselves, in that we are closer to uniting the spirit with our physical and mental consciousness," The Priest.

<u>REVOLUTIONS</u>
<u>AND</u>
<u>THE REDISTRIBUTION OF WEALTH</u>

"The problem with Revolutions is that all they do is redistribute wealth. It is the system of wealth that we must break away from. How do I lead a revolution where wealth is not desired? How do I build an army without using greed and power to entice them? Only the Best of HumanKind would choose to fight a fight for nothing. For Equality. For Freedom, by itself," The Father.

A RECOUNTING:

I would train only at night. Punch at the dummy through darkness. I knew that the majority of my enemies would be encountered when the world was dark. And if I fought anyone in the light the advantage was all the better. I made up a Reason while speaking to you. I trained at night true, but for no Reason. I have no Reason, I have reasoned myself thus. The advantage is mine because of the circumstances of my mind, preferring to train in darkness, hidden. But I could see every advantage to everything. Even though I never sought them. Situations have been presented to me throughout the course of my life. I judged these situations based on many things, with more depth and levels to thought than anyone could know. And I gained advantage to building the society of myself. A Free society. With the only person that would never oppress me, myself. Advantageous yes, but for no Reason, just to do my best at making a world I believed in. I believed the lies of the Teachers that told me I could be anything. I know they are some of the ones that fear most the people that have advantage over them. Why would they gain advantage over so many lives?..I do not need society. I do not need to choose to live in this cell, and be fed and protected from elements. My advantages are great because I have nothing I need to control, nothing I need to seek power and place over. I rank highest in my world. And I choose to share my culture of myself with other nations that are another Person.

If you function from the place of purest intentions, even though you are advantageous, you will have to justify your advantage to the weaker minded...People don't like it when there is no way they can have more power than you so that they can feel safer. .... If there is something you need to do. I mean something for those you love. For whom you've vowed. Something hard. Then you can do it. You can do it because of your nature. I can do it because of my nature. From the root of Love. And you create your Reasons from that point than people will believe in your Reason. No matter what you do. This is my advantage. I do not use it for Power. I use it for Freedom. I gain no Power.

MORAL: The advantage is factual. The Reason is a lie.

MORAL: No Reason is needed if you do not have to justify yourself. You must not fear the power people seek over you. It means nothing. If you want, your will can destroy it. Take no power from it.

"No one will believe in you until someone else does. An authority must tell them you are valuable. Do not look to those you love for support. Those you love will always doubt you, because secretly they believe that they are the most correct, and their inferiority complexes make them create the shaky illusions that they are older, smarter, wiser, richer, cooler, than you. Why do you think they push their opinions on you so sharply? Why is everyone else always right? You can look at no one honestly that ever placed themselves in a position of authority over you. This is the disease of authority. No parent, no older brother, no relative, no older sister, no teacher, no commander, no boss, no employer, some masters...no one that could help you will help you. If people around you haven't been humbled enough to know you as a human being, to respect you because you are simple, than people around you don't really love you. They love themselves, and they are waiting for you to please them in the way they have been taught to as they respond to the looks of others. You should seek those that don't feel that they have to be in any rank, where no judgment exists, where right is not sought or enforced. It is up to you to muster belief in yourself. The road is long and stupid. You will not likely ever realize you have always been on it. It is too bad to be lost and not know it. Because when you do step to this path, but stepping away from all the rest, it really is much more beautiful, and it yields you the ability to choose any and all other paths," The Father.

"Meditation is the art of changing yourself to suffer less," Father.

What are your actions doing to the people around you? NOT what are your actions doing <u>for</u> the people around you? Is the person that hurts people that you love the most is you? Isn't it worth a shot to try and stop you? To save people around you? It is hard, but it is not dangerous to attack your own mind.

THE OLD ADAGE OF FEAR FOR/IN FREEDOM

"Do you remember when the government, meaning the police, convinced a world that it would be safer to everyone if they drove in clear cars. Remember. The best way to take someone's freedom is to appeal to their fears. Then you don't have to take it. When people are controlled by fear they give their freedom away. None of these showman that offer you eternal life can give it to you. Turn away from the Reasons stemmed from fear. Keep your freedom. It's too late. We drive in plastic, see-through cars. Do you know why people are such assholes when they drive? Because they feel safe. They feel safe because they have a certain amount of privacy. A piece of a barrier. People feel just a little invincible in their cars. Fantastically so. It is awesome to travel at speeds we were never designed to. To pull loads only slaves could. We designed the world. The world that will kill us all. This time is over. It came. And their was nothing you could do to stop it. You are one of the People. The Populace. A tool. A nobody. You have no army to fight it. You are no King, you've been robbed from too much. And there is no army worth siding with. This is the way to absolute freedom. These are the only ways to win the war to freedom. Turn away from cities. Take with you what you can, leave behind what you can't. Teach yourself survival. ***Live cheap and rural, keep your freedom in that community by working online. Start humble with idling ambition, always ready to rev.*** Don't assume in your arrogance that you already know how to survive. If you think that, you should be fighting in the wars, and if you think that and you are not fighting, than you are a coward, and a detriment to everyone that left, and if you come here you will be killed. This is the way of Heroes. One's that risked comfort and ease and no-thought. Those that turned back. Because their was no nature in man anymore. No. Not even I will leave. I'll be here, trapped here, in this remote desert prison, when the world ends. As the temperature rises, and the guards die off, I will cook and starve here. All I can do is let it go.

We always think we will live longer than we will. We plan our lives like we are immortal. Never accepting our own deaths.

What?

Where are we? Who has been talking? Was it me? I struggle so hard to find out, do I really have to know. No. My brain is passed its usefulness," The Father, the taste of Zarat in his mouth.

"I like to watch television shows that make me have new thoughts. Something so deep it creates things in me as a result. Those writer's are my friends." The father writing about The Industry.

THE GENERATION OF CHILDREN
To Continue at Length Elsewhere

"The lives that have fallen in the course of this war for deeper meaning have found a common enemy in The Generation of Children.
After the second great war the country began to live in economic abundance. And generation upon generation has deteriorated in wisdom. I was fortunate to know some that fought the great physical war, the last of the unspoiled, a generation enabled by the New Deal. However, it was this great generation that first failed their children. The baby-boom generation was the first to be taught nothing. If a child cried, if a child wanted and screamed to have, then the child was given. Given the desire. With no lesson. With no wisdom. And the shallow ways of thought and instant gratification began. This is the curse of Capitalism, of only money worship, of only self satisfaction worship. Everyone is in their way and it does not matter if they are in anyone else's way. Watch the nature of the bicyclist. A Dark Way about them. We must share the road, and they are in it. People bring selfishness into everything, like a child does. There have been too many generations that know nothing. That know less and less, because the world must be censored more and more so that they are comfortable, which gives them anxiety later. But first done so that they don't feel so afraid, or angry and then violent, but for some reason the fear continues to grow and grow. The selfish eyes of want assume more and more authority. And nothing prospers or takes more power in the childish system of Capitalism than the child that acts only for itself. The Dark Society must change everything about itself to not warrant destruction from the other children it robs from. They are doomed, as are the children that will whine for their suffering that will follow," That Father. ***Here The Father is wrong, but won't and couldn't apologizes for it. Perfection is in no way what he wants or could ever expect. Generations in a free speech society and education society as this one can be seen if chosen, are better and better than every generation before them, and the Youth should be massively enabled.***

The intellectuals cannot find the answer. They make everything too complex, too distant, not as basic as living what they read accounts of. They cannot understand simplicity, impulse, and instinct, interlaced with hone interactive training in multiple sides. Their own coveted minds are their trap. Constantly thinking, wanting to be the ideal they have imagined, but there is a path to the dreams of the imagination. The Police, the Military, the People that control are controlled by the assumption that an officer in assumed authority operates better if he does not know the law or that there were eight sides to it before the last draft of it. These are the mindless tactics of power and manipulation. It comes from the theories of Freemasonry and the pursuit of Power and CONtrol. Everyone who is supposed to help you is disenchanted and cruel and usually very fat, because they try to fill the emptiness with something, but for some reason... the emptiness is never full. Everyone that you can see that "can" lead you, help you and "free" you...every religion, every government, anywhere that there is power is the impulse to propel the institution. To build. To escalate the cause. It is the nature of every organization. A society has been made where Imperialism, the Will and Want to dominate, is programmed into it. An organized group always leads to oppression. Always a majority is sought and always are we that seek it so driven by the inertia of building it that we rollover and crush what is different from it. It is why our revolution is built to fail. So it doesn't happen again. Look at us, we're all dying in it.
What if there was nothing to follow, nothing to join, nothing to validate your existence? What if you didn't give these good intentions of mass organization power. Only you can follow nothing. Only you give power. But you can't stop. You won't stop. No one will. The world will be destroyed by the arrogance of everyone that wants to save it. It is programmed into HumanKind. You cannot save us. Any of us. You cannot save yourself or your family. We are destined to fail. And there is nothing wrong with that. Man is not supposed to seek winning. We are all losers. And we can only

offer ourselves to those we love to ease them. Or you can make it worse. Either way...I suppose...no amount of thought can justify it or dismiss it. That's the point. It is ultimately...beyond us. I cannot stop it. I cannot stop them. I cannot stop You. You are going to hurt and damage everyone you love, and build resentment for justifying along the way, because people of this Empire are Winners and we are ashamed that everything is not how we imagined its perfection. Convince someone that everything they thought they were they imagined. They created a fake image in their heads of their ideal, but not intentionally like an Us whom Exist can, and in a way that it controls them. Imagination keeps us from the truth that we don't have to be anything...we don't need a title or a job, or family, or a car, we don't have to be---anything.

If you are reading this book and agreeing with it than you are going to waste your life trying to avoid authority. You will criticize it and hate it, and you will never start the war within yourself. To not let authority condemn you to the scheming to avoid it. Can you just not be afraid of authority? Can you just fight off the consequences? Can't you know that you shouldn't facilitate a lie of power and authority by validating it with a fight? If you are good at Existing you can learn the ability to directly replace and crush authority that assumes unto you. And if you are a great at Existing and know the real roots of Freedom you will have reason to keep it. You would never let Power take your Freedom and force you to waste your life. Don't take their power so personally, it will not really touch you. The soul is unimprisonable. That is fact and your life is the precious, singular thing that the soul has granted us. And in the end we realize that we are the very thing that granted us the illusion of this world. Freedom is the truth.

If anything has a name you enjoy, or an appeal in the market, it is your enemy. Never follow it. It is designed to manipulate you. All of it. Anything on TV. I know I was in Television. Everything horrible has been dressed to steal money or servitude to a cause. You worship everything that harms you. And there's really nothing you are going to be able to do about it. Follow no one, especially not the most destructive tyrant in the world...YOU!. Of course. Be many things.

<u>Where it Goes is to Begin Again</u>

"When the People are over taxed the standing military grows. Pride makes them feel like brave men and women. And the People become oppressed. Militaries only oppress. The formation of them is always bad, even if they are for defense, the fear of another attack will lead to the oppression that sought power over the original nation. These are results. Clear results. A cyclical rebalancing of who gets to feel secure. Something is not working in maintaining the free society. An armed populace is important, an education in personal combat is important, the training of the mind to be able to release the animal that can kill and how to subdue it should be taught in a free society. And in a free society it can actually only be offered, but Equal training leaves no person above another. The world needs more education in all things, without biases or slants, to be equal. Facts. To stop the rise of power, to stop the security of all militant/armed forces...these are reasons a free man kills. Wars. And a tyrant seeks sensation of herself," The Father still fighting for his men. Still bleeding from his heart for his Cause. Does he weep for Physical Freedom still? He will never know it again.

NOTABLE INTERFERENCE:
"My x-wife would speak to me sometimes, and I would realize that she was *rap*ping up a thought, and she had been talking to me for several minutes, and I missed it all, my mind was *lf*uttering so fast, and I wasn't listening to her beautiful, loving, glorious majestic words. What wasteful thought," The Father.

Echoes of Her. Of the mind She left me to develop. To bring to this man, to this moment, to philosophize some answers. To try further. Mischief maker. Still playing her games for no reason, but it is nice to hear Her laughing so happily.

<u>I am No Man.</u>

I had to be 100% individual. Independence was a way of life for the necessity of the philosophy. I had to be able to go in every direction at any time. To be true and open to the randomness of the idea of freedom, and to fearlessly let great moments sweep us away, while we hold our heads up alert in our minds. Be the person that someone wanted to see so that they would trust me, always out-matched and expecting our failure. Make the image for their greedy, half-wit minds. That are offended when you show them the kindness in the comedy you used to coddle them into brazen Freedom. They got a little closer, until they were inevitably displeased. I never had the benefit of assuming an image of a group. It was not easy for me to join anything, which means get any kind of job. I could, but didn't like to emulate what people wanted, but that was different on stage. In reality I tried to be as genuine as possible, constantly busting myself on delusions of philosophy, even as the showman in me played to each individual audience for their joy and their pleasure. Something made me into what I am so that i could be what <u>I</u> am. Every interpretation sticks together as proof of my existence, and it shall all unravel, as proof of my non-importance. I was forced to yell at the dim and arrogant mockers and posers that I needed to use and I had to explain to those I needed to love. There was a lot that I could be, and I'm pretty sure I was most of it. That means, a lot of people Got Free.

"Spoke The Father," said the Priest.

"Sorry. I forgot what I was talking about. It happens all the time. When the path is toward complete peace and actual contentment, then the natural course is to let thoughts fall away. To not be controlled by the illusion. Though my mind is brilliant and it should be easy for me to believe in it, I must not, thoughts fade away. But the proof that this path is supreme lies in the fact that it does not bother me. I am quite aware how absolutely fine it is. I have no fear of what .I am., and how I may not exist. Most people would be bothered by not being able to try and be the most right all the time. But the practice of truth and freedom, without power, by use of the silent mind is most great," the Mindless. "And it saves you from the Great Tragedy as Buddhists say...in America we just call it serial killing and mass murdering. Heroes go BEYOND the nothing and leave the pornography of power, away from the capital you may wield." If Love and Compassion aren't used per Individual then self-worship and self-destruction while destroying all around, all that is now imagined as nothing, the wrong nothing, can occur."

Wrapped in a dream machine:
The rage in the flowers' screams for pandas to express a rocket into the moon bouncing confetti from microwaves into our brilliant sparkling eyes everywhere!
Shake that Paprika, Mr. Kon.
This would be one of those things, Internety-type side-quests.

"Throughout the course of a person's life the second phase of the beginning, the adolescence, is spent defining one's freedom. Healthily, one breaks away from shame. Healthily, one inquires questions to the deeper level of consciousness. One uses the mind to form idea, new idea, fresh idea. Healthily, a person grows. Until... until...that which propels society more quickly into darkness than anything comes and kills a person's mind. A person evolves until the shame of a life explodes into the life of a free person. Until, a person becomes a vast and terrifying hypocrite. People's lives die when their children are born. When they are trying to build and gain and have. When they fear death greater and greater, because they fear the death of their own children. Shame and fear have destroyed the natural course of human life. These children that grow that take a person's life and make it something it should not be because the parent thinks that they cannot be human they trigger programmed shame to burst. The avarice hypocrite parent resents anyone that does not make the same sacrifice and cater to the satisfaction and ease of their already dying children. The madness is hidden sharply behind the eye of the Dark Society's parent. And the growing children that will rebel against the shame, will lose their spirit to their own children. Because they will become what is familiar, and safe to them. They become oppression again and again, but hiding their masturbation in the garage. They create themselves as an authority. Children are the biggest threat to the world. The more spoiled, sheltered, repressed, they become the more their minds will mutate into deeper and deeper malice. Crying to have whatever they want. And what they want is constant satisfaction. The Generation of Children. Children that are shocked to see sex, to see penises, vaginas, peeing, shitting, throwing up, conflict, arguments, and yet worship these thing they repress...thus is the nature of repression. Thus is the nature of shame. It makes all societies dark. And it makes the weakest members of society breed for the right to care and be cared for. People have children now to have authority, and they think it is by love. Though love will come later...as a person nears and eventually accepts that the world is fleeting away; however, this is not the same as accepting death. People induce their own shame for the sake of their children, and they damage their children. Only as time goes on in a life and a person is forced to let shame go so that their children can wipe their leaky assholes do people begin to become free, and eventually they are forced into the freedom of their own feebleness. This is the way of Darkness, of the life that struggles against everything for dominance, and the gradual acceptance that they are not all powerful and that death is coming. This is the path of fear. And the most fearful always breed first, they want to matter completely to something, and this pride, this greed, this craved approval, that is enforced on everyone the parent encounters, is the root of Darkness itself. Darkness spreads and spreads and prospers, like un-insightful stupidity, because it is rooted in the family unit. It is rooted in the hypocrisy that crushes the lies of programming that a child is forced to take by the failings of every parent that has betrayed truth to create a more comfortable lie for the sake of a child. Children induce fear, do not fear your own death or the death of your family. Both are traps into shallowness. I am not saying don't breed. I am saying <u>fix yourself before</u> you do and do not fear their pain. They will know pain and there is nothing you can do about it. Don't seek authority over others for their satisfaction or to try and make their place for them. This is Darkness. People seek all manner of control for the fear that they feel for their children. Turn away from power. Do not let children curse you. Be stronger. Let the fear go. And leave a future where children do not have to rise up against hypocrisy," Father, "The best people I know never had children. They never clung to the desire to live forever, to gain immortality through the spread of genetics. Heroes will always be those that have the least."

"From the moment a child is born he exists in the den of another that, so long as it can breed, will seek dominance and control over it sexually. All children are banned and controlled through sex. No sex in the house. No girlfriends. No porno. The sex drive must stay down in the den. Why? So you don't fuck what is his. So you don't fuck your sister. So you are not the buck. You can't see his dick. He does not want to see yours. Repression. Repression of his urges to rape everything he sees. This is the nature of a man. A natural design. And when repressed it often grows angry and obsessive to the point that he is mad from it, and if it comes up he feels so awkward because he knows the child might find out that he is a monster. Society uses shame to control the world of men and woman that know that all they should be doing is fucking. But! It is also a natural, self-induced repression that is partially functional in the situation. However, as we know, our programming is not the best, but we can change it...by accepting sex. Then, the repression of it wouldn't give us all Freud's disease or the more fun, maybe just as fun, sister/cousin fucking disease. But none the less, it will not stop the human instincts that want to breed, by breed, I only mean cum. But if we let our children go out and fuck when they were nine or eleven when they should be, then the world would be far less repressed. Educate them in birth control and STDs, and everything besides sex, and teach them where knowledge is kept. What if we were all cured, and we allowed ourselves to think?" Zarat. Still within the Darkness. Still unaffected by his malice.

THE EYES OF A CHILD

I was taught in this life, by the eyes of a Child that was dead inside, that no one can ever make me offer my life to slavery. I know that no government can force me into being anything that they want me to be. I cannot be oppressed. Why would I serve anything that I do not completely believe in. If I thought that this system was harming people around the world by bringing them into a forced rank of greed driven class I'd not offer my will to fight for the name on it's cause. Where a society that worships authority figures (the news, the detective shows, The West Wing) reaches for power and more security at the cost of their very souls. They gave up the chance to live completely happy. Appreciating the little thing of life. Loving. Doing what is really important. Thinking on your life, understanding your kids and your wife. If you didn't have to serve Capitalism to survive, would you? No...We'd all rather be doing something else. To keep the feeling of artificial movement going. And you serve those that control this brilliant weave of slavery that drives on every peasant's base desire to want to be a king. What is the Creature from Jekyll Island? Why would I serve what I believe to be a world of money? If money is the root of all evil, and the world becomes money, what is the world? What have you given up to survive in this world? My life is all that I have that is precious, and I risk it, because I know that when it ends, I did what I dreamt to do with it. I understand what Her eyes spoke to me. I understand my holy grace, that makes me nothing, but equal.

<u>More Enlightened and Dealing with the Darkness in People</u>

"Within the Dark Society people have been guilted into believing that we must deal with all the different, nasty, cruel people around us. It seems nice at first; everyone getting along, but the ego is still present, still being used and still filtering reality. What this does is create a society where cruelty cannot be fought it must be accepted. What people fail to understand is that abuse and the assumption of power and authority over a person does not need to be tolerated. The arrogance of the ego makes people think they are invincible, and since they are not receiving consequences for their rudeness and self absorption their egos grow and become darker and more and more shallow. These often upper economic class criminals speeding and dumping and cutting the corners of roads and financial forms never see themselves as criminals, probably someone's parents. These people of cruelty not only don't judge others (that doesn't mean they don't become easily enraged), but they also do not judge themselves. And so not even the person of shallowness can check themselves and ease the lives of those they think they love. As it spreads the society grows in its dominant attitude to satiate unchecked greed and other cultures suffer. Cultures without the power, cultures that have nothing to lose. Cultures without the Darkness of Empire. And they will fight at all costs, make strong reasons to fight against their fear, and they may win against technology even while using it, and they will fall for the same reasons the last fell. On the person to person front, when someone rests in that den on invincible (false) non-judgment, a quick punch to the neck often reveals the feebleness of their false security. And god won't help them as they might expect. Only man will try and convince you that there are penalties for living. There is little reason to let oppression reign over you by the falsely reasoned," The Father. "However, it is important to remember that those trapped, that you can now see, remind you of what you could not see when once your mind was trapped in the same consciousness, which is the chance to know Compassion."

<u>Women</u>

"Let me tell you something about a woman. All of 'em. Every one I ever loved. Every one that moved me and hurt me. They moved me. Changed me. The one's I spent the most amount of time with... the one's I lived with...gentled me. Taught me. Made me realize the limits I had, and kept me living when I was at them. A woman can teach you to understand. To tolerate. To hold dear and precious. The right kind of woman, even if you hate her in time, the right kind makes a man and never tries to. They changed me by letting me care about them. And for a man like me, that simple act of being there for that love to exist, whether it lasted or not, it saved thousands of lives. I would think of them when I held a gun to a man's head. It did not always save the wretch that would just come to attack me again and get paid for it, but sometimes I could see their potential to love and to be loved in just a tiny part of their soul, and in that, I would see myself. When I let myself love, when I opened myself to pain, that is when I truly began to make progress in the strength of what I can be. If I could let so much of my arrogance and inferiority go, that pushed me to violent frustration, that I would risk such awe, meant I could do anything. It is when I knew Nirvana was attainable," The Father, "At the same time I realized I'd damn myself and kill the world if those rare ones would live happier. Love can only give you strength."

You will rarely love a person completely, but parts you will find vast value in, enough to even make you feel Love to spark mercy without damnation. The best of who We are will Love him completely, lifetime over lifetime, merging into the circumstance of the renewing cause. Your devotion need not be absolute, change prevents cancer and rot, by preventing excess. Love hard when you are near.

Their Mirror of Balance

"I was a leader once, behind a camera, a gun, a penis, words, images, metaphors, and a smile. I found the strongest. I found the best because I have the ability to push people to the peek of their limits in what they can withstand. I find humor in it. I love it. I like to bring people to the point where they have no defenses. To where they are so disturbed that they give up. It is a short course. The point where everything they could say or do becomes futile. They become futile. At this moment in their reality maybe they will realize that they are not gods, and that they are not qualified to tell anyone what to do. How dare they assume power. Simply, my allies realize this. Simply, my enemies become more frightened and desire more control and want to stop me from ever speaking again. It is a good way to weed out the weak or just primed minds, to make them pop up and shout. To stop those here to look the part from infiltrating my group that would assume power over others, and bring it through their good intentions into Darkness. Freedom is always the main concern of the war. To free Man from Man,"

Said The Father,

*Within my ability to lead I find great weakness. I find that I take betrayal very personally. I hate from it. I am hurt by it. It is hard for me to notice this about myself, because I don't want to know this.

I don't want to feel weak, or vulnerable. But I am. If I notice this, perhaps next time, I cannot be so hurt. And I can be happy with any service that anyone would graciously offer me. I would not think on past betrayals in the darkness I sleep in. Maybe this will give me the ability to handle the criticism of other people. I know people think that is what it would do. I know people selfishly want me to do it. But will it make me more free from the weak tendencies of my own ego? Can I ease this reflex to defend myself? Of course I can. But it will take persistence. And I do not believe I would lose my preference for the people that stick by me and don't mock me. And surely I mock others. Surely this hurts them. Should I stop? Should I not push? I do it to help them, they must deal with my existence, just as I will be forced to deal with theirs. A constant push and pull between the egos of the worlds. Between the natural defenses against our vulnerability. It is amazing how we are programmed to survive. It is amazing that we gained so much consciousness that we can pull ourselves back from it and see it, ourselves on our own stage surrounded by living life. The bottom line is that I cause myself suffering, I take my own freedom to be happy, and I can end that, by letting others hate me, and letting others choose a different choice other than what I think is right, and by letting people laugh at me and with me. If I Risk this vulnerability I will be able to do more with less hindrance slowing me down," he thought 50 years ago... this day too, and before that, something close, some of the same words, but the same reinforcement of his own reoccurring, impermanent identity. One side, many sides, countering and balancing a single source, a human man, another homosapien, with or without a penis, and any color that could or has or is occurring on Earth.

<u>From His Chariot</u>

"I am the kind of man that possesses a natural demeanor that frightens most people, but there are those that are intrigued by it. Those that would die to adore it. It is a strong intensity. I have it in the depths of meditation. I have it when I sleep. Always. Laughing, at peace, coughing. There is great energy in me. It magnified upto its utmost when the Girl's eyes stole my life and wracked me with the shattering depths of absolute death. When a man with so much power in himself realizes that he has no more self-induced limitations, what can he do? But exist, like Arjuna. It is strong what I am. Sometimes it requires great concentration to control. I have only succeeded in doing this by knowing that it was not real. I could not believe in my own magnificence that is present as a fact right inside me. By letting its power wane. If I had let it use me for the securing of power the awards from the other path that I have gained would not have been so great. The treasures of the soul are rich indeed. Better than what man has made up. Most people will not let themselves die enough to realize what sort of majestic incommunicable madness is within them and is manifestable as Creative Force. Most people that feel it get destroyed by it. Most people cannot face the death of everyone they love. Most can't think about it. But I have swam in it. I became what all men are looking for and all men constantly run from," The Father.

"The Rapture," The Priest.

Choosing War

I made war against the Dark Society of Failed Democracy when the government became more powerful than the People. When fines were exorbitant and penalties for accidents and happenstances and free choices were lifetimes in prison. The FBI kept pushing too many people to keep looking for what was "wrong," and that type of vengeful thinking rampant in freemasonry always leads to prejudice and the reason the man and Girl that can commit acts without a reason, the mass murderer and the serial killer and the political revolutionary, the Creationist, are all given the reason to end the illusion and assumption of judgement and authority the FBI freemasonist assumes when terrified. It didn't matter if I lost this war and was imprisoned for my positive nature. It didn't matter because I was already a slave to a system where too many people sought power. Where every side had power. When every opinion had a contradicting penalty to every random circumstance. The Prideful took every shape and chose every side of every Reason. And I too chose my Reason to follow my ego's natural nature to want to war and to want to have the comfort of Freedom for myself. I was part of the problem, because I had not fixed myself enough to not want so badly. But I fought power, and I justified myself that way. Choosing and unfolding a life that was identical in impulse to every other action of Darkness. When the Dark Society left me in shackles to be at the mercy of those nasty Prideful souls on every side that acted with cruelty and avarice, while driving, while speaking, while bossing, while stirring in anger...I was a slave because they knew that it was legal to be Prideful and cruel and they knew it was illegal for me to do anything about it, like end it.. The Prideful think, "What are they going to do about it? Kill us? Ya right." I loved that look in their dead eyes when I would become free from a single person's bonds. I loved the ease of knowing that I would be more free because that person's smugness was gone, and the world was slightly more free. I was not bound by law, or the fear of the law's illusion of presence, I was free to have cause and to end each life that threw nastiness

in my face and were offended that I did not eat of it. I warred for the right to have Just Cause, without prejudice or resentment. I warred for the right to not have to deal with their Pride. Death is the bringer of Peace and the cure for Pride. But...it makes prideful vengeance in return...and the killing does not end, because more and more Pride grows. War never stops. From generation to generation we are oppressed and vengeful and militant forces grow to support it and the world always suffers, because no one will realize that they are the Darkness. War...prison...failure...all inevitable goals of my life and my demise that I saw from the first breath of Freedom I had. In the Dark Society only the Prideful win and the Free and the Holy Powerless are crushed under the fearful random judgment of those that think God is as disgusting and oppressive as they are. The cycle roles on, and Philosopher after manipulated Philosopher fails again and again, unable to convince weak that find false and fleeting comfort in power that sets them preaching.
:Father:

THE HIDDEN TEACHING

"All people have the ability to think of any situation in a way that would frighten them. The key is to direct your mind in a way that is not afraid like a coach simulates to a team. The trick is to teach yourself how to do it. See how to raise the emotions of heroes or the peace of monks. The best way is to direct your reasons towards stillness you can feel inside yourself. It eases the mind so it becomes more noticeable and malleable. Everything can be affected by conditions and if you can change the conditions on your mind then you are a Master. Learn to let go of emotions. Learn that emotions occur as responses of fear, pain, survival, pleasure, etc. The body and the emotions are not who we are. We can release emotions as easily as they arise, and as we teach ourselves we can build a reflex for it. The world can be peaceful. What you think you are is only an instinctual reaction to dominate and your reasons and your beliefs and your mind, are a byproduct of the initial instinct to need to survive at all costs. You are free to end your war against humanity. You can stop having to make the world in your image. Know stillness and know god, know the inner world we can control. Know the glory of true reality, a reality of the soul controlling the emotions and tendencies of perception. The soul is unafraid and benefits nothing, so it is free to know love without the bias of seeking advantage," echoes in the annals regurgitated by dimming reflection, hoping that one ricochetting tone will break through your filthy crust and blind you into reality.

There were times when the silence would strike me in a different way. In a very calm, very slow, very masterful way. In a way where when I am attacked I see everything that moves at me. I stare to the center of the body and remain calm. I watch, I hear, the twitches of the body. It is as if I see the same simple movement a thousand times at once in a time limit that is not nearly as long as a pulse. Some of the madness that was attracted to the campo...Some of them influenced my reflexes to turn into this animal of absolute Will. Will is all one needs to succeed. I saw a nation of bullies. A nation of weaklings. Hiding behind what they see as invincible. Like I haven't been programmed, by myself and others, to go further than they would. Like all I would do was talk and maybe break a window. All I had to do to win every situation was have the will to see that I am no man's slave and I will be free and anyone who seeks power over me will lose their power. That is all. Yet I collaborate exceedingly well, with the exact same principle. I have never lost a fight, though I have failed uncountable times. And still I gained nothing from winning, save my eternal Freedom. That which was enchanted to me by something I cannot even imagine. Something with an echo that strikes you infinitesimal. Am I the epitome of what is Existing? Who cares, it isn't the movement. I am free and am free of the need to win. If I am not truly threatened nothing happens. I am not afraid of the frightened squawking of the (how do I feel about them) (what do they make me feel) (Feel your hatred for their animalness) (For their lack of Being) (Are you afraid of them) (Ask deeper) (No fear, Hatred without Fear, strange) fucking meat. I can end any battle whenever I want. Fear is all they have to survive on. I am limitless. I am their natural superior. A natural Over-Man. And they, simply, are not, but want to be, they want to not feel afraid. Nothing strikes more fear into a person's heart than seeing someone that is stronger than they are, nothing makes a person want to assume power over that person of strength more, nothing turns them into more of a frightened rat. And I never even did anything. But when they rise it to a head, when they push too far.. I end it when I see that there is no way for them to recover from their inferiority complex. How sad. Unlike them, I would have never thought to have hurt them. I never had the fear to think that. My mind is stronger, my soul is wiser, and my body is quicker. I have yet to be proven wrong. And if I am killed I lose nothing, but I fight like I have nothing to lose. My Philosophy is Stronger. My Reason Greater. Freer.

This Audience got The General. One of his most impressive forms when set to absoluteness. This is the camp before the revolt that anointed the Girl with the sword and baptized The Father in innocent and Universal blood, that you witness inevitably led him to right here.

"Always, throughout the history of societies, the one thing that has led to revolution by the people is the darkness formed by the standing armies. The police forces. The forces that are used to invade other countries and care nothing for the rights of another country's people. The Dark Society, the one you live in, has always used it's standing armies for the profit of the few greedy in power. The Bay of Pigs, Panama, all wars in the mid-east, WWI, WWII, Vietnam, The Spanish American War, the Genocide of the Indians, etc., etc., every war the Dark Society has waged has been for profit, to open a market, to exploit someone else's resources. Before the Dark Society was corrupted by freemasonry 11 years after the Declaration of Independence was written by Thomas Jefferson, the Second Amendment granted the People the right to keep and bear arms, so that these standing armies would not form and oppress anyone. Now the guns are being taken away and given away from the People's hand, whom want less and less to do with the uncomfortable thoughts of reality. Fools and idiots become richer and richer. The standing armies are abused more and more. The armies, like the FBI, the DEA, the ATF, the military, are all mostly concerned with their own growth, power, and publicity. Darkness. Standing Armies should be the populace. Each person trained by its government (if it must exist) to defend themself. We war against all armies of all governments that assume power over anyone. These types of organizations are the root of all corruption, always, in every society, and the cause of every revolution. If the standing armies are disbanded there would be no more oppression. The oppressors would not be able to join these groups that use pride to manipulate idiots------and I would not have to kill them to defend my Freedom," The Father.

<u>Veils</u>

"The most threatening thing to a soul is the mind and the subconscious. Either can trap a person in a state of fear and pain. Either can mutate a person into weakness and strife. We must reach for the base consciousness. The state beyond this state of dreams and illusions. We must force ourselves to open our eyes and awake from the nightmarish suffering our own personalities force us into. Return to the state before a personality was laid over it. The deeper mind that can see the personality. That can see how the mind exists to carry out the function of a person. Believe in the state that exists if this personality that you currently believe you are was destroyed, be it from a blow to the skull or a blow to the nervous system or the nerves. The personality can fail, malfunction, but still consciousness remains in the body until the body fails. We may not know where we are from delirium, but we are still there. If we can shut off the mind, disconnect it, bypass it, if we can remember how to do it while in this state than we can be at peace with the dysfunction. But we must learn to do it before the time of this malfunction comes. Or we will not be able to learn. Only that person that is jolted into a state where the surface consciousnesses do not exist, such as death, or near death, or a type of projecting shock, will be able to find it in a malfunctioning state. It is much easier to find the path if you know what you are walking into, it gives us the state of faith. Individual faith heals us, no one else can," knowing this, but still hoping on the surface of reality. Hoping he can accomplish what he knows can be accomplished. The subtle wanting of a warrior. Like a bug on the water. Prayed the Father.

"If you believed in God you would believe in how he made me and what It is making me tell you. Or, are you only believing in yourself. See what you are seeing," The Priest. In a floating thought. Disjointed.

NOTE ON THE FATHER'S BEHAVIOR:
"There always comes a thought that occurs so loud and vivid to him that it makes him stop listening to me," The Priest. "Sometimes he notices when I stop talking. Depends on how long the thought is. His friends cannot mind, they lose no value, they only must speak again. And sometimes he must talk and then answer a question you asked when then he changed the subject. His mind was like a minefield, running out of it could lead to any manner of explosion, or chain of explosions."

"I have began to notice a change that has occurred in me as time has passed. I believe that the world tells a human the path it wants it to go. I believe that if one pays attention, If one is wise in how he sees events unfold, If one is deeply in touch with the spirit, And if one does not need to fight the natural course of this world's design, then one's own joy will take them to the greatest moments in the greatest places. Of course, the Existing know that it is because of the individual joy within them, makes the best of the greatest situations. Another person might not even notice it happening. But still there is a will that reveals itself to me as I delve deeper into the path of emptiness. Of no ego. Of silent soul. And when the dice roll, it will give me perfection, because I am at peace with my path, no matter what it is. I cannot lose. I always prosper, from the inside out, if anything pulls at me it will be what loves me and what I let myself love," The Holy Father.

"As in the physical world, things do not always go as planned in the dream world. Events that are not happiness inducing spring forth. Sometimes from the subconscious, sometimes as a warning, sometimes influenced by an outside energy...it does not matter for the most part. What matters is that, as in the physical dream world, while in the world of the projected body things may come that are supposed to frighten you. "Supposed" to frighten because one would naturally be afraid (of a fake threat to a fake life). But, in both worlds of perception, one can be within these more difficult events and feel no fear. One can think clearly and try to understand why the dream is happening. One may not be able to find the answer, but as in the physical world when harshness comes, the Master's heart remains calm. He can notice the rise and fall of emotions, if any. This is not the same as feeling nothing, which can be a common place to visit on this course of overcoming. One feels calm. And if one feels nothing, truly nothing, the void itself, then the technique of the Inner Smile is most useful. It is a technique where one creates a smile, a sense of happiness, across the void of nothing. This is when one realizes the powerless control of this path. It is up to the Master to make his emotions, to form his thoughts, and not let any world, or any authority (no matter how advantageous) take control of him. This is the way," The Father, awaking from the stillness of despair. "Things do not always go our way, but our perceptions, our inner peace, dictate our true reality, and what we will see with our own eyes. However, one should pay attention to what is happening in the dream world that is springing from the sub-conscious, it is likely telling the mind that a change in the simple path will be making the road more difficult, completely unnecessarily, like having to hide the truth."

Title Directed Toward Light:
COMPASSION AS RECALLED BY IMPERFECTION AS SHAPED BY PERFECTION
(Those that have)

Title Directed Toward Darkness:
A DREAM, A HALLUCINATION
(Those denied and those that must get)

"In a cell one has a natural path to growing detached, to overcoming the need to belong. All heroes want freedom most when they are in prison. And they defy oppression with the laughter they hear inside themselves. It always happens. The masturbating. Most begin ashamed and jerk under a blanket. Some become enraged and hurt themselves. Others shoot it into the walkway so that someone has to clean it up in front of them. My style varied. Or varies. Mostly I lay on the bed and turn towards the wall," Spaketh I, deliberately confessing.

PEN ON TOILET PAPER SQUARE:
I remember him...The Priest. He got me those red sheets from the monastery he lived at. No stains. If they were white sheets there would be huge yellowish stains that couldn't be washed out.

"I would turn against the wall and slowly stroke until I came when I was younger and people were about. It is easier and more kind to not make a mess, or flaunt it too much. We travel lightly, our bellies are tight. The past is saturated with beautiful events a free heart and mind remembers fondly, a mind at the end of this therapy we pursue. I become conscious of the guards as they pass. All of them look, at least occasionally, as they pass. The trick is to enjoy being seen. Other people naturally do, that means you can too, right now. That's a fact, if you weren't afraid and ashamed of a reaction with an audio vibration but no physical impact, a comment, an opinion, a fear the FBI put in their heads about their genitals and their children, and if you unleashed this sexual freedom now, you would likely lose control of it and harm someone or yourself, thus is the penalty to the techniques of shame and fear---repression. No one stops no matter who they think is out there watching or listening to them cuss, moan, or cry. It is hard to stop and easier if one chooses to not be concerned," myself.

Holy Shit! What the hell is this? A memory? Holy shit. I'm dead. I am remembering this event. In flashes. But...Oh No! What? How can I remember this if I don't have a mind? Where is this tattooed? How the crap am I thinking?? When will I know peace? When will I stop searching for myself? .... Who is that? Flowers without time never wilt.

GLOBAL WARMING, THE PROPHECY

The panic of global warming didn't come until the sugar crops died. When the flavors of the modern gluttony changed, when the people couldn't have exactly what they wanted a great cry of financial support and research began. Far too late. Not that they ever had the capacity to stop it, just the arrogance that made them think they could. As the waters rose across the lands, the wealthy began to build great pillars to support their new societies, bringing them closer to the hole in the sky where the stars now shine through. They used those poor to construct them and left them behind to live in the muds to live in the sky. If a "mud covered" came to the "surface" of society he was persecuted, sometimes dropped all the way back down to the gravity of Earth. It is foreseen that there will come from the mud to destroy those that live within the sky.

"There is a simple explanation presented for us within Catholicism that explains all of this. This life and death, this crying for our loss. It is in the often misunderstood Holy Trinity. The Father. The Son. And the Holy Spirit. There is a Father, a great essence of the universe that gives life to living beings. There is a Holy Spirit, that which is within all living beings, the portion of the Father. Then there is the Son, the incarnation, the living being itself. The Son, the human we are, is a functioning earthly body. It wants, it cries, it suffers, all for its primary purpose, survival. It is this survival that preserves life. We cry when life ends because our humanness naturally wants, it wants what we have built love for to live, and we fear death, so we want to live forever. However, the body, the Son, will die, whether you want it to or not. But the Holy Spirit, that which does not need to want, because it does not need to survive for any purpose, will continue on. For it was the Holy Spirit that gave its essence to a living personality, that was able to exist on Earth in a functioning form. So, at the end of our incarnations, where we embodied these personality types, we are released from the body in the form of the Holy Spirit, which we have always truly been. It is at this instant that we realize that we are that tiny piece, that essence of all things... we know that we are God. And we know that God is Love. God does not judge or condemn, it has no fear, so does not need to protect itself, because that form you don't die from but you're born from and die to. Human consciousness is supposed to not understand why it has been forsaken. We are supposed to be angry and forsake God in times of suffering, this is the nature of natural human survival. The suffering of old age is our opportunity to surrender to this truth because we do not wish to live anymore. We realize that we are not this body through the course of pain. The Son is supposed to ache. But the Holy Spirit knows, without want, that it is free and it is light with love, because it does not need to survive, it never needs to dominate. The trick while living is to realize this. This is the path of Holiness, when we get past the want and desire of humanness and know the calmness of the soul. This is how to pray, how to be with God. We will always be with the person that has died, because they too are the Holy Spirit, they too are a piece of ourselves. They too lived the journey of spiritual consciousness within a personality, facing circumstances falling randomly in time In our body, in our soul, in our omniscience. Never separate from life, death, or God, regardless of what we might think.   This is what we are…The Father, The Son, and The Holy Spirit. The Holy Trinity."

Peace be with you.

Being with him is making my voice stronger as I am simply there, performing, the words that Audience needs to hear to make the same feelings of pin shattering Equality their enemies need too.

The Consummate Romantic

"Do you think that it is possible that you could love someone so much that no matter what happened to the soul that you would be naturally drawn to that person? That your desire to just be with that person, led by the non-selfish reasons of love, would put you near them, just so you could have the honor to serve them?" The Father.

"The soul does not care about the sacrifices made in a life. A soul cares about love. It loves it. It worships the very purity of what it is. To a soul it is the only thing in the Universe that is real, undying and possibly not subject to evolution. So, yes, I think the soul can go wherever it desires. I also think that hatred and absorption in the desires of the body can trap you and damn you to the trap of being human. Trapped by the life, by the life, that you believed in too much, that you sold everything valuable for. I believe that selfish desires, regardless of action taken or not taken, weigh heavy on a soul and cloud the unity with what God is, and can't be named as," The Priest, "But how do you convince a human being that being a human being is not important, and that everyone they damn with disapproval or imprisonment, or better as worse, did not deserve it?"

"How do you tell a society that tortured the Earth, and every civilization it has come in contact with that it is not God. And why, why, why! does it happen in every society? Why is man programmed to destroy itself to regenerate the planet? And why would I be cursed to be one that can see it? Why can't I blindly have and want and need and desire? Why is there always a Socrates, or a Nietzsche, or a van Gogh? Or the other countless we haven't been brainwashed with by those making speculation of the great and dead," Father.

"The majority of the Dark Society doesn't even know what it serves. It serves because it is easier to buy yourself off with what you want. It is easier to not think. And when they do think, they think from fear and greed and oppress us all," Priest.

"A great man serves. He never leads. I think a lot, so I worry a lot. I worry that my thoughts need to be thought out more. But I have always had the ability to instantly silent my doubt. I have always had the wisdom needed to bring myself into a higher consciousness to act. Most people can never bring themselves out of their fear induced thought to finally do what they dream to do in that moment, the secret noble and may be vengeful, fantasy the mind has waited for all of a person's life. I can ignore the exaggerations of the penalties. I know that exaggeration is the main way to control. I know that the illusion of presence is a tool of the tyrants that run on Militant Orders. I know the world is not as dangerous and my enemy is not as powerful as people think it is. I have led men to die because they knew that I would act whether they were with me or not. I would fight. No matter what. I don't brainwash people into fighting with me. I never manipulated the easily controlled mind with lies and illusions of glory and stature. I showed genuineness while I bled and bruised, and sometimes vomited, with them. No man ever fought for me. He fought for himself. And we fought beside each other. Both of us choosing to live better or die," Father.

Neither spoke for a time, just because neither had anything to say. It was noticeable that there were no other noises. All happenstance of the normal life of the prison sealed away by a large white steel door. Both men took such shallow, gentle, slow breaths. Sometimes not breathing at all. You can tell a lot about a person by how they breathe. Trapped, and free to walk...but The Father would not walk away from the medical care he sought when he chose to surrender for crimes he won't ever confess to. No Hero confesses, madmen confess, and these Heroes have never been them even though they have played them.

"I never feel trapped in here," Father, "Well unless I find myself noticing it, but it is easily released so that I don't have to be burdened by the illusion of walls, there are so many walls in my mind I have had to break, I have never been free. I know it is an illusion because I know that we are never ever truly free. We always serve something. Always. Even without a moral or governmental opinion. We would still have to serve the body. Serve it food, often sex, we are forced to breed, forced because we want it so bad, crap and piss. And all that. I find ease because I know reality. We are all slaves. So it is all right that I am here. I am finding out many great things by studying myself," Father.

"I live by what I have learned. Not by something that I fabricated or believed on "faith" or manipulation so that I could feel slightly more comfortable in my unknown life. People fabricate direction so that they don't think about its futility. Their conditions are so fragile and life strikes them hard when it shatters their lies. Reality is too hard for the entertained society to think on, even though reality is simple, but there are many minds and few opinions. But the observation of your true reality is the only thing that can lead you to truth. Even with a guru, or someone of spiritual caliber, you can still only trust what you can teach yourself, maybe they didn't go far enough, and age is zero proof. Maybe there is more. And absolute honesty is the only way to know it. Gandhi said to conduct Experiments with Truth. Reaching to discover that we, a mass of individuals, in the reality are what we are all fighting against. The clash and the dance of the egos, " The Priest.

These texts are like a castle. Cold grey bricks, by brick by brick, adding to a known image thought far too long ago. I know from ancient texts that 2000 years ago the mindset of the world powers and the world's impoverished were poised in the exact same arrogance. And Philosophers emerged to reason. Many by the armchair, reasoning with whom they knew. And some golden spewers of secret holiness and forbidden light strode high and hard and left echoes. And why are we Philosophers creating the same works and expecting the same results of poisons and stabbings and shots from psychotics trapped in images of power and place? Power cannot be glorified above the simple living form, people are believing too strongly in things that people made up. And they made it up for power and for peace at the same time. The ages of trickery and corporate visage must end. Or, I am sure you will murder another Messiah.

Get over words, stop reassuming a pride to die for, they are just sounds, it's primitive to be addicted to them, religions are trapped in dogma and the imagined written words that could have been made-up anywhere, suffering Jews. Release the words, silence the mind riddled with words, and see the familiarity in the breathing breath of another Living Being, without words, void of pride-stricken shame-enforced tradition. Dogma is Dead, or it continues to hang on to what it should just let go. Be free to move to a better neighborhood. Defending complexes what is simple to do. Youth can let go. The Open are Free.

RAPTURE

The churning chant of war in peace can't slow,
the emotions still manifesting in swelling whirls,
drowning the Witness while he floats to the surface.

Father held her bloodied head,
witnessed the dragon.
She had pretty eyes.

Stage of Alzheimer's is moderate decline.

Karma

"There are lies in Karma. Karma does not appear to have a ranking system. There is no penalty, but your own lack of peace. There is nothing better or worse than any other animal. One still has to deal with circumstance of their own physical reality (their "fortune") and they must deal with the setting and conditions of their own personality, be it any kind of animal. As any creature one can direct their thoughts to the center. But it is easier with a mind that can produce various and conflicting strings of thought. But then again, a simple man can know it precisely. All Karma is dissolved when we go deeper into the subconscious and we are able to see that we are the Cause of our lives. We are its purpose. And every reason we add to ourselves covers a reason of the subconscious. Why are you choosing what you are choosing? What insecurity triggers it? Find the insecurity and allow yourself to not be afraid to be different, or wrong, or punished. Exist calmly in every situation, with the knowledge that you can direct your mind towards stillness and experience your suffering with grace," Father Priest.

Think of Karma as any habitual behavior. Karma can also appear to be a societal sway, as deeds can weigh on the stress of other people and that can make them violent, meaning you were creating bad Karma. One thing Karma is not is a revenge system. It is not like heaven and hell or rewards and penalties. Karma can be over come in an instant when the ego is overcome. The feelings of others is not real Karma. And Karma can never catch up to someone, just the persecution of society can. Good Karma is no Karma, being free and Enlightened.

THE GOOD PEOPLE

"The more good, the more right, the more satisfied you feel, the more you have worshipped Pride. Darkness. The better you think you are the more people you have hurt, by not noticing the Yin that exists throughout your Yang, while being blind to your naturally occurring hypocrisy. If you think yourself good than surely you have never looked into your true intentions and reactions or you would know what a horrible person can be, and certainly has been. It is noticing this that allows us to change. Through the force of will we can let go. This is a technology for the future. It is not for sale. You can have it. Just choose to be a better person. We are born with egos, and egos are destructive, they consume and they survive and they very naturally defend. We no longer need to be so controlled by them. We Can Overcome. Forgive yourself for your natural power hungry nature, and start working on it. Come closer to the soul and the ego will have less control. Be 'good'. Be Free. Good Luck," The Father.

These are people, characters hide people's true intentions. These people exist, your opinion of them does not effect their existence.

"Within the realm of relationships, most people spend their time avoiding, hiding, pretending to be false, yelling, controlling, trying to not be taken advantage of. Darkness. Anger. Fear. We all need to stop being afraid of being humans, we need to admit that it is difficult for all of us, and we need to stop trying to make others please us. We are all dealing with the thought processes we can produce, riddled with the conditions that have formed our neuroses and idiosyncrasies. Stop fearing, lying, hiding and yelling. Then choose to be there or get out. Stop fearing what security is lost or who allows themselves to be emotionally damaged. We are angry when we are not free. We are in pain when we avoid pain. Truth always eases us. Speak," The Priest.

<u>A Heist</u>

There was one job that went down gracefully. I generally only took from the wealthy, as it gave me an illusion of righteousness that did not change the non-condemnable act. ***Non-condemnable because the authority of one moral over another moral is a lie. Judgment is a contradiction to morality, exactly like survival. Morality does not exist in a system that damns and punishes, as it is a logical fallacy in the meaning of a Free and Equal country.*** The heist came long after my financial victories in entertaining the mind so that it flickers money from the hands to get more and more. An old Teacher that fell prey to the image. An addict accusing others of being an addict of anything else. Like most of my crimes I stole the priceless piece to scar them, easily, without ever touching them. I cut their pride. I damaged their sense of what was theirs, and violated an illusion of secureness, of what they could own and keep forever. And it meant nothing to them. nothing. It was an object that is in no way themselves. But it was theirs. They want so hard, the arm of want has a hand that holds tight that clutter they want to define them as imaginarily as a tattoo covers an illusion. I could have lived on what it was worth for a year. It was worth 12k. And that would be living well. I would cut them because all they needed to not feel the wound was humility. Balance. But like others they too began to see the reasons for oppression, as they gained and wanted and believed more and more in the visage of the comfortable. I loved them this much to do this for them. I can love what any man can. Which means I can shape myself in a natural instant to use the reasons you thought were unique, but are common, to be what you are or to be anything. Everything We do is greater than the meaning you touch in the greatest deepest moment of your life.

I understand the many hearts of man. And I see a way for them to be free from the pain they cause themselves, and everyone else.

"People have lost the benefits of the loving heart. People do not have the courage to talk to another person about themselves. They more prefer force, or behind the back bickering and gossip, wasting their efforts in contempt and anger. Instead they could speak to the person, share their concerns, then listen to the reason for it, and try to understand another. Try to understand the self that is concerned of the method of living. Maybe you will find benefit and become something greater, something you did not understand," Blessed Father of the Clear and Caring Light.

***

"Someday you will die and your spirit will be free from your personality," he said once to an awkward boy.

***

"To learn anything you must utilize the technique of absolute faith, to become wise you must learn to doubt what you had absolute faith in," rules came from his sense of absolute equality where life would live beside one another without a need to take, control, or belittle to a place that doesn't exist. The tribe was monogamous mostly if paired off, but not if The Father was around. His sexual energy that propelled him through the hallowed annals of Studio hallways, that which his creative energy flowed from, that which is the source of his new material, would often find a Muse that someone else thought they owned, but he would remove fear with compassion and since the land was ultimately The Father's corporate sole's, love could occur quite naturally for this Hollywood man, never bound by a mother's and a wife's rules or threats to stomp off and cry, and not ashamed to mount and milk the imaginary owner either on a California coastline.

***

On a porch he thought-off: "The most surfaced of the consciousness seems to delight in torture. It seems to fall prey to torture. One should never trust any person that is on this level of consciousness, but this does not mean that you should not have compassion for

106

them. An example of such torture are chain letters, especially chain e-mails, that predict bad luck, or that if you don't forward it you don't love another fake God, and people feel wary, frightened, nearly terrified, because they fear misfortune so greatly. It is the same as fearing failure. Or fearing poverty. Or fearing hunger. It drives us to do great and horrible things to survive. Depending on the amount that our psyche can interpret, meaning at how many levels of consciousness it can see a situation, will influence the choice made. But the fact is, no matter what fate this life forces or you choose and take (it doesn't matter), if there is no fear, there will be less suffering, less avarice, less revenge, or resentment. We must not fear death. Except its inevitability as absolute and a closing fast fact. And prepare yourself to understand it, this will…" well, he can't give you the answer. The answer doesn't lie in words.

***

To a fearful dying man whom did not have the peace that comes from the cowards heart where a life was spent uncontemplated in the fashion of doing what one is told, "Forgive yourself. Would it not be easier for a god to forgive you if he can see the smile of an unburdened man?" Knowing that there was no judgment for living; knowing it would set his mind best for what was about to be. I laid my hand on his faintly beating heart. My eyes fell gentle enough to see and smell the light burning of his spirit rising. Burning up the last of the energy to give us the force to move out. His breathing, in the instant I touched him, slowed and softened. He knew no fear. He knew the peace of the spirit that he was realizing he has been all this time. Happy for the life of experiences and choices he got to make to unfold a story as significant and equal to all others. All amazing. All beautiful. And I wept for a man whom I would not care to know in life, but I wept for the beauty I felt his soul to be. For what I remembered in that instant I was. And for all he'd could have been should he not have stayed afraid when he first he became it.

***

The seconds that mean nothing that have no power mean so much in the stream of consciousness, in how it all felt and where the reverence fell for what we could see in front of us. There is a way to see this world in the state of perfection everyone wants it to be in for the comfort of their bodies. It is to understand that the perception must be deeper than the perception of the body can comprehend. Though difficult to understand if you do not know it. The way to understand any of these words that confuse you, or perceptions you just can't understand, is to do the following:

Sit. Stop trying to understand the words. Don't think about them. Be still. Exist in the very place that you are sitting in. For any thought that arises, use it to no longer have it, notice it, and release it. If it returns do the same thing. Focus on your body as an empty shell. A thing. Something you can be in. Don't be afraid. Continue. Focus on happiness. It is important to do this. Imagine a smile inside you. If you feel despair from the nothingness that your mind might think to be afraid of, silence it. Don't be afraid, focus on glee. Easeful glee, with the sensation of safety, you were young, remember joy you did not have to doubt.

You may return to your normal state by thinking of your human life, your body as a body. You can always do this. There is much to learn in the depths of ourselves. And you will know the consciousness these Great Books are directed towards. Remember always never to be proud of what you have achieved, always, always, always know that pride is the shallow-animal mind driving you into power and dominance. Never seek power, or you will suffer and suffer, especially with <u>this</u> knowledge. ~ **Spaketh**

STARRING AT A WALL, STANDING, HIS LIPS MOVE, HIS FACE AND BODY TWITCH, THINKING IN THE IMAGES OF HIS BLINDING UTOPIA

Every person falls into a realm where their logic is logical to someone else. Which means, every person has the ability and will use the ability to call another person that doesn't think with the same logic that they do---an idiot. My ego does it too. But I know it is doing it. But there are surely a great mass of people that are stupider than I am. Factually. Fools that cannot control themselves, people that cannot understand the deep complexities of the advanced emotion love. Those that don't see the logic in a smile and a long conversation. Those that can't sit beside someone and not speak to them. Their spirits are not less than mine, but I calmly crush their resistance to my single kingdom of Freedom. I wouldn't conquer their kingdom and I don't tolerate them conquering mine. I could leave here. I've thought it out. I might. But not likely. A cell is a good place for a dying man. In a cell I am free, I am alone, unafraid of my thoughts, free. I am naked. My old balls snug and warm in my hands. Never forgetting that I must live mostly in the realm of the spirit. The spirit that does not have a fear of someone's nasty reaction to seeing me naked in my cell. I have been beaten in three other prisons for not wearing cloths. Do you see? How they judge...how you fear...the vengeance you seek on others simply because you hate the human condition. Fear festers in snippety rule makers, that easily break rules. And rebels fight them, never realizing that they are using the same Pride. Endless is the wheel of shallowness. People living without Spirits. Cruelty in the smiling rot of teeth...Tell someone these things Priest...ramblings of brilliance. Peacefully dropped into the pit of dogs. Never realizing the pain they are making for everyone. Never realizing the damnation of thinking that Pride is God. But it makes no difference how the ego can construct the mind. Any ego can be shattered with the truth. Egos struggle to avenge themselves against my immovability. Every section of people seeking the ego and thinking it is the god of their random culture confirming them. A dark society breeds every entity dark, struggling to matter. Logic's oppressing. I see you watching me while I am thinking. Thank you for not hiding. I like you watching me naked. I've always loved to be seen. You think I might be mad, but I am just free from the other's fear, thank god that you see that. Dear Priest. Brother of honesty and light. See a world without insecurity. Behold.

Men have trouble getting laid because they don't know what a woman wants, because women, as a culture in a country, are so deeply vain that they expect a man to know what to do; meanwhile, if one might ask the woman they would not be able to answer, because they are not aloud to think that women have a system or a function, or are not completely invincible super women. It is the same thing that happens in many minorities' minds. So, here is the truth, as observed and experimented. A human woman's primary function is to get fucked so that she can breed, or feel as if she has simulated the function. Even women that are against breeding are pro the sensation of sex, and all sorts of situations arise so that they can have that strong urge satiated. And she will make up reasons to make it happen. She just wants to do it in a way that she does not feel afraid. But every woman, especially those that the man doesn't know, wants to be told what to do. They just want to get laid, they don't want to think so much of it, because every time they think about it it gets complicated and abusive, because they compare what they get and don't get. Once again, want creates suffering. Respect her, introduce yourself, stare at her, listen to her, make her feel desired...Women are seeking to be valued. This is why there is a "player," meaning a strategic rapist, that pretends to care, but doesn't. A master uses these techniques from the light, meaning he does respect her existence, he does listen and respond, he does desire her, and he would ravage her and could create the set of circumstances so that she would not feel afraid or inferior (as is the disease in the Dark Society's woman) and he will passionately rape her for the sake of programming. For the sake of breeding. All the reasons and motives and justifications people make to fuck each other are wasted wasted wasted thought. The ego, the program itself, just trying to survive. A master could do it all and not once feel power, control, or dominance, even though it is occurring. He can also choose to see that his personality is controlling him and that there are ways to stop it. Ways to calm and release the things that will lead him to cheat, lie, and steal to fuck, never actually harming anything tangible. And he can remain calm when the consequences arise, the results of actions, he can sort it and survive. And in the end, no matter what path may be chosen, the experience existed, and he enjoyed all of it," The Father. "I played the balance of egos. I can master every situation eventually by appreciating the way I can learn and deepen, because my interpretation is superior and without regret and without gain, even if I gain. I know that there is another way to see the world, once the dance of survival is weakened. And fear and inferiority do not need to be hindrances that a person has that makes them manipulatable. It is up to a single individual to become stronger. Seek out diverse training. This is how we gain Independence per Individual."

Sitting, thinking, "Sitcom's are the portraits of America. In them you can see so much. From the fools that believe neuroses are functional and beneficial to the avarice that feeds the sensationalism. Selfishness is funny because anyone can relate to it and is familiar with retaliating against it.

Thoughts brought. Thoughts lost. Thoughts that can accomplish nothing, bound by earth and brick, buried alive," The Father. "It doesn't matter if I can tell what is happening. I cannot stop it, but I shall endure it, simply by existing as it happens to my body, my mind, and the growing path that I grow larger than as I drift above it." Leaving function behind for formlessness.

"When the time comes and you wish to define yourself away from the Darkening Souls you will not likely know where to look. You may read the truth, the exact truth, the observation of actual truth, but you may not have the wisdom or intelligence or humbleness to believe it. You may miss the chance to use faith. Or you may devote yourself to something completely false. And misinterpret your whole life. This is why doubt is important. Deeply important. With doubt we can look deeper and deeper, knowing that we do not have godly qualities yet. No age of man knows when the world will end. It does not. Can't. And if a few could see...it would make no difference, they would just know. You cannot prepare yourself that fast for death. You will lose. You should have been preparing now. Not for the end of the world. For the end of your life, afterall, that is the end of this world as far as you are concerned. You will not likely ever have that personality again, that you didn't even try to overcome, ever again. KNOW THIS: If what you follow, what you subscribe to believe so emphatically, with such trembling fear...If there is pride for what they are...No, there are too many reasons...Can people give up reasons?...No, people want to matter too much...." grumble "... Even still, when you die, maybe you will be able to stop and see your spirit, what it is without the lies you will be killing for. You will take the steps you take in this life, even if they are the steps of a cowardly child that wasn't able to believe in <u>nothing</u>, so that they might be quiet enough to finally know something, to use all the benefits of religions without the dogma, shame, or lost time. If you feel a fear of death, if you strive to avoid death to try and live forever, if you do not embrace your death and see that there is nothing to fear just because you don't have this personality, if you cannot see that the cruelty and nastiness of all the putrid people around causes them great and maddening suffering that makes their lives crap, and if you don't have compassion for the plight of their useless lives, then you have some more work to do to on this path. No Father is devoid of Compassion. To be free from the fear of death. To know what omniscience feels like," The Holy. Damned to be heard by no one, thus is their plight, and their echoing frustration in prison alleyways. "If you are one who believes that they deserve then you are lost to ignorance. It is most likely that you will not be able to see that you are lost to the pride that you are. That is the nature of pride, it is blinding, all you can see is your own satisfaction. You will not know, because you will not give up and drop down to the greater consciousness, that which can see pride and rest it. Where you can see this identity you think you are, but are not. Look at your life... haven't you always thought that you were right? Don't you think you are now? If you did not think you were right, didn't you strive to be? Didn't you make up reasons to defend with rage? No, it is not likely you will have the ability to see it." Words fallen and lost, wandering into souls and leaving. "No one wants to be irrelevant, especially when they have struggled their whole lives to be something. And that is just the thing...notice it...you must want nothing. Only those that change their hearts through these devotions for liberation will be able to be able to know what I mean."

It's seeming like the more he lets go, from himself, from dysfunction, from trying to keep what is failing, the more he is as fresh as he was originally in this life, getting closer to a source that will erase him.

The majority of all organizations that try to influence government in the Dark Society come from an origin of insecurity. The organization is formed by people that want to be stronger or equal to another organization because they feel afraid because they are inferior and take offense to their degrading by the powerful. Every organization just wants to be just as powerful as what they are taking on. Power is a disease. Opposing power is the root of all cause, and it effects.

Authority Dies, and Should Be Aware of It

People are trapped by the desire to pursue what they know, by seeking security, by wanting comfort. One cannot change the psyche if one fears. If one fears change, insecurity, fear itself, then one cannot become that thing that is the OverMan, that thing that is a consciousness above, but it lies within. "Above" is a description of deeper, a more beneficial level. It is the same word to say "Over." The unfortunate thing about spirituality is that it is first presented by a person that knows death, a sudden person, (not random, but sudden,) because that person, through no fault of their own has found out a bunch of stuff that other people don't even know exists. His heart overflows with the knowledge he has gained. And a Hero will do anything possible to say it, no matter what other reasons it defies. He knows the absolute Reason. The unfleeting Reason. He knows that no man can damn any other man. That is what death is. It renders all men powerless. Every kingdom expires. Pattern over pattern, the world is designed to die. Every society collapses for the same reasons, (pride, lust, greed, sloth, gluttony, envy, *Anger* (**RRR! I wanted to think of it!** why couldn't I..?**)** These things, these signs, that show that a human thinks it is a god; that it deserves, that it can judge.) and the thing is...is that there is not much you can do about it, except stop yourself from doing it all like an addict. It proves that all power is only a glorification of an ego that was meant to function and die.

However, it is the strength of the OverMan to pursue without care for personal gain the transcendence of the preexisting physical condition by altering the mind from a deeper consciousness. Meaning, you can transcend a good amount of what one might call god, but only by letting your identity cease. Afterall, all the deadly sins are rooted in fear, and we can choose to turn to the path and methods that overcomes fear. So, as you can torture the earth for it to reveal its secrets, one can also torture the psyche to reveal its.

Death is the gift that God gave us to save us from Humanity's
authority.

Duel Mind

I have found, that as the Taoists believed, there are two minds. Clearly. Anyone who studies these arts of deep spirituality can discover it. One is in the skull, One is in the Belly. One different thought thinking through each. One accesses the spirit directly and brings peace, a consciousness that bypasses the brain, by relaxing energy away from it. The other mind, the "known" mind, brings war. Yin and Yang. A physical mind tries to survive, a spiritual mind is fearless and easefully benevolent. A person can think through both. Isolate and merge them. Great power is drawn into the body by thinking through the void-mind. This is a natural effect of it, from within your empty shell. When searching for this spiritual mind do NOT look for an upset stomach, as when looking for your "normal" mind you would not think of your skull or the grey gel in your head. Look for something that functions in the same type of intangible plane. For a world within. Without thoughts. Thoughts are a byproduct of <u>this</u> realm.

The birth of an OverMan can come to any family. There is no control of it. And you will love the child. Of course you will. But your view will not be hers. Bloodlines can end, when he decides she doesn't want to breed. He will not wait to be taught, he will teach his Father. An OverMan can vanish at anytime. She has one view, the salvation of HumanKind. And he has no concern for where that takes him or what it does to her or what it does to you, she will continue, expecting you to breakdown and accept her. Your son, your brother, your husband, you have helped them and they thank you for their and your service, but to the OverMan, Individual want means little. Yet she will pursue with avarice his want of Universal Freedom. Altering the world, rippling out his reason from person to person.

Those that access the Spirit Mind receive a way to reason that reproduces in guru to spiritualist to monk, that never met or knew each other's teachings or religions or atheism. The reasoning of the Spirit Mind will seem cyclical to the outside observer. In the physical world of Earth where matter is present logic is linear, and cyclical logic identifies a fallacy. But to understand the Inner Universe you must learn to think in loops, from a central point, the reasonings always looping you back to the source whenever you think out into a reaching loop of thoughts, re-reminding you of the simple density of Existence itself. The Inner Universe proves true and astounding as the reasons of Philosophers and spiritualists mirror the same contradictions to linear logic that the entire Outer Universe displays. The proof in the results of testing by Great Scientists like Tenzin Gyatso the 14th Dalai Lama. A King so Benevolent he stepped down and gave his country to Democracy. True intelligence thinks of all things around the line of logic that makes an engine combust, or a rocket fly, or the function of a beating heart illogically beating for a reason that cannot be found. The vastly achieved Deep Ones do not think from their point, or their line, or around either, but think as an Ocean that engulfs that point and that line over and over and an infinite number like them. ~ Think as an Ocean.

A SCRIBBLE, IN A RED CRAYON, ON THE FLOOR; PHOTOGRAPH ARCHIVED:

Seriousness is not hatred. Seriousness is not meanness. Growing-up is not something you should stop doing, old man, young lady, you. If there is a point, we won't beat around the bushes to get there and fill pages with fluff, or our mouths. We are your friends. We will fucking tell you. We are the ones that get it done while you talk about it.

"People are crushed in the Dark Society. Let down by the disappointment of the mythical American Dream." The propaganda to promote it is so powerful that people worship it. They will fight you and hurt you and they defend it absolutely, these people are so riddled with the illusions of what they get to dream about that they have become mutated to bring destruction and superiority to not feel like the slaves that toil in that circle of survival (eating, sleeping, flushing, oozing, eating, sleeping, etc., and the illusions over our function that imagine we are doing anything else.) It is interesting that the worship has spread through all cultures...thus is the Power of television. When the illusion is crushed it shatters the person that believed so deeply in their own Superiority. And they are never quite the same, differed by the repression of it," Father.

"Children wait for their parents to die so that they may think of them fondly. The tragedy of life plays out as the parents become more and more cruel, mad, and senile. It grows harder and harder for the children to keep their fondness for the dying. Fear keeps us from the grave. Fear makes us fight it. Fear creates this tragedy. Why do those that believe in God so "strongly" never have the courage to face it? Persistence does not truth make. Hypocrisy makes the fear of their wasted lives. When death finally comes it is only a relief for the children, like the eye of the storm...waiting...calmly...to become the same burden on their own children," Priest.

<u>ALLOW YOURSELF TO BE YOURSELF</u>

What is a great source of anger? What harms everyone? What would break a common thread of repression? People grow angry at people that stay in their homes for long periods of time. People grow infuriated by parents-in-law. All because people repress themselves in the presence of others. All because we are afraid of criticism. Afraid of a bad opinion. Afraid of a made up image of control and imaginary emotional consequence. We must allow people to see us as human. We are not all winners. Nowhere near perfection. Relax. Stop being afraid. No matter what you do people will judge you. Allow them to. People will try to control you. Don't allow them to. Collaborate. We are all the same animals, with all the same problems. Be the same with everyone. This is true honesty. Don't smile in someone's face and then complain about them with your mate, your secret conspirator. Stop complaining and be fine with it. Be fine. Stop caring about what everyone thinks. And feel everything relax. As you untie your fragile mind. Be as you would be with your wife if you didn't have to take out all the anger of your repression on the one person you have chosen to love most. Change the world. Stop being afraid to be natural and human. (And masturbate near drains.)

"Think simply to try and understand yourself. Do you drink tea? Do you like tea? Would you try it again if you could see if you would like it now? Most people do not like to try new things. They know what they like, and deeper, they feel good and safer within their own personalities by knowing what they like. Look simply at the everyday reality of the actions you perform and see the programming of your flow and know that when you see it you can change it and know the nature of the everlasting Spirit," to someone, with words borrowed, possibly believed, influenced by the slight nuances of a new blending of personalities in people. It is fun when both people in a relationship have new fun sides brought out in them that they can joyfully explore together. Do you feel joy? Will you try to feel it again? We feel it. Do you want to? How much will you give up to feel it? What will you let go of, you neurotic wanter?

<u>Police Aggression,
Our Right to Retaliate</u>

In the end, he remembered more of himself. It is so loud to live through a life with such surging power nearly constantly grinding the mill of the mind. The strength of this life will lay like an imprint upon his soul. He won't recall it, but it will effect him for several more lifetimes. He has done well in it. Gained much. But the child he will be next, again, will grow up too quick, and his chosen birth mother, probably a former lover which will conflict in her being, will feel slighted at the rejection as he rises quickly to become what will be far happier, due in part to his efforts in the Time line this time. An unknown mother's suffering, carrying a bag she can put down.

"Police these days are bad people when the economic sector allows for no chance of recourse. Unintelligent people. Cruel people that seek to fill insecurities with the atrocities of false pride. The militant way. To be disgusted and to tell the world how not to disgust you. So many people go to jail, pay penalties, suffer because of these people that choose to oppress. The reason for this is because all people in law enforcement have the same goal. To close this case and build the next one. And this Dark Pride in their efforts of "work," the darkest, like tar sunk in your lungs, gives them the painful curse of absolute faith in their dark dark, often foolish, and commonly lying minds. NOT EVERYONE IS A LIAR, just, EVERYONE LIES TO COPS, but they think wrongly that everyone lies. Dumb. They will do anything to vengefully prove that they are right. This pride.... this self-righteousness...these are our taxes for not stopping them. If they are wrong they will be fired. Do you not see the Blackness here? Bleed for the advancement of a career based on the most insidious sources of nature, fear and anger as the driving forces that control your actions and career advancement. You'll die to prove that their right is far greater than yours, and they will feel proud that they harmed you. As the enforcers grow, as the ego runs away, the armies rise to destroy their oppressors. Let people be. Give up on that sensation that gives you comfort in power, the power that clouds you when you think you are doing something great and good," Father Father Father --- Do we stop them, or do we turn our other cheek? We must fight to show them what they are doing.

Always fight. Make a war that never happens. To be free from war, finally. Try to reason. Only in this way will the cycle stop. Or maybe in this planet of life and death and survival of the fittest, maybe it is our programmed nature to destroy them. Maybe. It would be more effective but far harder to teach them how to see through eyes unclouded by hate. Hate cannot stop hate. An open soul, love itself, can stop hate.

The Constant Winner

I sat on a cement porch. My feet up on a yellow and red bricked perimeter. A cigar slowly puffed. The sound of the waves lapping the nearby beach. The heavy, near-still silence that surrounds you when you are beside your brothers. Your blood brothers. Those that know just what a piece of shit you are, yet die for you because you're their reason that's good enough for them to use to die and to kill. Like me, they exist in the silent night staring into that wayward feeling the black ocean of night gives you. I slowly began to drawl, "I am a big dreamer because I had no fear. I saw what could be done and could push onward through the fear that would stop me. I could try. Try like gods try, without worry for any results, with the calmness of the knowledge that the world is in a state of operating perfection, but man is too worried about survival to see it. Society must free people from the violent state of survival. You see how this heaviness in this air effects us differently? We know all manner of socially unacceptable things about each other. But I cannot care about it. I never have to have the insecurity that could hinder me in my free beauty that would make me worry about what shallow thinking people might think of me. I say shallow because people form an opinion without knowledge or an attempt for imagined empathy. People form an opinion just to have one. They want one. They want to feel smart. To have something to reference over cocktail wienies. They don't even know whom gave them the opinion, but it wasn't theirs, but they have it and there is nothing anyone can do about it. So that's what I mean. I could face and conquer within any arena, any system, any society. And I never cared if I won or lost. I would just play, just to have something to risk. Just to fight. But I never sought power or victory, but I could take it if it came. I perfected myself to prosper in it. I came to understand this whirlpool society. So easy to get sucked in to trying. So I did. And I won. But I also won the hundred times I failed. Never swayed my silent humble pride, because I did not have the kind of pride that cares about the opinions of anyone. So I had little conflict, because anyone could have theirs, so long as it didn't touch mine. Cause and effect of this mindset, of this change. Silent Power....I am going to go and stand in the water to see if the sharks are hungry tonight. Anyone may join me." They milled down to the water as I walked, but did not step in the water. Thinking I was mad. Not realizing that normally I would never do it. But I was delighting their minds. Bewildering them. Always entertaining. They could never know who I really was. And I was fine with that. I never had to prove myself. And some see this and see through themselves and think that there must be insecurity in the justifications...but no...it was not there and if it was it was not real to me. I was free to be anything at anytime and delight in it. Thus is the truly free heart. Free to Risk everything. The adventurer's form of Existing. How a hero's mind reasons this. The water was cool. Something sheer brushed my foot and wiped away my thoughts.

PATHS TO CHOOSE. UNINFLUENCED BY NEUROTIC FEAR

"When in the course of this thought path you should realize that you can be anything, you will likely first make some war. And as you continue to push deeper into yourself and you realize that only the ego defends itself, and that the defense of the ego will make you your enemy. The air of mystery is exciting and terrifying when the threat is so close and so unknown and only ends for the dead and a buddha. I pushed forward in the course, deeper, more still...And amongst it we choose the path of moving peace. It is obvious that the path that makes anger will often oppress to take care of its own longevity because someone will eventually control it that did not make the reason to fight and die for it and so lacks the compassion of those that have suffered to build it. Companies, like us, in our image with the sides of a full human; reaching out, defending, trying to get over it, but seeing compassion grow us. And some will feel prosperity from the success that anger gives. Those with the sense to build it will create success and lies to make an image that would conquer its opposing image. To gain power it is always better to lie. It is easy to want to war when there is no fear left. But it is braver to go deeper and carry the war inward. See that you are what you are fighting. See it, and save the world around you from your own intentions. We can see when the knots of a biased life have been untied that the path of least resistance is the path most untraveled, most would think it only for animals and never even see it," Father.

"These are things I have learned from experiencing them. The absolute only way to learn anything. : : Everything you see on television is designed to keep you here and afraid. Everything you see is to make you watch more of their, television's, experience. To make you think you are learning, when you are just being entertained. People don't really like to think that deeply. They think they will be losing control of their world if it is questioned too hard. Everything that puts forth the effort and massive amount of money for you to know about it in your microcosm vies for every penny you have. It is beneficial to create addiction, and you must be present to buy. This is a side effect of our current Capitalism. It must be fixed," The Father said hoping that the "them" in anyone's mind would dissolve to realize that "they" are made up of people smarter maybe than to be alone in this rocking ghost ship of reminiscence that when traveled by the sacrifice of The Father leads others to use the simple things already present for means wider than imagined originally. Learn the vocabulary and grab the ear of an industry that wants to hear it's own words echoing back.

Spoken as if they had thought together for a lifetime. As if their love had grown so long.

"We have the ability to perceive anything as good or bad, as right or wrong, whether it makes us happy or sad. When we let these preferences go, we can observe things, and find a solution that is effective,"

When you meet a truly right person. Someone who's sincerity moved you into genuine calm belief. Someone who moved you by shear reason based on what they had been and are. Those people are with you for all time. Connected to your soul with the bond of infinite love. Nothing holds stronger. And nothing breaks so sharp if warped.

"My basic principle is this: Man is Chaotic. Man is Chaotic because of the mind. The mind is Chaotic because of the pursuit of Power. If we surpass the mind, man ceases to be chaotic. And by result, man has the ability to stop seeking power, in order to save himself from the suffering he is creating, which leaves money, the inevitable root of all goodness, to ease the suffering of those without it, by getting it to them."

Did you ever wish that everything you said was like how words are written?

Reasons Have People Kill People for Nothing

"I have changed my mind over time. But there was a time............
People think that money is power. The pride they feel when they tell
you how to be is fed by it. When you show a person their own blood
they realize what power is. Will is everything. I cannot lose," The
Father Spaketh, "Yes...yes, that was a different mind, but surely one
I could find the path back to if I desired to."

"It is most possible for the mind and body to be controlled through
the void where death is not feared, and guilt, and remorse, need not
exist," The Priest.

Revolutions Are Born Wet

In the time of my GrandFather's, people believed, full of faith. They believed. But time passed. And one by one as their government broke promises it made to use people to gain something. We began to see. We began to doubt. We began to identify those that were assuming power over us...

THE WAR AT HOME

In me is great passion. I feel a torrent of life. A grip. A great current that raises with tides. And I feel a great restraint. The thing that doubts me. It's myself. One side is the side of Indian Blood, Scottish, a revolutionists'. The Other White Christian Blood, from slave makers, real estate dealers, and tax collectors. A lineage of time. Fucking to bring forth my destiny. A spawn with both visions and logic to foresee what he can make. Making me. Half man and half woman united in form. I became in the belly of time. A character created. It is unstable. The conflict. For everyone. Those minds that were supposed to war against each other now battle inside ourselves. Even though a man loses it's remembrance of history, a spirit remembers. Minds, souls even, bred inside ourselves over eons. It comes to make me think that it was unnatural to be in a world of conquerors. Invading areas of other humans. Assimilating them. Marrying them out of existence. I live in unity with them. That is my evolution. Every conflict you feel sounds like a million tiny bells, a full sound, and it feels like God.

These paragraphs, without quotes or tags, without physical description from myself, The Priest witnessing his sainthood, these are his pages, and his words that appeared somehow in this time in this place as you are.

"I had been with a woman. The same woman...for a long time...I..I.she asked me why I always said I was sorry, she'd make a comment about me and she said I would always say, "I'm Sorry." I said, "I don't know.......I guess it's the easiest thing to say....................................
.... That's funny. For most people "I'm sorry" is the hardest thing to say. I realized how deeply rooted in me the perpetuation of this spirit I had built from lifetime to lifetime *(oneword)* ejected me forward into each and every action. Slowly. Slowly outweighing the power of the body. The mind is just like the soul. Both propel us with illusion. Both the mind and the spirit call us to wake up. They both build in yin and yang, give and take, and create us into the birth of something even more impressive than this. Try not to be premature. Work a little hard. It will be easier in the next world, or from whenever your view will change. As the spirit gains dominance as the superior consciousness, the thoughts begin to flow through the mind in a kinder way. It is natural. That's how we grow, every time you have grown hasn't it felt satisfying? Keep growing. Try and you will become something, whatever it may be. Humility is who we are. Love is what we want. "But...god fuck fuaahhh..." I feel something else. A lot stronger than that. What the hell is it?" Into shadows and lights.

"I reason so hard that I hurt people. So honestly that I expose people. If you are not on the path of betterment you are only my victim," Thus Spake the Father. Thus your image dies before his wrath, Thus is your salvation.

RETURN TO THE WORLD BEFORE MAN SOUGHT POWER HERE, BEFORE FEAR HAD AN ILLUSION

"This is a delicate and specific revolution. A revolt for all people, under all regimes. This is a revolution where man comes to remember that there is no shame, there is no judgment. The world is designed some way or another for something weak to have to die so that something else can exist. All people want to rape, and all people want to kill-at least when they are children. But still it is animal nature to jockey for rank, to fight and compete to crush and conquer, low income bullies running away with stigmas. It exists in every society on Earth. Except for those that use the method of Compassion instead of dominance, and still they rank themselves for functionality, because those that seek power will always come. Those that are "right" will always return. The single brush made-up of many bristles carrying the same paint and ignorantly forming the same stroke on the same enormous woven tapestry. Most the world is blind, never seeing that they are what drives all suffering, all posturing, all power and cruelty. All controlled by an instinctual design that functions for the purpose of the preservation of the beast. Like any animal. The only difference being that man believes that a god might favor them so greatly that they are gods. It is why man invented judgment and said god did it. Judgment exists to assume power over. It is done by those that chose their animal controlling for power and security, which yields a natural hypocrisy which comes from insecurity to be judged themselves...never trust a police officer, a judge, a president, never trust anyone that holds and uses authority. Never trust anyone that would fight you to prove that they are right. Your revolt is against yourself to make sure that you are not the animal that hates being an animal. This is the disease. The mutation that is absorbing the life of an entire planet. Look at yourself. My weakness is lust. I am not damned because I have made love, raped, sodomized, reveled in, impregnated, orgasmed...this is what I can do...what I am supposed to do...and this is what controls me. I am a slave to a natural impulse. I think of what is beyond, what I can have, I must work to see that there is beauty beside me. Around me. Near me. But the programmed responses of my brain that make up the animal I currently exist as, until I die, make me want to fuck. And if I do not escape it, I will be driven forward by the raging ego, by the first consciousness of human reality. Making me be this person. And I will waste my vision on things I cannot see. Things that cannot be. Things that would take away the ease of a simple day. A day that I could notice that I am deeply loved. This is why we attempt to silence the illusions of the mind. This is a war only you can commit to. A war against yourself. A war that will yield a society that is not based on the surging ego, but a society that will yield compassion as a result of its function. People never realize that they are the rapers and the killers, because they are afraid of them, and don't want to see, even when tears get them off on the guilt, but they must see to fix it, but since they are afraid they want to stop all the other more overt rapers and killers and dominators and controllers, or rather they want someone else to stop them so that they don't have to think about it and possibly see themselves as the rapists and killers that they in fact are, and every second have the potential to realize a frustration and become them, whom they lie and say they could never be. You see, it is complicated to think of, this is why it is best to bypass it, deconstruct it, and then build it. ***Baptism, Rapture, Requiem.*** *It is a quick process, our method.* This can only be done by having the courage to see the truth of what you are and what you want to be, easeful and happy. It is even a Revolution (back) that has a Utopia at the end," The Father's voice echoed in the empty halls as victory upon victory overturned for his mind. More and more free from everything that seeks his servitude. He serves only the truth that he has experienced in himself. He is a free nation.

<u>Darkness</u>

"It is prudent to keep the People in ignorance. All that seek true power you have never heard of. Only fools seek fame through media. True power is hidden. People can only think about what they know about. No one can hate you if they cannot think of you. This theory is beneficial to the Existing that seek Freedom from oppression. When people in the government think, they think to harm or avenge someone. They get paid to make up crimes. While always hiding their own. All people are criminals from time to time. The worst are those that control the penalties," The Father.

"There is no more light. And no more dark. If you choose a side you have failed. Hate and ignorance and drive for success will make suffering for you," The Priest.

"No light. No dark. Only results of philosophies. Only failure. Save one. This one. The one that reconstructs the failings of Man," The Father. "A philosophy with a way to make the Utopia without appealing to the egoic hungers of Man. With a limitless tool, that must be constantly observed, the human we are. The war must not end until we die in it. This is the war of a lifetime."

THE FALSE IDOLATRY OF WORDS

Judaism, like the curse that stem from it, Christianity, were undeveloped Religions that gave up on solutions when they chose to make up a Penalty system that wasn't real, Heaven and Hell. It's why they made up Sin, because they didn't have a way to stop the Pride that controlled them from killing when it felt like something was taken from it, like their wives, like their material possessions, like the lives or health of their valuable children. These ultimately false bases for controlling societies still warp and control the minds of the unintelligent today, left unintelligent because they are too afraid to think into doubt. It is the reason that all who believe in Sin will be controlled by Pride and will make Hell itself around them, damning because the fearful and sternly yelling convinced them they should. The false religions of underdeveloped Spiritual Technology should be left behind, their reasons not even worth reasoning against. This is the only way for oppression to end its repressive family ways.

Praise the Truth of the Lord.

<u>Failed Lives</u>

Every society's basic instincts promote survival. Societies form so that the want to live and live easily is gained. A people always develop medications, no matter what the fabricated belief in a god is. Every society will, no matter what other societies have touched it, attempts to avoid death. Why? Because it hurts to watch someone die, and most of the time it hurts to die. It terrifies people. This thought. This pain. If we learn to deal with the pain. If we can let it go, even while it is happening. We can move forward and move away from the need for power; meaning, the need for survival. It is so deeply programmed into us, so perfectly, it is this, itself, that is the ego. This is holy definition. It is everything you are terrified of. If you can stop being afraid to die then you can be eased away from suffering. Life hurts so that we keep living, and when life ends the function of this body's pain ends. When that happens you realize how light you really are and that the gravity of life was an illusion.

WE ARE ASKING PEOPLE TO REJECT EVERYTHING THAT THEY
NATURALLY BELIEVE IN,
THE DEFINITION OF THEIR PRIDEFUL BEING,
IN SEARCH OF EQUALITY.
NO ONE WILL DO IT. YOU WILL NOT DO IT.
ALL BECAUSE YOU DO NOT CARE ENOUGH.
BECAUSE YOUR NATURAL ABILITY TO
FEAR IS MORE POWERFUL THAN YOUR
NATURAL ABILITY TO LOVE.
THE WORLD SUFFERS BECAUSE YOU ARE NOT
TRYING HARD ENOUGH TO BE STILL,
AND TO RAISE YOUR WILL TO LOVE.
YOU ARE AFRAID YOU WILL DIE IF YOU DO, BUT YOU WILL NOT.
CALM THE VULNERABLE FEAR
THAT DRIVES YOU ONWARD.

<u>SOCIETY WILL NOT CEASE WITHOUT FEAR.</u>

<u>Pen and Paper</u>

When they initially apprehended The Father he requested a pen and a notebook. He needed to write down an idea. He asked again and again. He asked again. "Please," he said. Idea after thought between visions...they came and went. Lost. They hated him. They hate him. Those that choose the roles of the restrainers, that see liars, evil, and cling to rage, and discrimination. Every person that he would see until the end of his life...wanted him to suffer. Speaking against what they chose to be. That was his life. And he knew that eventually they would find a way to imprison him for it. Obsessed by repressed fear the Darkness acts quickly and cruelly burying their guilt in righteousness, and what they "can use against" him. They knew what he was. He was open about his thought process, what he loved, how he loved...He became famous just to tell us, just so they would come and kill him, or worse, take his Freedom. Would the people free him? Would they realize how large an Army they actually were when willing to act with their own bodies? They will not, and for the same reason we don't turn each other in to the FBI, we pursue our own senses of happiness, and avoid all others for their inconvenience to our happiness, their choices and circumstances their own, and not ultimately ours, resolving to there's-nothing-we can-do attitudes able to accept just the way things are.

He had to learn how to let the lost thoughts go. There was nothing he could do. His genius wasted. He couldn't even kill himself. Tear into his own neck with a pen. He had the will, to stop the thought, the word, the sentence, from rolling over and over in his head until he could record it and move on from it. But he had no pen.

That isolation, this one in the cage, and that need to let go of what he could not hang on to anymore...It was the key to his advancement toward his oncoming majestic spiritual self in these later years. He let go of all, all that old men cling to and weep over, even if he needed to weep to do it. And he became more than a body. The physical threats couldn't touch him. Don't they see that their consequences are now futile to the holy? He will love you as you penetrate his side with your spear. Judgers. Vengeful. Rulers. He once said, "If you don't walk away from it, we'll remove you. Can we prevent this bloody, decapitating, revolution? Will they become what they think they are?"

Only I heard it. Maybe I can write it down for you.

Who am I? Just a black spot burned out on his brain that he won't be able to get an electrical current to.

Everyday I come, and every day there are times he looks at me, and I know he's wondering who I am. I start to wear my robes and full garments upon every visit to elevate the grandeur of his final visions.

Employment, Serving Fortunate Fools, and Abuse

"It eventually became impossible for me to get work within the Dark Society, because employers, though comforted by my presence, would not be able to find anything familiar in me. They could not see the Darkness that was within them. Those that did hire me were often slightly punished for that Darkness. Enough to disturb them from the security of their imaginary power. Their sad humility always had a good look on them later, and somehow they always thought it was even though they knew, and they seemed thankful that it was not more than it was. So, I was forced to convince people that I could do things that they themselves could not do so that I could get funding to try at Capitalism. No one can tell you that you can't do what you have already done. It is amazing how fast we can evolve to suit our strengths. But surely this path is not the easy one. It's results within the Dark Society are difficult to handle. But luckily, because of the path we are easily adaptable because we do not have to hang on to the past for security, because we do not fear the future," The Father.

A Bug

A bug. A fly on my Fatherly arm. For days it has landed on me again and again. I should have killed it. My reflex was to smash its soul prison all over, wiping its meaning of existence from my mighty hand. Destruction is so natural. We are an amalgamation of little destructions. Each damaging moment building on the past. "*hmmm. hmmm.*" All of us, myself, are mostly damaged from the first Repression. The forcing down of the sensation of wanting to feel anything's pussy. All are endlessly curious. Constantly plotting another way to see more. Untie this knot. *Yes I can.* Disrupt the discomfort. I do not have to feel discomfort. Pursue it. I feel a pressure in my chest. A close, a block, a weight, a defense. Relax it. Loosen it. Feel it, and know it is just a feeling. A fleeting thing that I hung on to because I thought I had to, to protect everyone from it. The deep stuff is like this. It was advantageous to me that I never acted on the impulses of eternal rape that rest in a man. But, it does create a Repression of a ravaging without destruction within the clear light in the obliteration of contracting orgasm. A pothole in my soul's natural flow. My soul is to be happy. To love. I feel again the grip of meditation. The sense of the glowing soul. Roaring. Purring. Letting me know that I am it. A beautiful thing. I see so much because there is no place I will not look.
So saw the Father.

The explosion of stories and fantasies that erupt from the mind is a situation that can be taken advantage of, but it is merely a defensive response to the cruelty of other human beings. It is a skill accentuated by charm. So we become charming. Each moment we choose to create ourselves in every way we will wind up. We are the future, clouded with defense mechanisms that we really no longer need. We have the choice to realize our ever humbling evolution. The meek are coming, preceded by mighty words that need to make sense for Us and not you, we don't want the generation's confusion that came before. Our reasons we learned now, in a modern quest for Universal Education.

"Following nothing is the key to a free society. If you follow something, anything, any religion, any government, if you would kill for something, then you are a slave to it. This is not freedom, if you were free there would be no reason to kill someone, besides randomness, or to pointlessly prove unstopability and "their" powerlessness. The problem with the empire attitude is that it crushes the open nature of a society to control it, because the advantaged person in the society believes in its own power and its arrogance that never suffered and always had been telling itself it can use a human better than the human can use themself... if that human were enabled, without the condition of servitude.

If countries are allowed to exist without threat of the assumption of power.. Without fear that they might lose something.. If people could change themselves so that their perception didn't make them so blind to what the assumption of power does then all countries would be allowed to form a reason through an uncensored world. And people would be able to travel between place and place and choose where to live. It must not be One Government. It must be many. Free countries. Where foreign aid is seen as helping a country build its sciences and engineering and technology fronts because one day as they develop we will be able to trade with what their best minds, far differently programmed than our best, that will develop great things we won't imagine. But we must not be a militant society that wants to control. We must be a society that can live next to any other. So long as everyone has a chance to make money and survive and have their wants too, then countries will not be so radically violent, as we deal with grievances instead of making war. We must not take from them. We must all share by building each other's wealth. That is Capitalism in its finest. But you can't want to be the most powerful, not even the best, but you should produce the best product because you honestly care about the goodness it can bring to someone. Human Compassion makes better products. See, Capitalism became self-centered, people became selfish. They wanted to enforce their ideas on the houses of others, because theirs was the best. The idea must return to Capitalism where you want your neighbor to have his freedom too. And you help him. You don't resent him or think down on him. Follow the ideals of the great art of Cooking...Your dishes will be better and you will please more and more people and your business will grow because you make the best food, and you will do this by adopting the philosophy of love. Make something so that the person you love will love it the most. This is the way to cultivate love, and to profit from it with the productive labors of love. With compassion the Perfect Society, a society without dis-rest of dissatisfaction, or frustration, can exist and it can exist with Capitalism. The wisest answer often seen most clearly in the contradiction that makes money the root of all goodness, able to start the feeding and prosperity of a planet of life, free from the slavery it once circumstantially created. In this way a free world utopia can unite, completely independently," Fa La La La.

I dupe myself. I think and think and think and come to a reason and so I begin reasoning this reason and within the course of reason I develop a thought that proves the reason wrong. And I easily start over again. (No. How strange a tiny lie of minutia. I do not easily start again. I fight hard to remember where I was going. Oh. I see. It is not a lie. I just don't mind the devastation of my idea, so it does not weight heavy on me as a problem. The ego is ever trying to take control of me. I conserve my energy by not letting it run too much.)
Thought Father thought backwards.

"I remember when I first prayed. I recall it. It is moving when you feel the flow of emotion. Your feelings just below the feelings you portray as to lie to everyone around you. You know, when we know it is significant. I was poor and desperate. And I wanted. I wanted so badly. I began to bottle a holy form of spring water. It was holy because when one drank it, it would blank the mind. It's subtlety was so great that to even notice the moment of silence you would have to have studied the Still Arts for years, maybe lifetimes. I don't know. With little money I was forced to cut a lot of corners. And I prayed. I prayed that we would hurt no one. I hoped and hoped that no one would get sick, everyone would love it, we'd have no complaints... it made me work hard to make sure the bottled product was extra clean. So that no one found out we didn't have the eight permits we were supposed to have. One mistake in the Dark Society and the government organizations made-up of individuals that sought jobs that paid and pushed, will take your house, let other people take your money, and you will likely be imprisoned. There was no money to fight or attain the permits. So I prayed. Hard enough to feel the tears well in my eyes and the warm flush of tenderness seep to the surface of my facade. It felt good but it was no time to cry. I had to be strong to earn my freedom from those that thought I had to earn it, when the right was mine from birth. I pushed it down to where it needed to be. Like all of us. If we let that first identity go, the one for everyone else, than we would see that we are all emotional weaklings underneath. The first facade protects us from the pain we feel from the emotions that know we are failures and cowards. It is hard to choose the life of the deconstructing ego, because a hero must journey through those feelings that tear himself apart and travel all the way within it, again and again, until he does not fear it any longer. And so I prayed. And want controlled me when I did. It controlled me and I was stuck within its current. For now, I thought, for now I will endure this, test myself, suffer in it as I hated its bindings, I felt I should face it. My goals were small and I believed I could reach them. I, unlike others, never needed to want that much and I had the ability to endure suffering. And when I was done I stripped my shoes, scarred my chest, chaffed in wool, and bled, in hunger, through the mountains and their cold. All so that I would feel God again. I realized in that time of walking and starving that the desire to want led me so far away from God that I was forced to pray. To want is to suffer. I never had to pray again,"

~The Priest.

"My Prayer would later have nothing to do with want, but only to be with that emanation of pure living perpetuity that is the energy we cultivate that throws positivity at us. And we MUST feel this with no guilt. Feeling good is good, let yourself, trust yourself, trust the journey, you are your only danger here."

The Father did write this:
NOTE: Was the Priest real? Can your mind be so strong that you can create an alternate reality? The answer is, yes. But usually we are controlled by that. The hero figures out the way to manipulate it, to go beyond the brain, separate from it and see it.   We use drugs the same exact way. We manage ourselves. You may use illegal drugs, but they are not a replaceable reality for any other one that is impermanent. All, and every type of illusion needs to be overcome; in the beginning, at the middle, in the end; to set our behavior free from angrily controlling what we claim to love.

Take a Sad Institution
and Make it Better

"Overtime, an astonishing thing happened. Although I had been with so many woman. Although I loved sex. After she died her triumphant death...And after she loved me the way she did. After I saw it in her eyes. Felt it in the flow of her blood. I was never with another woman again, not all the way. Why would I want sex without that amazement of beauty? Why would I want anyone that didn't love that way? As savagely and certain, so completely in control of her freedom. Everything else is less than that. It spoiled me to the world. Knowing that love as supreme, knowing that it is so easy to give, and knowing what people offer instead, made me hate them all. Funny, what life makes us, if we choose to act normally," so spoke The Father.

I can see my path to Hell. It will come when I am unable to tell people what I am thinking. When I lose the capacity to write and speak coherently. It is the Hell my grandfather faced. Struggling, struggling, fighting, fighting, to just get things out, and not be afraid of what they never had been before. But the Alzheimer's held him. This is my path to Hell. You must know what you would fear. If a writer writes, then what does a writer do when he can't write? He suffers. Why do I suffer? Because I cling to want. I want my desire. My desire is for my mind. I worked long to develop it. I want it. Desire is the root of all mental suffering. So, to not go to Hell...I only have to stop wanting it. My training when I was young will let me let this brain go. And my consciousness will still be able to dwell in this body, in a state of stillness. Then I will not pull my mind to fight the mind. I will not need to use the brain as hard as I want to. It is similar to being conscious in a dream, when you realize it's a dream. It is possible. I feel it. When my mind hallucinates, and won't shut up with a song or something, I can bypass that first level of consciousness, thought, and move to another deeper, denser,

nonpermanent state of being. "Maybe I can let you know how it is working, or maybe I won't be able to speak," The Father.
I wondered what The Father had been thinking before he suddenly spoke. The Father went on:
"Our revolution is a failure. People will not turn from Power. It holds them. Control's their actions. But if the problems with the Capitalist Democracy are not addressed it will crumble. I see it crumbling. The self righteousness is too strong. "

"A problem within Capitalism is that to prosper in it you have to make yourself an authority in something. You have to manipulate people into believing that your side is right. Or they won't respect you to try and sell your garbage. This is why people in the corporate worlds, the heart of Capitalism, are people that suffer. Darkness comes over them in a heart beat to justify their paychecks. You must always be doing. You must always be winning. Or you will not have your job. That equals death of painful stigmas and regulations on your time and behavior in a Dark Society. It is worst seen in the system of the government, because the same corporate thinking people, those that seek Authority, are dealing in people's very lives, and they seek immunity to do it. It all makes an equal People... Unequal," The Priest. "Equality is the concept it is based on, but unequal is all it has been."

They sound like the same person talking. We are not the John Hughes' characters we think we are, criminals.

Always Facing, Never Running--
From Myself

As people age, even those that fought systems, and challenged minds, come to fear death so greatly that they come to think that the terror, pain and sadness of death is so terrible that they think it is better to be alive than to be dead. But it's not so harsh. The cross-over. Of course in my journeys, alone, deep in the silent Mountains, or it was on an expansive stretch of beach, I reached into the stillness and pulled myself from a lower level of fear and moved far beyond what I could handle. I knew that passing into death was only like walking through a sheet of falling water and winding up without a body on the other side, a lot lighter, because we aren't pulling the weight around anymore, literally too. Death is getting splashed on the Log Ride. It's scary, but you only wind up soak' and wet. Big deal. You'll dry off. And most of you will pay your three dollars to ride it again.

"The Girl forced me into physical war. The Girl forced me to murder her. She forced me beyond speculation: to take the veil right off of her," The Father confessed to me on day 153. "Now, Zarat chose to make himself a face-to-face operative, something I never wanted to experience so personally. Honestly, I am a never-official general, of a war that never happened, that people murdered people in, that I entertained people into, and The Girl is the only kill I can confirm beyond the shadow of a metaphor."

"Most people that have hated me have done so because they were unable to dominate and assert themselves into a position. They sought definition and I did not give it to them. I did not live within definition. I cannot give what they expect. Cowards live within definitions, in imaginary boxes, so that they can feel that they belong to some sort of group. They are proud that someone else believes like them. When we, the Became, find someone that believes like we do, we Become grateful, because it is so rare, and all too precious is a person that can push our strong wills deeper along our unmappable, but recorded, progress. And we try to calm ourselves so that we may hear these Ones' beauty strumming from their souls like the pluck of a harp resonating through a church. It is different to be brave. It is calm. Those that know God do not fear It," Father. We are dead inside and we are calm and free to love without fear of sacrifice or repercussion. We are the greatest lovers to ever exist. "The smart and the brave, in one person, strives to see what they are. If you look into yourself you face devastation, because the question that provokes it is teetering in the pits of us all. Look for it, and know that it doesn't matter, just as much as we don't." How hard it will be for anyone that needs to understand these preceding straight and logical sentences. How weak are their minds if they cannot seek with the logic of the soul through and by using the mind. What a waste, what destruction and pain it brings everyone that will ever know them..

Doubt makes us better. We silence it completely when we Act. After we trained, after we rehearsed.

In dreams again I see children. Children running through my parent's old yard. Screaming. Scared of a Siamese cat chasing. The cat runs too. Near them, not after them. I wonder what the cat did. It must have scratched at them. On the porch is a large man. Bald with a hairy face. He is angry, with a narrow mind, cruel, an idiot I was free to think, like most people, oblivious to his selfish serving rage. He is the father of the children. He is so stupid, but he uses my mind to coax the cat towards him. He is in my mind, it is available to him, in this dream. He grabs the cat as it chases after a raccoon tail on a string. The cat is frightened, as it must have been when it attacked the children. He smashes it against the banister and is overcome by his righteousness. The cat, so pretty, becomes a kitten again. Kitten. Stumbling, gurgling. I wake up.

I could be anyone, at any time, with this soul influencing an intellect, warped by the conditions of an ignorant life. I am sure that I have been a shallow violent man smashing life for my own satisfaction. What made me turn away from the instinct of selfishness that drives all other people I have ever met? Why did I choose to be as genuine as possible? What do I think is real? How long until I'm an idiot again? Mercy to the idiots...I may be one, selfishly.

I miss being kind to a living creature that is not a human. I miss expecting nothing from it. And I miss how every time I showed simple kindness to a "beast" and expected nothing from it, it chose to give me Love.

When life is fleeting out of us...perhaps this is when we want life around us most. This is my most hated thing of prison. Life is locked out, away from the imprisoned, from me...fear pops, makes me feel like puking, and I feel the consequence of my terrible mistake and my allowing this cage to form around me when I surrendered...how weak I was...to want to die here. ...We're all such cowards, all of our actions, just running from fear, hoping for a quality of life.

There were always lots of women to love. Goodness grew in people, just under the dust of shame. And I found it easy to cultivate. A Joy to use. People wanted to be touched. And my Lovers loved to be loved without an identity. Expecting nothing from them set them free to be everything that felt good and never destroyed. They lived in a world where there was nothing that could be blamed. And they were beautiful. Sexy and enchanted. And when I told them what I was doing, they thanked me for not using them. And that's what it felt like. It wasn't intangible. It was Freedom. And it was naked. It was a masterpiece of movement. And every doubt any woman ever had when she was with me, was quelled into peace, by the reason I gave them with specificity to that abstract path of ours. They just wanted to be calm. And with me, they were. They knew peace and sex. Humanness and Spirituality masturbating without doubt that it could be done, and is happening in this present. And we laughed about everything. Because we were vulnerable and unafraid. Both of us using each other and wanting nothing. Two branches of reasoning working towards the same thing. She, whomever she was, would receive whatever she wanted from me, and all she had to do was want nothing. She could have things, and she could appreciate what it was like to not have it. And in return she received the natural Father. The calmer. The one that would care about her. And she rises to know inherently how precious it is to be cared for because she is not reasoning for herself because she wants nothing. And she got sex. Her body taken like it was for pleasure itself. And it was. And it could be and that was all the proof that was needed to do it. A woman feels spun around by the meaningfulness, as she begins to accept that it has meaning because it is devoid of it, so all great feeling can surge over the experience. And life goes deeper, until she sits in a sea of thoughts, so many of them her own. And holes begin to open as the mind opens, and I filled them comfortably and she loved like she will never love again. And I greatly loved as I always have and always will.

You do not understand, unless you have been able to love me. Only then would you have let me convince you of True Love, and it's instant and spontaneous existence. I could make it all right with a joke or a reason. And that's what we've wanted. We wanted to feel like it was all right. I filled them, and I sent them home to leak it all out, until I suddenly fill them again.

The Father, "As my anger has fallen away. I have seen hope within the roots of the system. And I think that the system can survive an overhaul with the Deconstruction of Power. For example, One thing good about this system is that a single human being can keep what he gains, with only a small tax, if you consider the grand scheme of things. In some governments, if there was a gold strike, the whole of the claim would go to the government, and not mildly taxed by the government to ideally aid the common equality. I can see it when I look from certain angles. There is some goodness here, but we must change the impulses of the People. We must refuse the pursuit of power. We must reserve our desires for accomplishments. We must be sure that no one loses freedom and that no one infringes on anyone else's freedom. Hard, when you think of it on a grand scale, but simple if you think that you must be the one to do it. Surely you can make yourself change. Lead by the example of kindness. Change by the witness of rooted humility at the very base of all your mad actions. You must be good. You do not need to become a devil to fight The Devil. That is something that people that lose their souls to what they did not want anyone to be say. From goodness they come and into darkness they fall, with intention of wanting to help people, but their force crushed them."

THE TRIGGER PULLS EASY

After long periods of poverty, after starving and almost killing ourselves, our rise from it was so miraculous, so elegant, so prayed for and so answered, that I felt that I would not fall again. I would not be so close to doom again. It felt promising. It made me plan for what would come, for what I could dream and be happy about. That was Faith, a virtue of prosperity. But I could see doom peeping up over the end of the bed. Its eyes waiting...And would my doubt be what triggers my loss of favor with whatever divinity is aiding me? Is the wavering of Faith, the loss of my Luck, the joy in my eyes, is that simple change in thought that might damn me into suffering and despair? But I realized all that...and I built onward with my dreams, and somehow we didn't nearly die again. And somehow the despair slowly faded, which made me know that when it hit again it would be strong because I was not used to it or tempered by poverty anymore. And I will be weak, and it will be heavy. And the beat goes on. Our energy being expelled towards the whims of our creation, reaping our impending failure that specialization brings to us.

My economic fortune saving me from the True Becoming that Zarat was fated to. It is not The Father that becomes, it is the children as they defy hypocrisy and note every honesty.

The Father's First TV Show that Followed the First Pitch

The ultimate joke of "What the Fff?!?" is the irony it portrays. For the right people to enjoy this show, our true audience, they have to be able to see the manipulation and therefore not be able to be manipulated by it. Meanwhile, the general watcher will regard the show with a series of mixed emotions. No one being able to tell you exactly what they thought about it. Because they don't understand what these emotions mean. Because they believe they are their emotions. Philosophy is written to be appreciated by other philosophers and the best of it includes a benefit for the most people, places, things, and the more life and consideration that can creep into it the better. Don't you see, that we are just making up Reasons. Images in the whim of your emotions. Thought. And Entertainment.

<u>This Road</u>

"This road is a hard one. Rough on the soles and enjoyable to wander. A penalty of the journey of conquering the ego that my mind had to deal with was that...(pause)...I had a genius' mind, I could think deeply and movingly. I could see and dream and imagine realities that no one could. Inventions, theories, plans...I would run free with them and feel nothing anyone around me said. But. My Holy Choice would arise. And sometimes my mind would stop and notice it. Whenever the mind stops and notices a spiritual state of mass imagination it stops it. Once you stop to think on it, it is over. And you must remember it if you want to think on its meaning, or its cause, as if one was remembering a dream. (Everything we are telling you, you have done before. You just need to learn how to direct your focus and where it is best for everyone for you to point it once harnessed. This is the fruit of life, babes.) So, I would stop my advancement by researching my condition. Most people do not do this. Most people are ran by their programs and never have a single idea about how to stop them. How do you make yourself not sad? Or not happy? How do you stop anger? How can you be what you actually want to be? Happy and secure. Eventually I came to realize that what was stopping my flowing thoughts and pulling me from spirituality was doubt. Deeply rooted doubt. From the beginnings of my life. It was programmed into my basic personality by the simple situations that occurred around me during my programming years. But, it is not most beneficial. The program is perfect to maintain balance in the Universe, but it is truly not best for me. I can change it, and the deeper I go, the more I am willing to give up in this world, the less I want or need, the more I can fly through reality by controlling my perception. Dodging and laughing, as my enemies sneer because I wouldn't recognize their sense of force and remained unaffected. Letting go to gain control...if it sounds like an oxymoron you will not be free in this lifetime, you are not smart enough. And the superiority you feel, the smugness you fall back safely into (in the fool's realm where I can't just kill you) is darkness and pride and proof of my truth, that I see because I foil myself and point my thoughts with will towards constant victory...because I don't need to win, and so, I hang on to no weaknesses I might have had pride in keeping," be drown by it. So what if you die?

Idiots

"Overtime, especially through my 30's and 40's, it became harder and harder for me to be able to talk to people. People were so weak that no matter what I said I would hurt them; meaning, hurt their pathetic pride. I would say something wise, and they would say, "What's that supposed to mean?", and I would say, "It is not something people like you, in your state of perceiving, can understand," and they would be slighted. It would come across their face. The stun of their mind not knowing how to defend itself and regain a sense of place the person literally never moved from, or was ever near, the entire conversation. People take such easy offense. Such nasty egos. Always jumping to wars. Wars will only end when people are able to not take life personally. It was impossible for the fool to understand. They were not smart enough. They did not know, nor could they be taught how to make their mind think without the ego that is blatantly wanting to be validated right now proving the point. The insuperiority of those that want to be superior is obvious. Their insecurity is laughable and sick, at all times, in every time, in all of history, and RIGHT NOW. Those that want to matter and belong ruin all the world. They cause every war. Do nothing from insecurity. Guard yourself from your natural tendencies. This is real therapy," Who Cares? "Funny part is, *they* would take offense to everything I just said and not have the goodness in themselves to stop their offense and cease all the nasty thoughts they have for revenge to make themselves the greatest again, the greatest that doesn't feel afraid. We, your superiors, don't have to matter."

Your prosperity hinges on your ability to be with other people and collaborate with them with effective communication if you walk, and you will, in society. Reach for Compassion with these people whom will try to hurt you, these fucking idiots, your momentary enemies that will remain dull and attacking their whole lives, unless we shatter their ego and give them the peace they fight viciously for and never have.

"Father, I once kept a ranch. On this ranch we grew a great deal of hallucinogenics. Sometimes while I was on them I would be tortured by my mind. Especially as I came off of them. My mind would explode in anger towards me. At me. Within me. Loudly. And there was no way to plug my ears. My ears were not hearing it. But it echoed within my skull. It would come in voices of people I despised. It sought vengeance sometimes. It would happen sometimes while not on the drugs, and it happened far before I had done these drugs that can open a pathway of limited understanding. The unfortunate thing about drugs is that most of the hallucinations come after the drugs have been taken as people make-up false reasons to believe in them, and to believe in themselves. Reasons based on insecurity. They don't use their souls for guidance. Well...we know the Darkness. Throughout my time, that I alone pass through and observe, I have discovered that these audio attacks are my own assaults upon myself. My fears showing themselves to me. And I have the option to ease them. To not have fear of them. To <u>feel them, not fueling them with reasons, and let them dissolve</u>. To not be concerned with the world being in perfection for my approval. The Earth accepts me, and I can accept it. Without defending myself meaninglessly. Now... these voices are different than the Other voices. Voices found in the border world, between this physical world and Nirvana. The Other voices are of those that seek power and control. Demons, for lack of a better fear. These demons can send a sensation of fright across a person. It is the fright that makes them powerful. It is what invites them to access. There is a simple way to render them harmless though. Do not accept their power. Resolve to wanting nothing and there will be nothing for them to use to control me. This resolution is at the heart of the path. Stay true to this. Take no power. Seek no place or dominance or pleasure and Freedom will grant our salvation from these temptations of Darkness and Ego and they will not be able to take control of our Simple Path," The Father. His breaths heavier and more labored as the spirit becomes stronger than the dying body, opening his sensation of ever growing peace, regardless of the babbling mind.

His Trial

I remember his trial. It wasn't national, everywhere, kind of news, but it made some news.

The Father said, "You seek to punish me. To take me out of your society so that you may feel as if you've preserved it. And you've created this power structure to do so, assuming it is right to try and make your people as safe and secure as possible. And you justify your judgment by it. And you hope that I will accept it, so that you feel right. You feel as if I am in debt to you for betraying your beliefs and you must be compensated. Debt does not exist! And you do not deserve anything. In a true land of equality how could it? If there is power and penalty for surviving and not being part of a society than a land is not free. So I fought against it. To have my freedom survive. To not be a part of slavery that answers to circumstantial satisfactors, like yourself. And you will condemn me for it." You should have seen the judge taking this. Wisely letting this side fall into the record as a Warrior Poet's passionate grievance. "Your need to feel right is what tyranny is. And your safety is false. You will never be able to escape the death that makes you take away the rights of the free. For some time I have walked this way, refusing to be reigned so that you may ride for your pleasure. And for a long long time you have sent hunters after me with chains and guns, dreaming of the day when they will feel more safe and more powerful and maybe even make more money by capturing me." ***You, you, you. You did this. It is personal, because the man is a person, and Zarat could choose to be his vengeance.*** "No matter how strong the mind of a person, to live in crime, to be hunted, to see <u>everyway</u> that I could be caught, to know every path that a crusader may stumble upon and find me and prove his satisfaction, is a great penalty. It binds my stomach, it enslaves my mind. I never hunted to take away another man's freedom. I never threatened a person with the fury of the damnation I thought they deserved. My path had violence in it, but it was always walked for the sake of peace. Actual peace, not just my own in front of a big screen TV. But, to end the tyranny I saw in every justified, frustrated face. The irony is that I ultimately fought and stole and cheated this society in order to create the works that I thought could save it. So, send me to prison, and feel your fleeting sense of goodness, but know from this day onwards that your goodness is an illusion that puts shackles on the whole world with its terrible results. Your power and use of fear will eventually take everything away from you, while those near resent your hypocrisy and grow more silent, year after year. And your satisfaction will be gone. Prison a respite for me where I will receive medical care for the end of these days I've been keeping. And I will only gain more calmness by knowing that I don't have to worry anymore about the justified, the vengeful, the judging, the cowards struggling for a foot hold on a sense of security. My freedom has been gone for some time because the Prideful, the damning, reign supreme with hearts that never see the reflection of their fury. If there had been anyway for me to be free from your judgment and your power and your control then my path would have been very different. I wish there was less fear that makes more power in this world."

If there were keys, they'd have wanted to throw that one away. The judge let him have his final scene, she was an old fan of his show. But, what now felt like her condemnation left her with a defending look, too hurt to love what she now reasoned was not like her, and she returned the blow. The judge only sentenced him to one year in prison. If The Father was to die with the eased burden and hydromorphine of medical care, then he'd have to be quick about it.

Pride is insecurity. The fear of death is insecurity. When pride is damaged it becomes vengeful, it makes wars and suffering. Overcome pride to be free. We are not our reactions, so we can stop them.

At my rolling finger tips was the will to be able to have any woman I could ever desire. My great holy nature enabled me to see into the true heart of every person. To feel the true meaning in their inflection by simply being willing to notice. So, not just women. Being naturally sexual I naturally applied my skills to anyone I wished. Old girlfriends, new ones, relatives, your wife, you. Thousands have dripped for me. "Do you remember that time that you told me how wet I make you? You'd just gotten off the plane and you were only with me for about ten minutes." "Remember, when you were fourteen and I had just turned seventeen and you told my friend to get out of your room because you wanted to have sex with me." "Remember when you heard me fucking her above you and it began to turn your mind towards the majesty of my sex." "Living next to me you listened to me call her a whore as you masturbated in your bed, so high on what sex is." "You asked me if you could wipe me, like you did when I was a baby. You said it would be something to see." "When you were ten I would so often stick my hand down your pants. Just twelve but I throbbed for it." "Laying beside me you bared yourself. Hairs just growing on your virgin and open pleasure. Ten times I touched you as you slept so sound and so safe beside your cousin's hand. I didn't know you did this for everyone, hypocrite Catholic repressive whore." "When you rubbed yourself against me and told me we should just do it. And I knew, since we were so young, that you must have been born that way. I guess I was born the way I was too." "Did you always think that your daughter should have been with me? You had the passion. A fire. A sex. Unafraid to eventually have me." "Dog could smell you when you told me you were pregnant. How the lies soiled you." "Daddy's girl, older than me, but a child in her skull." "Watching you smile as I rub you down, knowing you shouldn't, but a man's desire pleases you. Our titles mean nothing, there's no sin, there's genetic mutation. You can feel me against you. Enjoy my beauty as only my well produces it." "Resistant, and wanting, repressed, daddy hating, and so, forcefully grinding and denying." All you had to do to see me throb was see the complexities and push through it so that you would know I smelt you. Don't defend against it. Don't fight it. Be happy that we had it. "In the car, you told me you were glad it was me. So was I."

I am the pleasure of creation. Everyone turning for love. Betraying every standard they clung to, to have the pulse I create. It was my great satisfaction that only openness and the veil and gaze in sexuality triggered in the rise and gush of many.

"Though Capitalism can yield its certain advantages, especially for the Desirous, it leads towards the final outcome. The Great War. Fueled by greed, by expansion, by accumulation, lust and shame. Capitalism has created a way for too many people to become powerful. Those that get money realize it gets people to do things. The small guys can't afford the big guns. Those that have no power to lose will risk anything to have power. To have their freedoms honored and raised superior against any other ideal. All as un-thought-out as all other ideals. The only way to stop it is for all people, everywhere to stop pursuing power. To stop pursuing comfort, superiority, and desire. The world is doomed, and no one has the power to stop themselves in order to save it," that sensation of peace, like you feel when you're dying, follow it, as if it were true.

"Desire used to only have to struggle against sex, food, and power. But the climb is much higher so we increase our desire. In the course of the Desirous Society the Dark People takes pride in their weaknesses and insecurities. They embrace what makes them imperfect. And they build that Pride to feel powerful in their lives. They build it to gain a sense of self-satisfaction, their own ere of superiority. And they develop the Will to enforce their personal philosophies. To turn all others as weak as they are so that they won't have to be criticized any longer. But they will criticize no matter what they make. And the desire to belong and overcome will continue and rot everything they inhale. This is the curse of Society. The curse of formation. It is what the most desirous system to ever exist has created. You are its byproduct. Dysfunctional. Imperfect. Not as good as the other cogs. No matter who you are you feel this way. Unless you are one of us,"

It doesn't matter who began speaking. It didn't matter who suddenly ended it. Just two philosophers talking themselves into oblivion, as is philosophical tradition and unorganized ritual. Who are they talking to? They possess no point to distract them, to make them lie for their own advantage. They have nothing to gain, and so, are Holy men in the instances the Unions occur.

Figurative and Intangible

People always pray with a feverish fear when they are most immediately facing death. No matter how death is facing them, they will pray or at least hope, which is praying, to try and avoid the moment. They want to live, to rule, to love, to revenge, to succeed. And they will want for it. And they will suffer, and be confused by their fear. But not us. We have already faced the loss of everything we could want. Even if we have, even if we strive, we never care that much, our want is only a hammer to bend life properly. We die at peace. You die at fear. Prayer is the final tool of the desperate, the weak, the gathering of illusion to build and sustain. But prayer done without want is holy, and you gain something that can't be proven, or written down literally. Feel the thing we are praying for by looking into the person you are. Now look way deeper.

"All personalities are fake. All personalities are only a mutatious response to the types of situations that have dominated a person's life. The society is dark because every personality within it is a response of weakness, using dark tools to justify their lives and feel superior in their own right. In a dark society superiority and dominance and control rule everything, democracy mixed with Capitalism increased the odds of those that can have power and Democracy created an easy portal to achieve it. The desire for power, even personal empowerment, must use the tool of Pride. And Pride always lead to darkness. To want. To desire. To belong is to compromise all things. We are men of crime, because our chances of being a slave that way was less than that of joining society. The society is imprisoning. It oppresses for the will to be right. The security of control.

<u>Beyond Relationships</u>

"Everything I have ever done has had a positive effect. No matter what the outside bias. I allow people to feel happy without shame. My grandmother was dying. Her body was covered with some type of orange rash. She had no one to help her. It was random that she had me. I had to rub her body down with lotion. I had to cover her body completely in it. Sometimes she slept through it. Sometimes she was awake. She loved it. She loved it when I rubbed it on her pussy. She loved to see the bulge of my dick, because she was a woman. I covered her ass, her tits, her feet. My cock pressed into her arms and legs, the side of her ass. She felt it. Neither of us said anything. When it first began she said, "I'll get my breasts." And I said, "No, I already have this on my hands. I'll get them." Sometimes she would close her eyes and dream of men she had fucked. And men she had wanted to fuck her. Without shame, there was happiness. There was orgasm of the mind. Without shame life was not pain. And she lived for three weeks. And I did my work," The Father or The Priest.

The Priest, "I was with a woman for seven years as came to me in a sudden obscure vision that I could not interpret at the time, not exactly. You. Know. that feeling that you get when you know you're in a spiritual circumstance. Like when a prophet makes a prediction about you and when it happens you swim in its slowness. Though the situation is extreme, that's why you were warned, but you are gently calm for no reason."

"I know."

The Priest, "Well, I had been incredibly desirous of women that have the ability to love deeply. That was my type. God, I'd kill for them. My distant cousin's types were women with insecurities he could manipulate for the sensation of power for the sake of control and slothful satisfaction. We all have a type I guess. So I had been writing a lot of love letters. Letters I meant. Deeply. To women I knew, through experience, would never ever be with a guy like me, but loved me and would lie or die for me. The passion is my ecstasy. Still, if I see that beauty of a truly loving spirit I want to get inside it, and feel it, and worship, and protect it. It can be hard on the people around me. It is my ego propelling its cause. I remember when I first felt my mind running away. When I was completely consumed by thought. Nothing can grip a Man's mind like the chemical tidal wave of lust, so I noticed it because of its strength. It's torrent. And I saw what it did to everyone around me. I saw that everything I do, everything that is programmed into me is my established response to the human condition. I desired. I took. I saved. I loved. I was human. And my soul was set in this body. When I thought on the soul the soul told me. The soul told me that I could stop the course of this momentum, this fury to survive, by focusing on the stillness of the soul. We are infinity, expanded through the expansion of consciousness that is my feeling of God. You will not understand the awe in it, until you truly feel it. I thought I felt it so many times, but I knew when the sensation began to really deepen. When it feels like you're swimming."

"I know. Our egos are of the same type. If people focus on our loving spirits, and not our pre-assumed personalities, if we can show it to someone that appreciates it, it is the most satisfying earthly delight to those that love like us. Truly, Madly, Deeply. It is the three things we try to get out of life. Our most treasured gifts from that which trapped us here, and keeps us returning to slavery," Spake the Father, "But we are Great because we are free from the propulsion of the ego, that which throws us into our duties of creating suffering everywhere. What will Existence do if man breaks all of his controls? What if spiritually advanced man with no religion, the Philosopher, moves in the same exact direction as science? And what if this was the way it was all designed to be? Everyone thinking they are against everyone else to increase the fury of the production of our own end, or our perfect world, saved even by the things we thought would destroy us and saved by nothing but ourselves and will to realize."

The Priest, "The answer is in the soul. The name of God is "I am." We have the ability to speak to God by feeling our own soul. And God says, "So what." So what if it is that way. The soul knows it doesn't matter what happens here. And as far as I can tell, God has no problems. And touching *god* in the soul, *h*e loves it."

"It seems that our ultimate programming insists that we discover the Stillness of creation. Humankind feels the need to want to stop tornado of knowledge it has yet to sink-out into," The Father.

Page lost...

REQUIEM

Every communion like an individual episode
of a now very serious sitcom.
The situation relatable to millions.

A large hand reaches to hold,
a stranger and friend.
A firm grip falls limp.

Stage of Alzheimer's is steady at moderate decline.

Some unusual signs of spontaneous improvement.

Enlarged prostate, chronic kidney failure evident.
Bi-monthy rectal cancer screenings.
A chunk of his intestines if cut away for being cruelly deprived of steady fiber.
These moments of pricks and humming machinery and icy cold steel were met with a state that allowed it. The Father easily resolving to needing assistance, from people whom he could not remember for it, or pass more than a second of appreciation for a wipe, or a turn, or for a cup of water, but the moments passed beneath halogen lights. Humans removed from the decisions by the evidence and results of Science and action and result, and in that fact of results without human perception and personality coming into treatment, seemed to give the man some peace in these times, when the cold becomes hot, and we start to gurgle, rattle, and drown. His friendliness and kindness to staff nurses and compassionate doctors made him a model patient constantly, forcing sweethearted nurses to find janitorial closets, cars, and lunch breaks, to weep at their futility and reassert their need to ease.

<u>Visions</u>

"I have had many visions in my life. I have always known that in the end I would be viewed as loving and kind. I saw my own face when I was older, I may have been in a wheel chair or couldn't walk. I don't know. But my face was gentle. Prior to that vision I saw my business partner's face. It was full of rage. I would have lost my soul with him, wasted this life. The only advantage to visions is that you are given the chance to not fight your natural course like everyone else does.," The Father, "You can flow with gentle fate if you are not afraid of where you are going."

The Enlightened are trapped on a pathway that makes one love deeply and want to help others, while also feeling with even greater strength the need to be away from the rampaging egos that shroud the kindness in people's souls. What if we don't need to fight, who's side do we choose? I would choose a meadow to befriend, quiet and soft, with hearty spongy soil to lie in. Wet and squishy would come the sound of porous soil, but no water would touch my back. The air would be warm. Of course the Sun would not care for a meadow. And it would burn it with heat. Dry it and kill it. But no matter, a field burns without care of its death, and it will suffer to die.

A Leader, A Nation, in Fluctuation

"I'm the kind of man that would fight for himself the whole of his life just to prove that the road of strong freedom is still possible. I'd fight and die, and never be so afraid that I would be afraid of it. Fools. They will never understand what I got, and they never knew existed. I don't care though. How could I? It was theirs to miss. I became what they dreamt to be. A hero. Loyal to a great nation. My Self. Sovereign and Strong. It will hold its independence for its entire reign of humanness. I have no fear of death."
Spake the Father

Flexing in the Universe.
Knowing he can bend it. Knowing it can feel him.
Curving dimensions. Warping Time.
All for the awe of unworshiped glory.

The Father

Speech Before Battle:
It's been a long time since any of you have seen me. (As he scanned the room.) I just want you to know that everyone that I invited, straight to your face...I found you, remember...has shown up here tonight. I thank you all for that. There must be Hope within you yet. All of you have been involved in some sort of action with me in the past. Whether it was a production, a heist, or a conversation. And the special friends know that it was many things. I talked you into facing Risk. All of you know what you showed me in those situations, and it was different and the same for all of you. You've all made dire decisions. And that is the past. Now. Now is the time to put the past behind us. Now is the time to step up out of our adolescence (his voice rising, rising, like a monk flying into the sky) and be the men we have become. Equal on the table of life. Our social and economic standings are unimportant. Alone it is hard to fight forth an empire. But many of you have built small things. But once...you all believed in that pie in the sky! That golden something you saw that you believed I could take you to. True Believers, when we come together we have something to fight with. It's called Capitalism. I seek success to bring peace to suffering times. I don't care why you seek it. You are here for those reasons. Many of which are basely the same anyway. But will you step up, and listen to more? Will you let die the Pride that brought you here? Freedom is the point here. Freedom is the goal of this company. And we can develop a publishing firm that will prosper. And we will have the chance to make Philosophy meaningful again.
(Now, would he flow into the plan, or would he let their faith decide? The Father didn't care if he lost, he just wanted to see what they would do.)
Who will come up here and take my hand? Will it be you? (His hand moved inches from faces.) You? Cowards. You!? Murderers. Failing everyone in this room. Because your hearts aren't good enough. None of you are brave enough to reach for Freedom???

No one say anything? Not enough to gain, you losers, now that you imagine you have something to lose? File out. You don't get the plan, I can do it myself. I just wanted to see if there were any good hearts left out there that were still light enough for any of you to lift.
(Like a knife a woman slid up behind him. Her arms sweeping up from behind to grip him in calmness. And he smiled, and then he laughed. And all left, save one.)
((Or did they all stay? And was there a war??))

Society, ideals, feelings, the concept of the spirit, are all abstract, furtively, and never literal. The Father fought for and against his own causes, checking pride, making opportunity anywhere there was a chance to ease the frustrated and bring them into a passion that will move them into any action at all.

THE FATHER'S MIGHTY FORM

"My form is the Hero. It is what I become when I feel pride in my personality. Because on my route I have overcome many fears and my ego has developed an even greater Will. A Will that can defy anything, and would. A Power stronger than anyone. Mostly I keep this reserved. But sometimes its machinery runs constantly in me. It is felt in the pulls and powers of sex and lust. In my lust for the bare souls of young maidens," The Father said as a wind chilled the floor, "This is not good or bad. This is factual. If it was used for your advantage you would support it and not taint it with the fear you have for your security. Both good and bad are wrong ideals. False ones. Emotional ones, that do not need to play into this ideal. Both control. Both prevent. Both create things to distract you from your truth. I would be shaken...shaken...by the thought. Noticing the disdain that rises in a woman. At first the Intellectual Woman is fascinated with the opportunity to use me. At first. Then as time continues she grows to hate me, because I always believe I am helping people. They grow tired of my constant preaching. Even though I meant no harm from it, only good intentions. But they will not be told what to do. They will not listen, they are self defined. Independent and strong. And fools because they believe so deeply in the ideal of their built personalities that they never humble themselves to see that their strength is their weakness and keeps them from every ounce of love they desire to quench their empty wanting holes surrounded by a vast vacuum of emotion, where logic cannot exist. Pride murders all people in many different ways. I do not deny that I use its full force from time to time. It has yet to fail me when unleashed...In time, I suppose I would have killed Her in one way or another, from within or without...she is deeply fortunate that she got to die so young."

When any of them says "you," they don't mean the person they are talking to, they mean, us and themselves. They mean Humanity.

WRITER'S WRITE

Everything I ever wrote has been based on some sort of fact, even if the fact was an emotion, or a made-up reason. I have never written about anything that I did not have some sort of understanding of, even if my understanding is wrong by being incomplete. People are wrong all the time. The facts are the things that have existed, even if wrong. I gave my knowledge formed from experiences and imagined with them. I gave them to eccentric beautiful souls. It is like they have my soul in different personalities. They are my other bodies. Personalities the energy of my soul can give power to. Just like my soul is doing with this body and personality right now. I accessed something that can create, and I chose to trust it. That's why <u>this</u> *is fiction, my heart will always be the heart of an entertainer bound to the reality of the obviousness in the metaphor. For good or bad, I cannot lose the essence of the being that holds this soul. I want there to be a joy in things, not just the facts. I love to let myself think beyond what happened. Adding what their lives could have made it. It allows me to see from many different views.*

I am the Priest, and that is not me that writes just above. If it mattered at all, I'd point out that some voices seem to give our minds and mouths the words we only mimic and think that we thought.

THE DOGS

The beast moved slyly, slinking across the floor, dancing to display the majesty of his prowess, showing me how beautiful his wolfish sleekness is, and letting me know that he could kill me, but loving me, so he does not. His respect is a great honor. I don't know why it does not frighten me. These visits. All of them come to see me. The canine brothers I walked with, fed, and taught. All of them dancing for me. Some things worry a person, some things don't. That is the nature of being human. But if we notice it, we can always let our worry that yields fearful persecution fall away back to nature.

Oh, my brothers and my sisters that I ran naked with in the forests... you whom gently laughed with me in our bloody panting animalness. Great friends, ye dogs that knew no shame. Within nature there is no shame. And we are free. Free like wolves. Free from fools.

Dancing. Speaking.

Laughing.

THE FAULTS OF A HUMAN

"No matter how deep I go...no matter how far I push into my spirit... when my mind runs I can feel the true weakness of my programming. I can feel the inferiority complex of my mind. It was hereditary in my family. Over justification. Over explanation, constant review, so that people understand our Reasons, so that people think about us the way we want them to. It is my trap that I have overcome for those that bled their minds before me so I could hear them speaking over the babble of my own mind waiting to speak again. It is a programming of the body, as much as addiction, smoking; it is the arrogance of man that thinks he can so easily overcome the weakness of the body; however, we can surely go into anther consciousness that can see these things far differently. Don't you see? What we are striving deeper into is beyond this programming of the mind. In the "mind-set" we are as our egos plan us to be. But we can go deeper. What we are reaching, is not reigned by the weakness of the mind that vies for power, and imagines a place, in this state of Man. This is why it cannot be understood through thought. Thought uses the mind, that uses the brain. Deeper then. There are levels that I do not have this weakness of inferiority. No need to fight, control, or defend. We must sit, work hard, and get deeper," Father.

Their war began, as all rebels, when the teachings present weren't delivering enough. The brain and mind itself did not give them the balance they required. Finding no religion with truth they dived into themselves, and as the truth was revealed to them through researching and experiencing themselves, it led them to others that found the same truth, and made the lonely less alone.

To The Father these thoughts randomly occur, but for you there will be made a pattern, a random one, thank Truth for that, never ever him.

Beside handwritten pile of brilliant waste that has written itself and stacked itself beside me, I recollect, not my own, but, The Father's thoughts:

I see the faces of the women. I see them willing to use you cruelly, and they are ready to condemn you if you dare do it to them. I see a nation of cowardly women. None willing to accept that having nothing is fine, and then they wouldn't do anything to have everything they want all the time. American Woman. But quickly my thoughts shift. To another type. To that woman that wants my power, me whom does not care about the rules she has built around the good person she was when she was younger to be good for her mommy, her daddy, and the men to come, and for her god, or anyone that had an opinion, made up or real. I wanted to strip them and give them the vulnerability that would let them see that goodness that has been covered up with what they doubt. It is too easy and too majestic to resist. It was an addiction that played like a master brought harmony, without pain, and she got to live with the happy secret of having had the man of her dreams. The man that showed her that that goodness was and is what she is. To make it, so that she could fondle her very soul and orgasm a smile across her mind, and so, though wars came and went, she would always come again, thankful, respectfully, serving the kindness that set her Free. Grace. And deadly rare, was the martyr that offers all to ideal. A Powerful Grace. And we may fall side by side a thousand times, in a thousand worlds, in a thousand causes, all of them fighting and falling, because my soul wants everyone to know it. She shares me with the world, and/but gets to hold my heart in her hands, blowing gently on it, to keep it burning blue. She accepts the reality I make will be, and she marvels at the craft, and she learns, and she teaches, and she breaks what I use to help everyone, and she tells me that the soul knows what it is doing, and that I may be calm. OverHumans come together and gain the power to feel what others feel, it is all based on the mental lies that cover the soul. We connect so deeply because we do not need to defend the connection you give but block over. (Deal with me talking in every direction and focus me into your soul and mine again.) WE ARE NOT AFRAID TO SEE WHAT WE WILL BE WHEN WE ARE DEAD AGAIN.

<u>FAITH</u>

"I discovered a great secret to Humanity. A lost truth. I realized that people that believe that God put us here for a reason...that God granted to us life itself...and it was a gift...an undying, forever alive gift...feel very happy. Very energized with a certain glow. This is also true to those that believe that God is absolute Love and that we are a part of that God that is absolute Love within us. The belief in something so pure and good triggers a reaction in people. A sensation of bliss. The wanting to believe in Love itself as an ultimate reality points out the path to bliss. It is a natural phenomena. If you want it you will find it and when you find it you will realize that you never needed it. When this sensation is felt, when hope and light abound, we are given the chance to stop believing. Let that man-made explanation fall away. When you feel only the sensation of the bliss.... Focus deliberately on its great sensation...then we can be led to the reality of what this is all about. Let the illusion of what people have made up for you to believe in fall away. No organization, religious or governmental, can lead us to any salvation. Only you can choose to let the mystic of something stop distracting your mind. God is simple and you cannot see it if you are looking too hard. You can know that you find it if it feels like absolute and massive peace. And if you pursue it...if you let your mind stop making up its ideals then you will be led naturally to a peace that will leave you in awe. This is not made-up. This is something that I <u>experienced</u> directly and witnessed without a judging bias or any fear...This is what I have learned from my continual research.

We all have the ability to put any sensation into anything. We have the ability to feel any ideal, any ideal, as a God. People put faith into every faith. It is faith that heels us and faith that leads us away from God. Faith does this to us because we are too afraid of the penalties that might happen if we do not pay homage to God. This "worship" of God was made-up. You don't have to "worship" any God. There is no penalty for it. If you believe in religions people can convince you to serve them and you will think you are serving God, but you are not. Know that there is no penalty. Know that there is no reward. We are all an absolute part of living, constant, creation. And, You have to feel that yourself. If you believe in these words I have written or someone else has told you...you will not find it. Your faith is keeping you from absolute salvation. You will not find God in a church. God is in you. A church just makes you think you have found God, when instead you have clouded your relationship with God because you sought a shallow, instant, egotistical relationship, made-up for you to order on a Saturday or Sunday, convincing you you are worthy of praise and victory. How do you feel when someone assumes they are getting something from you? There is no favoritism. No bias. Be your own church, the desire to know God is within yourself. Use it. Don't try to tell anyone about it. Or your habit of worshipping faith might return as you inflict your beliefs on another. The goal is further reached by always focusing on freedom. Freedom from the cruelty of yourself...that which is there for your survival...God is not only absolute Love but absolute Freedom as well."

The Priest

Faith is to be used for all its benefits that carry us through hard action and various poverties. Religions cause murder, persecution, and false education, and should be abandoned, but the spirit constantly remains for us to use faith with.

A hero faces his full spectrum, as he or she must to be prepared. The journey of diverse, and masterfully felt emotions, can feel the pleasure in the reasons of every lover, beauty, rapist, murderer, politician, tyrant, saint…all for the burden of loving and reasoning on behalf of all of them. Nothing could be real to me, so that I could move amongst their thoughts, and feel the sink into the heaviness of their feelings, that shit which they think is real. That shit that they will die and damn to endlessly justify the correctness of.

We now have the ability to understand why. This is the next height of Philosophical Beings. Existentialism is the door for the "West." But Rapists…when I see you close by. And I feel you passing me. And I feel the glory you feel in the domi-Nation. You are so easily stabbed to death. And you stare at the woman I took time to seduce, that I mastered, and honed a hum of happiness and tantalized value into, so that she walks beside me laughing, forgetting, dreaming, and dripping through the folds of her lips that I split as I pushed into the tightness while I was kissing her last night, while whispering, "I hope you think about me tonight when you're with your husband." See, loser rapist. I'm raping her, and she knows. It's exciting, and there is life involved, laughter.. And when she doubts I calm her. There will be no one to calm you, rapist, when you are alone in the coming dark. When the power fades. But even your own death gets you off…doesn't it…Is there a way to help you out of the tiny cave you are in? Running as fast as you can, waving your elbows, bashing and smashing the blood and the marrow, tearing yourself, ripping just a bit of the soil from the hard wall, never realizing that there was a whole world with light at the top of the earthen shaft. How rapist, will you touch Calmness? Without the power of a Mountain Lake, or a Redwood, or an Ocean. Without love, you will only soon be mush on the floor, only proving your point to yourself, that you did not matter. And so you spent a thought. Like a huff of smoke in the night. You made Mad people, called cops, to seek vengeance to torture the rest of us with surveillance. And you were proud to be a demon, but you never really believed it. Your demon heart, letting you feel good about destruction. The animal is in us all. These weaklings, just couldn't face the vulnerability that rests plainly beneath every false demon, as weak as their prey, but weaker and forced by themselves to act. We all rose from vulnerability. You are ignoring in a woman what you don't want to realize you have always been and will keep being.

A Rapist turns Hero when he realizes he can never be strong. And that is the cure for who he has left behind. Let's call it Acceptance. Seduction begins when a woman is either empowered by "nastification," eclipsing her vulnerability, or is willing to indulge her vulnerability, or she loves you which eclipses and embraces her vulnerability and opens her. But if done cool, she'll always love you. And if you're cool, you'll always love her.

The thrill of sex is Risk. The root is vulnerability.

No matter what you think you are making yourself, you will never be more than human.

I have come to reason that man is meant to ease its own suffering and the suffering of other creatures. Medicine is not defying nature. Every organism, even a planet possesses something that helps it and something that can kill it. Man is interesting because he can choose which to be. He can change the shape of the mind.

I possessed the genius (it always amazed me how simple a word genius is, yet I always put an "o" in it, like genious. A true genious, one that can see how he is, and that can travel so deeply into the complex that he can see how simple the word should have been.) ***to be able to create my own style of writing when the genre did not possess a functional way for how my mind worked. That is true love for what you want to do. This is the only life I will be this person. This does not live forever. Just your soul does. Just these Great Works do.***

"There is a simple way to sustain a relationship. There is a simple way to live a life where someone loves you completely. Do all that you can for the other that chose to be so close to you. And never have resentment for the other person that sacrificed their heart in the hopes that you would be there. Don't hate a person that is trapped in their own personalities and their own limits and abilities for not pleasing you. It takes two. Two wills, two positives to make balance. They try as hard as they can for you, that is why they resent you too. Suffering...because what you want reality to be is not what reality is... stop seeking power over perception. You should be seeking to alter reality for your pleasure. The "should" is to your advantage. Do it and make your life easier and far more beautiful. All you have to do to get everything you want is to give up wanting and the resistance, the fighting, that you do against all aspects of the world...as they will fade and love will naturally drift compassion into your reality... because you no longer fear its vulnerability or compromise that makes you think you are unfree or reigned. You never have control, and eventually your angst, your want to be winning, your hand, will force you into discomfort again, in any situation. You, each person, is the one that makes them suffer. No one else. Not really. We choose to want to matter," heeeeeehhaaaahhhhhaaaeeeeeeeeeeeeeee, hissed that Father, knowing of the power that weeps through him. "Do not struggle against your frustration to understand how a completely different mind works."

Did you ever write anything that makes you feel magnificent and beautiful, original and helpful to everyone you truly deeply love, to those that will cry for you when you are only dark emptiness in their lives? Did you? And did you witness the disappointment in another person's eyes when they read the majesty you wrote and they say, "eehhhhh," because they were not in the same mood as you, or could never understand the glory of the ineffectual mood you were in? Well? What have you done?

Possibilities of the Guarded Mind -- The Possibilities of Ignoring the Security

All men are capable of sacrifice and all men are capable of survival. All men are capable of running and all are capable of fighting. And all men can create reasons to justify these actions. A person holds the ability to have the only perception that counts. The perception of the self. Man has come to think that he can place a function on everything on Earth. However, he cannot place a label on himself, or any action (since man has become a definition of actions and justifications for those actions), actions have results that are both negative and positive on the physical and psychological environments: The reasons for these actions are irrelevant, the results of these actions are important. The negative weighed against the positive, the created and the destroyed. As a result of people's greed and selfishness to build their own tiny empires of glory, wealth and stability and to believe that it was their great reasons that got them there...oh the tyranny rains down from the self-righteous, from all that would force us to be as pleases them, for what is best for us, for lies and reasons, misguided from a comfortable place. We are a nation controlled by the psychologically diseased. The fearful prosper in Capitalism, and they work hard for the proof to show that what they believed in mattered while they took education and jobs from people that made their place and whom they will never know. The managers, the teachers, the tellers, the users, the controllers, all the same...all unable to break the bonds of fear that crank the neck to peek further into the uncertain near future or the lazy ass that weighs them to a surface of a plastic chair in need of more stuffing. Lives of fear. Lives of fallen slaves and lazy heroes. And always the tyranny in your heart, that makes you this way, is the fear of the loss of this body. Always the fear of death. Always the glorification of your justified Reasons. The arrogance of the ego.

SERMON OF THE PRIEST
ADDICTION

Are you one addicted? Addicted to pain? Addicted to your destruction because you cannot see the worth in your life? Is it shame that drives you down? The heart loses faith in itself when it does not live up the expectations of the mind. If one is trapped by the illusions of self-inflicted shame, if you want to be perfection and feel you can never be so, then the insecurity that causes this will always draw one back to self-destruction. But! If you can see that there is nothing one has to be, that there is no real ideal on Earth, but those made-up by other inferior insecurities that sought power over those people and situations that made them uncomfortable, if you can take yourself back to the root before these problems existed...if you can learn to be still...enter into a state where you can accept the world's natural loss and accept the warped interpretations people may or may not have on you...if you can let it all be...then addiction can be overcome. You can be free from yourself, and possibly without even quitting it. Free from the insecurity that makes real addiction. Most people that are addicted just want to stop hating themselves. They use excessive drug use to not face themselves, or at least they keep using it after the social world gets a person into it. You must be able to face yourself and see yourself honestly, and sigh, and see that all the world is as imperfect as you are. This is our opportunity to create compassion. Return to the point of stillness and laughter, before insecurity, then we can be free of psychosis, so often called disease. But psychosis is not normally disease. It is normally fixable without medication, but medical chemicals can help and they should, and you can leave your fears in science fiction films. One should never mask addiction with medication for the comfort of others, that only feeds the insecurity, the having to live up to the expectations of others. Wanting to belong...wanting approval...desiring position...this is the way to many addictions. Want is always the path to Darkness. Desire to matter and the desire to not want to want to matter and to not know where to turn but obliteration...this is what kills people, not often

drugs. Psychology kills. This Dark Society's greed to matter kills.
Surrender to meaning nothing. It is all right to not matter. As you
realize it does not matter, you then build equality from the point of
nothing, until the whole world stands in your mind as even. In the
end, as death sweeps us away, clearly none of us matter. And that
is just fine, we don't need killers to prove it. By realizing that...we
see our simple worth...a value that does not have to be anything,
but has a value by simply Existing. To be free from addiction, stop
being ashamed of who you are. The ideals of Darkness are false. To
follow the false ideals will lead to the addiction of wanting others to
value you. Value exists only when we place it in something, and this
includes ourselves.

THE PRACTICE AND DEVOTION TO CELIBACY

"Every man must choose between debauchery and love. I choose love, only because it is easier to reach my goals in such a way. Sex is so time consuming. And most people are not worth even cumming in, because they seek power for the whole of the time you speak to them. The truth cuts deeply, and people scream out in pain for it to stop, but what they should do, must do, is tear deeper the wound and feel its pain. Pain itself. Pain alone. And it leads us to nothing. The answer....But I can bring the lust forward and raise it. There is great power in it. I still get hard when I shave my balls. ***Intimacy.*** Most weak souled people choose love. It is less risky, more comfortable for the lazy. Some can choose both. They can easily compliment each other. But most minds can't handle the balance of differing communication styles for multiple woman that rest in differing emotional states within the mind. The man that simply takes from the same pool constantly is sick and depraved because the water gets stagnant. But a Lover takes from all sides of the track. A Lover devours what pleases his deepening sense of self. A Lover finds the next gateway for his talents. Lovers gain. Never use. Always elevate their mistresses. Always loves his mistresses. And leaves his mistresses with warmth and hope in their hearts. That is the Lover Artist. A rapist and a king," The Priest.

"Love brought me some of my greatest breakthroughs. Sex too. But love is more powerful to someone that is paying attention to it. Listening, valuing, responding, or at least trying to, even if he fails because his mind is strong. I remember once I spoke to a woman I had been with for some time. And as she spoke I heard her words for the first time. Surely, I knew she loved me. She was devoted to me. Probably still is, but there was a moment when I was struck. I was having a personal sexual revolution at the time...so I happened to be very sexual...and vulnerable...she had just fucked me really hard in the ass nights before. ***Thank you for risking your humanity and fake place with reality.*** I was united with peace inside myself. I managed to calm my mind and I heard her. She was lonely. I was all she had. I was her only friend. If I did not slow myself to give her compassion and deep moving love and shattering sex, than I was nothing of the glory I am capable of making myself into. We sixty-nine'd a lot, boy, she could eat an asshole. What can a relationship be when there are no expectations, true devoted mutual unselfish love? *What?* You deal with the shit of life, but...I did anything to be with that love for as much time as possible. My life is important to me, because I know it means nothing to anyone, but for their own satisfaction, which means far less than nothing," The Father.

The Hardest Revolution

This Revolution is the hardest one in History, yet it is for the reasons as every other one in History. People feel restless, they feel controlled (by something, anything, but they are). They suffer too much and they must find a way to stop it. Then there comes a revolt. A revolt that destroys the Revolt's People, and everything around them. Man is most dangerous when he is doing something, and creates more for himself to do. This is the Hardest revolution because the goal of the revolution is to stop ourselves from having it. We try so hard to imagine the revolt, make up reasons for it, lying ourselves into belief, meanwhile the other side, whatever it may be, plotting and scheming away their lives. Wasting the joy of life. So how do we stop it? That's right. What? The answer. <u>We</u> have to stop. My mind drives forward on a million thoughts a second...so does everyone's... it piles forward building and building a Tower of Babble. Forcing you into every action. From the beginning when you had your first thought and you began to retain knowledge it builds and builds. And in this society it builds fast. You learn so much, and we are so smart that we know to be afraid of everything. And we know that if we learn we will be safer. So we stop the cycle. We shut down the system and take control of the mind. We must learn how to not be controlled by the mind. And the way to do that is to learn how to silence the mind. To sit and work at it. It is hard. It is so difficult because it is the rampaging mind that must find it. And the mind wants to think up a reason. But there is no reason. The mind can't think it. You just have to give it up. If you had given the mind up, you could not have had the thought of where to find it. If you have the thought you need to go further. It becomes a game. And as the mind silences we realize more and more that we are not the mind. We exist without it. So what are we? Don't think about it. But the name for what we are is the soul, it is unowned and untouchable, even by you. Though, when you are the soul, you cannot name it. But you know that you are the very essence of the universe that you worship. You learn that you are the manifest of God on Earth, like all living beings. Your soul is a part of God, like all living beings. And it is all the same in every person. This is the truth of it. It is not to be contemplated. It is factual. You cannot make up fact. You must experience it. And we can. We have. Just put the brakes on it for two hours. Everyday. It takes at least that. I recommend four when you first start. When you are at war against yourself you fight all the time. Like in any modern war. But nobody dies. When you are fighting this Revolution, you won't appear to be doing anything, so you can certainly not be killing.

We are not the mind, we can silence it, but the mind must be exercised and activated directly to perform and create. <u>Our</u> Revolt just gives you a real sanctuary, a blissful heaven, that you keep with you and can access at any time.

"The Priest chooses this Revolution. He bares witness to the Saints that went through hell, to get to heaven, so the rest of the restless, the frustrated, and the violent, will have a sanctuary to achieve," The Father anointed me when he knew I had become his friend when I joined the cause of his mind and his unfathomable heart.

Growing Fear, Choosing to Stop It

As you age you feel growing fears. You wander home, again and again, and back to that early feeling when the world served and feared for you, before they developed the instant diversion of their eyes. You seek more and more familiarity as everything moves beyond you and everything around you becomes less and less familiar faster and faster. And you want. You want everything to stay the same. You want to try and control it and change it back, back to when you felt powerful. Back to your time of control. You want and want. And this want makes you ache. It makes you suffer. It harms you. And the want will grow and grow as you have less and less control. And you will suffer more and more. But those of our Revolt, do not feel this want. Though it is natural. And it arises, and we can notice it warping us. All types of yearnings arise, all types, sexual, violent, frightened, but we can notice them. And we can revert back to the Point of Stillness. And all these desires that swarm through our heads are calmed. And we do not have the fear that makes you suffer and makes you absolutely need to survive. Although it is clearly programmed into our being to struggle, lie, cheat, etcetera (or abbreviate etcetera)....(wait)...So much is programmed into us from the habits of the generation before us. That is why as societies grow we grow more and more and more complacent and spoiled and imperialistic, because there is more and more comfort and more and more wants that can be satiated, less and less humbling, more and more Sloth as the relativity of having nothing and having anything is flooded out by having so much from birth. It leaves one not realizing how close the filthy forest is, and how much it took to simply survive, long before we had to think sooo much to feel stable. Unless we stop the momentum of growing money we will rot, destroyed by our own want that you won't stop. Life is a better prize than victory.

<u>A NOTE ABOUT ZARAT</u>:
However, Zarat chose to feel it. Chose to Reason. Chose to fight on and on, until he wanted it to all stop. Profound and poetic echo found in the reverberation of a large and empty church. A bullet hole left in through the pane of stained-glass shaping the form of St. Christopher. Quickly repaired, quickly cleaned, quickly shaping the image that death must be feared and comfort must be had. Teaching children that they live in a world that they do not, a world of a perfect comfort. It is why people suffer so much when they find out it is a world of suffering. It is why there is such mass repression and avoidance, so much true cowardice. Zarat knew that a beautiful passing, a great treaty, would be warped by the Dark minds. He knew they would create suffering. He knew there was no way to be able to be concerned with them. He knew that they must free themselves by stopping their wanting. Zarat knew they would not.

The Father thought that Zarat had killed himself until the day he died. After Zarat's book came out, everyone thought so. The imagery is simply the poetry of The Father and his obvious respect for the way that killer boy that loved big and deep would strike himself out and with whom he'd like to leave the strike.

Life's Carnage and the Practice to Ease Suffering in the Face of Our Helplessness

"We watch violence from afar, it sterilized into our minds by television and film. But to be amongst it...To see the randomness and ridiculousness that brings the mangling of a human body. The more I have seen the more I wait for it to happen to me. The more I wait for it to happen to the people I care for. This fear, overtime, is what has driven too much Darkness into the Church. People turning to God to be saved from this suffering that leads to death. But this is not what God is. It is not serving God; it is begging for a magic biscuit. That salvation of greed and pride never comes. I believe that a Servant of this world comes to it, chooses to continue to live in it, to fill in the gaps of this randomly perfect sudden design. To ease the suffering we will have if our hearts were cowardly, like most hearts of civilization that know only the slight touches of death that have shattered people into franticness. I became a Priest for so many Reasons. At least it was a chance to guide people towards peace and not fear. It is good to see the face of death in the panicked eyes of a fool that knows nothing of the Spirit, it surely teaches us that we are not gods. And that the knowledge of God is devoid in the lives of most people that claim to know it," The Priest

"The face of death is a terrifying one. The screams of half limp bodies...I can see why people are so afraid of dying. Especially after someone they love dies in a suffering way. Most of the religious and political leaders that support wars of any kind have never seen one. Anyone that wishes that type of suffering on another human... hmm...The Girl had no fear of it, or if it was there we couldn't tell anymore._ But as I made her body meat with my blow... Oh! I remember the moment her soul was ejected. I remember her body going limp, the kink in her neck the second before she collapsed. I had already began to remember what little she could. I had killed before her, but never since, she taught me what it was like if I had known everyone that I had killed. Why does the mind remember so hard, what it wants so badly to forget? She stopped the war by making me kill her," The Father.

"We work again and again on the thoughts we don't want to remember. We bring it up and bring it up to try and keep it from our consciousness. It is a bad cycle to get stuck in. It helps most if we could think of it and make ourselves fine with it. But often times Man does not have the wisdom to," The Father, "That Girl's message that came to me in an instant that I have been forced to translate into words in order to warp it has taught me that we do not need to be afraid. It looks bad before we get there, but when we leave here, we know it was all nothing to worry so heavily about. There was never really anything that could actually happen to us, just to our bodies, just to our minds, just because of malfunctions, the soul is where redemption is. It is through it that we can know the peace of death, without the lies put to the terror of its face."

"If you hear a man that claims to be holy speak like this, then you know him to be holy," The Priest.

"That Nameless Hero, sweet Girl, is where I needed to go. She was there at the end. It never could matter that I was older, only pride is so stupid, she is the Holy Spirit that at the end we are to realize is exactly who we've been, and it can keep no name," The Father.

Contrary to what I might Think

"It is logical to believe in hope. Things will go bad for a time, but something advantageous usually eventually happens. A man never knows what surprise is around the next turn. People believe in the possibility of a better. Because of this it is easy to raise an army and convince them to kill." The Father's Words, "Funny. I think most things I've said in my life would be against that idea. Man can make a Reason for anything. How could man ever figure It out. There are so many paths...but few currents."

"We shape the world in our own image. It's like a zoo. We are all animals living in the cages of our rampant methods and conclusions. Every type of person, industrialist or spiritualist, is just trying to overcome nature in their own way. Fighting with different tools. Running from the way nature would have it, all of us living and dying, bloody and laid. Both afraid of what will happen if they do not try. If they are fully engulfed in life in its full form. All slaves to that Fear of Judgment, from anywhere," Holy Words from the Church, "Where is real Faith? Beneath the camouflage of what we think we should be doing. There is no Fear or resentment for what faith did not give you. There is only what you have left. And if what is left is fear, your faith was always rooted in fear, choose to believe in something because you know it is true, not because you want it to be."

Both have stood before legions. Spoken softly. Spoken sharp. But the ears that heard could not listen. The words of the wise cannot be understood by those that have a shallow perception, for those too filled up with the air of themselves. All they wanted towards the ends of their many speeches was just a single person that might understand the depths of their endless thoughts. One person that could echo back a single positive rational that was hard to get to. But lonely is the leader, weak his heart grows, he's the only one that good, no one is smart enough to get It. How fortunate that they get to be so intimate with each other's passion. To preach their thriving wars to ears that could truly care.

CONTROLLED BY PLEASURE

"Can we help our selfishness? We know we can. But what about the base selfishness, for food, for sex, for survival? Especially sex. We don't have to breed, but we want to breed with most things. It obsesses us. We think about it always. Some even more than us. Do you know how many children I knew I could have been with?" The Priest.

"Do you know how many women I have been with? Over and over, and I loved it every time, at least until I came," The Father.

"Most of us that aren't programmed with thinking that a family makes us adults don't want children, but it does not stop us from wanting sex. I am not even supposed to jackoff but I must, or I would have taken it from too many. It is so strong. It is my programming to want," The Priest.

"I love it, there is no doubt. I love the interaction of it. The force, the vulnerable power, the lust itself, the orgasm to a lesser extent, but I'd work so hard to get there. I could see it though. Controlling me. The pleasure was taking my life. I only thought of who I could fuck. When and how. What I would make them feel for the massage of my mind. It is an easier and holier path to escape the need for pleasure. There is more time to love what is with you, as opposed to thinking about what else you can fuck while you are fucking, after I orgasm this next time," The Father. "Actually though...and truly now...there was that One...that time that angel of ecstasy flexed her powers on me and showed me the bliss of the all consuming orgasm. I had no control. Not a single thought, nor did I need one. I couldn't speak for a good two minutes. I couldn't move for a great five. It was a pleasure to be paralyzed by her talent. (Yes...a relationship where one would do anything for the other is always in perfect equality.) She drank every drop. I have known magnificent souls with marvelous mouths that they used with me."

"We must let it all go. Everything that pains us and pleasures us. Everything that controls us. If freedom is our desire we have no other choice," The Priest.

"But how?" The Father, "When the force arises, stop, and direct it somewhere else. Force yourself to not act on it, or avoid it. Face it, feel it, and realize that you do not have to act on it if you don't want it. Don't feed it with the fantasies of the mind, silence the mind. Then you can do it or not do it. It won't make you do it. Well, it will, but you can shut it off if wanted. But it is best for holiness and freedom to overcome it entirely. It made my life more sufferable, more difficult. I had to leave it. Pleasure causes suffering."

"Any woman, in any situation, be she married for twenty years, infatuated with another young man, twelve, fourteen, seventeen, twenty-seven, from any culture...I could make her want to open her folds," The Priest.

"Me too," The Father. "I never had to rape a woman. Every woman is a whore that wants to howl. One just needs to know how to turn it on. Sex is perpetually present."

"Even now. I feel it. The arousal. The surge of that energy. I would have you. Any fantasy is create-able in my head. All acceptable for the pursuit of my pleasure. This is a benefit and a dilemma to this path. We can do anything, and we must overcome that," The Priest.

"It will be a greater science of freedom if we can overcome it now, not if we pursued the experience of sex. There is nothing to advance beyond with it. I have orgasmed in every way," The Father. "Sexual energy can be directed toward any action to make the action occur more frequently. If you want to meditate a lot, do so every time you want to cum."

THE HERO

It is never the "coward's way" to fight back against insurmountable odds. The freemason Society that seeks to have no conflict against its tyranny will always call those that oppose it cowards, but to fight the situationally-powerful supremacist is True Courage. The Revolutionary that seeks to free himself against the "justice" of Darkness is an actual hero, because he did something, not because some tragedy happened to him. Just because you are killed does not mean you are a hero. Just because you rule does not mean you are a hero. If you fight against those that seek power over you or your friend with excessive penalties, then and only then, are you a hero.

THE HOLY

All ethos, every philosophy, even atheism, is derived from the belief of what the afterlife is. And each side attempts to enforce and spread its "proper" imagined knowledge. Maybe it is a battle for Heaven? We all fight to prove the way in which we are most satisfied.

THE LONELY AND THE FREE

The Dark Society spews forth from the mouths of the greedy and secure. When everything is said to justify yourself, to prove that you are right, this is the Darkness. This is the suffering for those that believe they are the ego. They will fight and fight to wrongly prove that they are right. It is the root of every political and special interest entity. This is the formed Dark Society riddles with good intentions, and enemies we must befriend.

"The People of the World will not be able to understand this through intellectual description. They aren't smart enough, but anyone can be taught to understand the Spirit. Anyone can see what they really are, and how this world is not worth fighting over, and compassion will keep it alive," The Priest

"The whole of my life I have stayed devoted to the One Desire. I always made sure that I wanted nothing. I expected nothing. Even though I could take, if I chose not to, I knew I would be fine. I knew even if I died, I could do so wanting nothing. Because of this...A result occurred...I was free to Love with the greatest of intensity. Give myself without fear of losing myself. Even though I knew that if I lost myself and got betrayed, the pain would mangle me. I knew...that pain is something I could gain...there was nothing to lose. People have loved me with absolute deepness. Even if they betrayed me later, as most hearts do, still they kept with them that sting of love for me. I always heard it in their voice. Even if they knew I betrayed them. Because they knew I truly loved them. And so a second result occurred...because I stayed devoted to the One Truth, I could give much. I never needed much. I took enough, certainly what I needed, but I was never greedy. So people never felt taken advantage of. I always, naturally, as a result of a previous action, gave more than I got. These are the effects of choosing to not need," The Father. "I often sought more love. Often. I craved it. But still, it was not so greedy a love that I would betray a love I already had. If I wanted sex, wanted a new experience of it, a new expression, I would bring my new lover home. Give them to each other. Or, I could. For my pleasure, like anyone's that could let go of what the society tries to program us with. Sex. A pleasure. Without power. Just play. Dominance. And Submission. Loving Intensity. What love can be with a free heart that is strong enough to stay together while riding from plateau to plateau. Don't you see, I loved her so much that I didn't want to be without her. I wanted to share my lust, my experience. Even if she wasn't there, I kept her love so close to me. How could it ever leave? Because I stayed devoted to the Path, my life, even parts that make others uncomfortable because they desire them but do not have the courage or intelligence to manifest them, I, my life, all aspects were in an absolute state of perfection because I expected nothing from anything and was always pleased with what

I got. The risk, the consequence, the advantage...nothing. All equal in the majesty of what I can gain. Because my perceptions make a perfect world for me. This is how we can win this New War."

<u>Our Parents live to long. Our Parents do not leave us free long enough. Our lives are too short</u>.

"I find myself wanting. Praying. Loudly. Fiercely. Forcibly. It does not last for long. But as I age my body begins to cry out. AGHHYAHH. It spasms. It howls. For the lasting moment. This body begs for it. It wants to see her face again. To have her, smiling, never withering. Never falling. Always rising. It hates that it is gone. That something is gone. It weeps in my depths, drowning me until I want death and fear it deeply. This is the nature of the ego...As I transcend the illusion that the weak have not yet had the courage to release from, I explode without noticeable action and shroud the gentle veil of peace. I know no fear. I am certain of my outcome. I am positive of my swimming laughing existence. And I want no more for my Right to Freedom. I expand. I am calm. And I suffer no more. I want for nothing. But surely, the ego will be there, somewhat, always grinding my mind, driving me mad. I wait. I wait for the moments that my body and mind are uncontrollable. Dying. Mostly dead. More dead than alive. But still, not Nothing. I await that course, and I await the depths when I will be able to access myself. Though it is so near...I will know a better sense of spiritual density. This free life, The Existing Mind that transcends the belief in itself...unto those that understand what that means without illusion to advantage. Huh.?. Will this fear inevitably make me cling to this world? Will I be able to let this world go?
I don't believe that my constant Practice in knowing a deeper, freer self, a holy me; I don't think that I will ever forget the realism of my spirit. I will always crave to find its Stillness again. With Love reoccurring at the actual root of my striving struggle to cope with our inherent animalness. No matter what mind or personality I have. When the fear is too much, gripping my malleable mind with tension, I will automatically dissolve into the truth I have always been. And I will have the opportunity to remember what I am. The unspiritual should not feel afraid of their lack of knowledge. Don't

feel insecure. Don't dismiss and mock. Be calm. Do not be afraid that you are going to die. Don't retract with cynical scoffs. Please stop killing. Please let us stop fighting against those that want the "best" for us," Spoken Unto Us, "Why did I become a Priest? All because I was afraid. Afraid to not be able to be still enough at the moment. I needed time to focus. I needed my time back. Or else I could not accomplish it. I had to overcome fear. I had to be without fear. I feared it. There is no path without fear. But how will our souls choose to bravely use it? When will we be brave enough to surrender and no longer make ourselves fear and seek to make comfort for our fleeting times?"

When we all stop taking up arms to prove that we are the wisest, or when we stop wanting to be the safest, then we will know that we are free. A world without fear.
However, I am 100% man, intermingled with 100% Godly Spirit. Both in full reality. Both conflicting their truths. I also, have the power to be the strongest of the lambs, and stop those that will not stop their vengeance for the injustices they imagine. My compassion is absolute, it has nothing to do with my own comfort. It will help those I can love. Help the world ahead be more free. I am a warrior, that is free from the old weaknesses. Because I know I am not these weaknesses. However, since my concern is actually for the good of all, not for my greedy, self satisfying Self, then the Reason, or sudden action, does not normally swing that way. There are many paths, some of them bloody. Many paths oppose. Many fall, but one is always more free, for everyone. Let Go. How could you be right, if everyone else is too? You, like all of us, are a primitive psychotic. Your Reason is not the one that should be supreme.

"I was always amazed at how comfortable she always was," The Father.

"Why did I become a Priest?" Me affecting him. He can let me in and feel me, but for him not to notice makes me think his spiritual walls are crumbling.

Deaths

"I held a gun to a man's head and I watched the fear shake within him. I saw in his eyes absolute terror. Complete fear. Most men die with this fear. The fear of what they have always known was capable of being turned against them. The thing man fears most is himself. It is what he sees the world as. And all holy and non-holy people know that they too could feel the fear when facing death and the coldness that comes over you when you hold a gun to a man's sweating head. And then it happened. Instantly. So Beautiful. His eyes grew calm. His shaking ceased. And he felt it. He used up the fear within him. The emotion reached a point where it was simply not useful to have it. He knew peace. I smiled as the sound of the gun sent a bullet ripping through his skull. I hardly noticed I even pulled the trigger. For all people that enter fearful situations, the great strong ones, push beyond the fear. This man used that technique on me to save his soul from madness. He used it quick. Mine was tempered into me by each time I killed another person. It's the same reason I don't fear another woman's bullets. When the fear stopped I could see that I did not need to have it on," The Father. "Every situation holds the potential of peace and the ability to see with eyes unclouded by hallucinations of majesty."

WHAT CONTROLS YOU?

Priest: "My Friend, I can see the source of your ego. The single strongest point that holds it and swings it. How you believe you are right. How you turned from the simple path and gained the quiet rumbling voice that rolls out stories that are true and hard. How you sit there with no fear and with contempt for what you must expect to see in people, but when truth is shown to you, honesty and purity, you'd vow, fight, and die for it. You are lucky it is rare. But this that you serve, this kindness that expects nothing but appreciates everything that does not try to use it...this path that you chose...is what binds you. The Pride that you have for the Reason that you have formed. Though less than it must have been, still you must let it fall, you must fall deeper into what is more still."

"Yes." :Father, "I have always had to use the stillness to push further in my cause, past the doubt of my abilities. Without concern of the canyon that the river of my life leaves behind. That is not my concern. My concern is not where the water winds up. My concern is nothing. I can only be water. Only sit and flow and be what I have been. Slowly ripping, seeping, and splitting myself into the rock of my ego that traps me. Everything I am doing is my natural desire for more than this. But yes, you are right. Pride. I can break its programming even more."

"Look deeper My Friend. I am challenging you. See it in your actions now that you know it. Why do you expect other people to live up to the expectations you have made for yourself? Don't you feel slighted by it? Every feeling that brings discomfort, that you want to run away from...any discomfort, is an opportunity to change. To remember the stillness. By doing this we go deeper. And we see God. We return to the essence of consciousness. You see, when you come through and others don't, you have contempt for them and elevate yourself slightly. You define yourself. This is the ego. That which dies. That which should not be worshiped," The Priest.

"You are doing well. Seeing deeply. Seeing yourself and telling me about it, because we are trapped by the same things, you know that I will understand. That's good. Wise. Ever deeper and we shall be free. Where we see even more than now," The Father.

"Anytime we turn to the anger that justifies us...Anytime we grow angry when anyone disapproves of us, and we make their degrading word our pride...When we follow our causes with this passion.... When we need to be just as good as anyone else...When we need to be better than anyone else...When we believe in rank and class... When we sell ourselves for approval, especially our own...When we need to belong somewhere...Anytime anyone follows any war...Or any Reason...and knows it is right...even if that sensation fades into the reality of a longer life where many causes rise and fall...This is the ego in action. This is the root of war and suffering...and it lives inside you...And it all comes back to the same root, the fear of the death of the identity built and slaved for...it stimulates everything. And the neuroses created by the threat of penalties lying after death stirs the cauldron of confusing that continually keeps the People from knowing where to turn. Naturally, we must turn to ourselves. And find approval for being human there," Priest.

<u>Minds Change,
Don't Cling too Tightly to Belief.
Believe Lightly</u>

"What people do not expect about this path is that their minds will change, while Physics remains the same. It is important to let go of the mind, the identity, so that the mind is free to change. This is the whole point of silencing the mind. So that it may evolve by deepening consciousness into something that is calm. This is also where we use Faith. We choose to travel the path because we believe in the sincerity of someone's words, or we were struck by God and made a slave to happily tell people about the truth of death, forced into it because the perception of it is so false and imagined otherwise. It is sad when people believe their imaginations are deductive thought. It is more and more common. The curse from the modern school teacher. They pushed imagination too much and not deduction. But anyway, faith is used to go on. And it is the belief that the individual has in himself, the faith that he isn't going to not exist if he doesn't have to hang on to what he wants to have live forever. Know your thoughts die along with everything else you think you are," The Father.

"It is common to see/feel a quiet pride that is often doubted when one goes against the mainstream, or primaryriver. When one fights the criticizers head on. It is a natural way that the psyche deals with the brave. But one must be strong and not believe in the identity that the mind wants it to take. This is the nature of evolution," The Priest.

<u>RPG</u>

"Have you ever played an RPG? Have you ever played an RPG? Have you?...ever...? A <u>R</u>ole <u>P</u>laying <u>G</u>ame exists in a world with numerous fabricated societies, economies, and relationships destined to be controlled and broken free from. I knew a girl once...she showed them to me. When you play one after another person you really realize that there are other minds in the world. Different ways to think one is right. You really get to see: 6 Billion human worlds, all with the ability to constantly perceive and explode into violent action, all for the single goal of living through life in the absolute most beneficial way for their own preservation. At least, that is what I got out of them. I liked to speak about what she liked," Sometimes I would write merely to delight her. Knowing she is here. Knowing that she came back to sit with me. I sit or lay, thanking her for being here. Silent. Pure. Anywhere in the Universe, and she came and sat with me. Holy Stillness...Dead beside me. The Spirit of a Living Girl. Touching me. Laughing at me. Knowing that a human becomes anxious when a spirit is so near. Continuing to remind me that I am here because I feel the gentle buzz of terror. Knowing that I am afraid, but I am what she is now. I just have a body that fears. I will know it soon. I wonder if we will get to choose where our spiritual technology will take us next. "I remember that she would gently wake me from my stupors by laughing, or telling me she loved me, when my auto-responses would grip me and I would run around in circles, not remembering how to encounter the enemy, but surely set out to fight them."

Did you ever speak yourself into rapture and tears?
Have you ridden the strength of this world?
Only those who risk are Free.

<u>You are a Tyrant. Stop Yourself
before it's too late.</u>

"People are beginning to get over propaganda. They can see from the lessons of our past that the people-filled government has not been perfect, and within this democracy the Darkest of people sought power. Those that wished to build their glory through their life, those that felt that they mattered most. Police, politicians, all militant orders, freemasons...when the order serves the pursuit of power, the pursuit of control, when there are those that create and enforce massive penalties for free choices...when Freedom is taken for the sake of a few people's views and sense of mattering...Then you live in a slave country. You still live in a slave country. Where people, upon person, upon fool, sought power. Sought security. Because someone constantly reached for it over them as a penalty for the help that is subservient employment. See it in the coldness of people's idle chit chat, its genericness, feel it in the emptiness that drives you deeper into shallowness to try and escape it. We must see that we are responsible for how this is. This is the society that sought power. It is the society that tried to please and satisfy those that controlled it. This is the result of the idea that we all had to be the best. It has limited our minds. And if you seek to change it...if you believe yourself to be right...if you want to join it and change it from the inside...then you will easily lose your heart to the wanting of your cause...you will want to make it important, marketable. You seek to belong to a group, just as your enemy did, you pursue the desire of wanting to make your idea more widely accepted. You want a place for yourself. You need as many people as you can get to believe like you do. You will seek power for your Reason. You must pay attention to the Reasons that you use to seek a place of security like your enemy already has, you must pay attention to the feeling you are wanting, and you must allow yourself to stop wanting the sensation. Always see what you are wanting, truly, deeper, it is not your ideas, the idea was made just to reach the sensation of control that is our security here. Look past your mind to the reality...you

are like your enemy...you are your worst enemy in this war for Real Freedom...stop wanting...stop being trapped by the same impulses that you hate, and that made all the people you must push against. Stop seeking a place. Notice when you feel slighted, notice when the anger arises to try and make you matter. Notice. But that doesn't mean don't try to reach out into the world of many others. Just make sure that you are not gaining power, make sure you are freeing people. To have the sense of Freedom we must actually be free. If you feel that the controllers can fine you, can imprison you, and that they aid each other unfairly, if you see that people have lied and exaggerated, then maybe you need to change yourself, and then wipe;
Pride (The sense of mattering, the feeling of success),
Lust (The blur of calmness, the pursuit of dominance),
Anger (The justification of your soon to be dead mind and its Reasons that make you think you are right, that which makes you matter)
Gluttony (Craving, Wanting sensation, that which tries to distract us from the void we should be calmly exploring)
Sloth (The sense that your comfort matters above the comfort of anyone else)
Envy (The desire to matter, again, still, always...we are not as important as we want to be)
Greed (The pursuit of power, purpose, fraternity, stability, security, dominance, lying for all of it, faking compassion, lying about your true natural image, repression for comfort, the pursuit of pleasure and pain).
 And if you do these things do not feel that you are bad, do not know shame or guilt, be calm and try to notice it again and try to let it go more so that it holds you less. These things are not evil, they are quite natural and highly functional, and universally common, but they create more suffering. Never believe you are good. All people have the natural potential to create suffering for other people and themselves...All people can do these "sins" that have been used for control instead of Freedom, but were created without Science to attempt to stop murders and mutations. And if you are controlling, if you are satisfied with yourself, you have hurt hundreds with your pride and must change or you will never be what you want everyone

else to be.

If you lose yourself to Darkness, you will miss the lives of those you thought you were protecting, and you will harm their naturally free spirits, and everyone you love will become a liar to you just to avoid your rage and sense of self-righteousness. Stop trying to matter so much. <u>You</u>, the enforcers of morals, have lost all spiritual progress. Pride makes you think you are right and makes you hide the truth of your god-given nudity," into words...into dust. From his mind, into space. "Success on this path is rare. But these are facts, there is no lie here that wants the power to matter. Just what we have seen within the peace of Stillness."

A Fighting Reason

There are many reasons to continue. There are many reasons to fight. Many choices and definitions-- taken and given. And somewhere... no matter what your choices...you will fall in the fight. Age, time, you are ever closer to the fall. Why do you fight? Do you fight for yourself? No. No man fights for himself. He may think he does... but he cannot. What is the point? He cannot live, he cannot win, he cannot keep or see anything he has built, stolen, or kept. So why are we fighting? So hard. So fiercely. We are fighting for our Reasons. Having children for our Reasons; to teach them. To spread the power of the Reason; from a life sustained by the participation of millions. A tiny, ever spreading echo of what we had thought that made us who we are, an individual world. Echoes build societies, until the next echo knocks it down and makes its own creation. We are manifesting wars to prove ourselves right. Man shapes the world in his own image. Bleeds the world to take it. Sacrifices himself to the world to give to it. We are propelling ourselves into destruction for the sake of the Reason. Your Reason of Taking. You chose your reasons because you cared for them. Because you worshiped yourself, and your reasons justified your nonpermanent emotions. You believed too deep in them. Time has taken you. And in the end all you have is that little Reason that shapes every world to come. Slightly. A life of demanding for a prideful Reason, you probably can't remember at the end.

If man seeks power and authority the world is as dark as a man's heart can be. If a man seeks freedom, without power, free from wanting to spread his Reason, then the world can be as light as a man's heart can be. As happy. Do you care enough about your own futility that you can give up your Reason, and save the people around you with gentleness, and save the world. Or will you eat the Universe under the weight of your greed and non-ending ignorance. What will your Echo make? When will your war end?

Although my Reason means Nothing...I am so fearless of the world, that I never had any inclination to ever stop the war to stop warring. I bled the world for it. Sacrificed myself to it. And I know no lasting grudge. I know no hatred or resentment. I want no money. Want no power. Want only freedom For people. for Myself. I wonder if I can fight until the last second.　　?　　?　　?　　Maybe I will try, or can try.

The Path through The Mind

Most people travel in the mind. It twists a lot. That's why so many people are lost(, which is fine, even if they use power over you). Even if one goes around the mind, they must still go through it eventually to reconstruct themselves from the center of our being, which is passed, beyond, the mind. It is just easier to find where we are going if we know the destination.

"Every person I have known, every woman I have loved for a moment, has struggled against me to try and carve a place for themselves. All of them struggled to have power and place. All of them wanted to be the strongest, especially when vulnerable, and all of them failed to dominate me because they did not realize that their Pursuit to Matter stemmed from the weakness of being afraid to not matter. Because of this insecurity that every one of them had I was easily shown the side of betrayal. A gross thing for my type. A side of failing that reverts a person back to a hissing, pissing runt of a beast reaching for another moment of supreme life. All of them are seeking a place, a place where their weaknesses, cruelties, and insecurities are catered to and quelled. Instead of overcoming the weakness. Whenever I feel discomfort I dive into the emotion, I contemplate it, I explore and lessen it by feeling it and not fueling it with reasons that justify it. Usually it is the same few complexes (like the bother of other people's rising anger to their ignorance) emerging again and again, deep from the root of complexes, and each time it loses its grip on my will. Always I came with open love to all people I knew and always their insecurities masked the vision of their mind and they saw themselves in me. Dark People only seek themselves in other people. They only seek the same mirror of insecurity instead of seeking love, they seek want, satiation, someone that will see that they matter. Live in a world without rank, seek only people that are free from the desire to be anyone. In Entertainment, I never worked with anyone that ever called anyone a "Nobody." And you will see that these <u>Positive Enablers</u> will take you the furthest, and not for any reason, but to work with you. If you want nothing from them, they will give you everything. But want, and you will lose them," deeply into caring, The Father.

Every Smiling Mask

I traversed the heaps of crowded mingling socialites. Bouncing from click to click like a snapping finger. Truly, honestly, kindly... assuming the position of the personality that would most please them. The skill made me a great Director. Not for manipulation, for conversation, for pleasure. For rhythm and rhyme. Drifting in and out of smoke filled lighting and laughter and the shadows of the room; in which I collected myself for the next encounter. Ready to take on the next topic. Always, I was different, but always I directed the type of identity towards the same point, spoken for the same topic that only I could hear. Talk about your house, talk about your dog, talk about your job, talk about the end, the beginning, the lost, or the found, and I will ease your anxiety about it, all the way back to Calmness. I could show them the prettiest of the funniest part of something. And their distress or their excitement is calmed and their appreciation is deepened. And maybe eventually they too become deepened. I leave them like a rock dropped into a silent black pond of water.

I move their psyches to a better place.

So, like them, I pretend to be something, but because my center is honest and unchanging, people believe in me and want to like me. Or they are threatened and weak and fight me randomly or secretly, but still I'm smiling when I am stabbing with considerate lube on my knife, directing them towards equal oblivion, towards peace, freedom from their fears. It's better, words don't work for them anyway, so I direct them most effectively. Returning them to peace, without a sin on either one of our souls.

<u>Dark</u>

"The Dark Society is so dark that it is not likely it can be turned back around. For example, if I say to the public that their souls are sinless, that heaven and hell don't exist, then it is most likely that people will come forth with anger and vengeance and tell me that people will do whatever they want if they think that. And many people that would hear that would. These people are effectively known as trash, they are rich and they are poor, it doesn't matter. They are unchangeable. Everything these types of people hear warp it, transform it, make it dark, and keeps false education in. They polish every thought they receive in the turning and turning of their working machine powered by insecurity and fear of having no respect. Thus is the nature of darkness. Guard the mind. The Dark Society must be calmed before it can be freed. It must be taught what light is before it can see it blinding it. How do you convince a person in darkness that it is better to be blind than to see everything? Will we ever be free again? Or will the militants keep thinking they are right?" spilling.

The Existing

The hardest burden for this Evolution of Our Reality to overcome is the deep sensation of inferiority and insecurity that springs it and grows it. The Existing aware, are often times self loathing people, or are too weak to fight. Their minds are often times very ingenious, and vivid, and very busy. To a state of almost maddening proportions, as if it can be too much for the human brain to Reason forth. The shame-society lies heavy on them because they can understand everyone's Reason. The Dark Society and its ways of power are hardest on them. I can have all the power I want, I am limitless and can do anything, but I know that there is a step beyond these initial thoughts. But. Don't you see? There is a way beyond this. Beyond the failure back into the system of power. The bravest person in the world is the awakened and resolved Master of Existing. He whom is beyond inferiority. He that bled from his mind every thought against himself until there was nothing left to kill. When grace takes you and absorbs you. When your Reason is no longer needed to protect you, you can see into the expanse of a real Utopia. The OverMan is free from man's weaknesses. Free from the weakness to protect himself. Unafraid of the consequences of his truthful fictions.

It is most difficult to defend a Reason that one <u>cannot</u> believe in.

Only a Master of Existing can. Only he that has seen IT could fight so hard for IT. A Warrior with no country, no religion, just a soul and the will to examine its knowledge, and battle it forth forward and up into the conscious mind propelled by his ultimate love for all HumanKind. Just another even soul.

From Dawn til Dusk, Turning Over

My feet are falling asleep because I can't move much. I can't work. I have to lay here and rot. My calves are turning to mush and it hurts. Sharp jolts shock me as my nerves pinch. Everyday, I wake up and determine again, and again, what the pain is, and decide once more what is causing it. Constantly reviewing it, forever rerecording it. A part of my everyday experience. Sometimes, I can see bashing my skull into the wall until I split my bloody casing and hush my thoughts (She had a pretty eye), but then I think that I may gain some sort of grace if I should suffer on longer, if I could become calmer in the fury of the anxiousness, the spin of the waiting. Fuck! my legs hurt. fuck. kicking against the wall i feel nothing. I guess that means I'm not suffering that much...

And just then, the wave came across The Father. Heavy it held him. The stream of consciousness that he realized again was constantly washing through him. His mind pulled to observe the phenomena. And his body he could feel less. Less could he feel his body. And Silence came:

For some time the Silence lingered in its space. And thought by thought fell, not needing to be kept and identified to see if it had merit. The structure of the definition of the image that he needed to prove could be built and dismantled to reeducate the forgotten.

There it is   the goal   it
arises.

I see it again in my mind.
It came up when I let it calm. My stream of Reason. My stream that did not lead back to me, but instead blanketed cities and

nations. My Existence. When the Reasons I must think against it, to defend it, can stop...And I don't need to defend against the Whole World of Reasons. All believing the Capital R in Reason.

Shhhh.

All seek happiness.

(deep slow breath, surrendering to not mattering. Accepting his solidarity.)

People are violent against others that they feel threaten their individual and group ideal of Freedom. Also, if people fear what they do not actually have to fear, the goal of the movement is to encourage to let people bring together their happinesses. We all have every piece of all people, we choose what gives our coward hearts advantages, so we must make ourselves brave and seek to understand and allow ourselves to relax.

Ha. We are like a bunch of hunched backed weasels, squealing at each other. Well of course we are. We are Nature. A Formed part of it. A sign of the passage of its time.
Freedom burns strongly for Americans because Native Americans are so present to let us know that it was not always like this. Our guilty gash is oldly scarred, but theirs' is new. And this relativity from the heart of our always oppressed minorities that come in all colors makes us curable. Savable. There is a Spirit that touches us. And minds go blank as they want to think what they want, never understanding that they must think all of it. That's what we did. We filled in the gaps and linked our contradictions with logic. They call this stream of consciousness; strange how it comes from a stream of non-consciousness. Non-Being. Nothingness. Fearlessness. Calmness. These are our words of Booming power. Presented for your Liberation from all that seek to get something from you, from all that we just cannot satisfy, and may we all be happy about that.

The stream sweeps him away   .; ..   ...
..

Say what you will, but
all of us, all of us were Americans at war to survive because death is
the constant threat to motivate us to work. Of the U.S., we existed
in a time, and we came to conclusions to counter our suffering
and we lived glories and made Faith and showed people how to
break it. And we loved and we hated and only as we loved as we
suffered and we spoke and were many things and we died. By the
sword, by the pen, to the Conclusion and the point. And we were
Westerners. Fighting, even for nothing. Strange, the veins in us.
The programming we defy and cannot escape.

Surviving the Body

"First came a craving. When the stomach aches the body tells the mind again to feed the body, to sustain it. To fear it's demise. If one doesn't fear it's death then one will be in pain. All living creatures would simply rather not be in pain. So the body controls us. So it's consciousness tells us. We don't seek pain, and we medicate to lessen or alleviate it, but when we have it, we suffer in our anxiety through it. How can we say we are the body when one can be controlled by it? It controls a deeper consciousness. This is what we are trying to do here. Let go of the first consciousness and reach into the consciousness that does not have to worry about dying. Then you can control the body, even when it is malfunctioning and failing and oozing, you can ease your own suffering by letting go of the belief in the body, when you reside your consciousness backwards, out of the body's primary control. Why not try it? Everything wants to ease its own pain. You will suffer less if you do it. There you go, I just appealed to your ego. I gave you a reason of greed, of pride, of sin, your reward...and that is what it takes. And that is the reason that no sin is punishable, because all paths to God...to Stillness... destined for he same non-judgement. To not having to be so afraid of dying. To know, and so have calmness about the impending situation.
Don't you see? The level that Zarat reached was pure enough to fear nothing. To know that superiority is a lie made up by man so that a populace would believe in a leader or an organization, so that people let something powerful and corrupt exist. So that they can justify the mistakes in a ruling people's judgment that harm the populace. To ward off revolt. Darkness. Zarat, while within darkness, allowed himself to become unaffected by it. Peace in a violent world. Peace because he had no guilt, no shame, nothing that he worshiped that would give a person those dark tools of control. But still his body had reflexes, he was pained by his deeds from time to time. He did not let go of the control the body had on his deeper, more powerful, consciousness. Zarat was no master. But he was a great Willful Man. He mustered strength with the use of will. But still, in his situation

he probably had to focus so much on survival and he felt so much nasty murderous fear in people that it just prevented him from being completely still enough. But at times he could reach it. Burn in it. Offer his soul to anything because he was not afraid to lose it. What real Heaven is. And that is when he was able to kill himself...within the heart of freedom, where we are limitless in the possibilities of our future. Holy is the Path of the Martyr," The Father. Speaking into a camera that wasn't there.

These are humans knowing other humans. The story is in knowing them as we know any human, by knowing their minds and everything deeper, the personal remembered as a false sense of shame.

We fought wars so you wouldn't have to. We talked and talked so there was less for you to justify. For your Freedom. To cure the imbalance in the inferior mind that feels the need to reason toward violence and supremacy because it got so afraid, your mind and my mind. We walked the perils that could have turned us cold so you'd know the risks that kept us warm, and still continually dying for each other as easily as we accepted survival. Know your Friends. Beyond the sociopaths and the successful. Beyond Bounds. So untouched by anyday circumstance that the need to kill someone doesn't even come up. You accept that you can kill, but you overcome the obsession with the Law of Compassion that replaces a thousand pages of any of your mimicking religions.

Religions were trying to prevent fear and death and suffering. To stop death, we try to make up reasons to stop it. These Heroes, dying in the Manifest of Utopia, carried only one sin, they killed, but not for the reasons that are any other sins. Not for envy, or greed, or any, not any that everyone else is controlled by, but these Ones are most condemned because its all been about avoiding death, and the inferiority complex that develops against living itself, and killing is the made-up sin, and old solution, that has to be what the afraid fear and condemn most. Fools will hate Heroes. They killed only to end power and cure imbalance. In your society, perhaps far from the Dark Society, you just can leave the situation that creates the opportunity for someone to control you. Economic Liberation is key, by any opportunity of your time that keeps you from bloodying yourself again, like us, for pointless Nothingness.

"The problem with the war against the ego is that all egos act with the best intentions. It makes it easy to believe in the reasons of goodness. However, all egos are false, and all damage humankind. All make pride. And all make the want for power. If a society wants to succeed it must give up on what causes revolts. It must not want to be the strongest. It must want to be the <u>most</u> functional, and that means as little power as possible. Compassion and caring is enough to make us work hard for each other. Egos make bad results. It doesn't matter if you believe in them. Pride causes pain for everyone around you. It makes them angry and violent. Do not elevate yourself. Stop believing in your great intentions, see what it does to so many. Everyone is not great," Father.

"A Spirit can be instantly realized, especially in a near death experience, but it takes much time and much conflict against our own egos after these enlightening events to know in full and real faith that you are forever, but the body will feel fear, the more fear with the less training, even if the Source of ourself was realized. It takes a special understanding to know what real faith is, while the identity that is our shell is shed back into the earthly dust from whence it arose," The Girl.

:)

<u>Identifiers, like Her, like Him</u>

"The Him the Her, the It, the That, The whatever...it never occurred to me to care so much about my identity that I had to tweak and screw with myself so efficiently. Who were they anyway.. Just humans, not even fit to have names. Worthless, and wonderful because of it. It let them not struggle so hard. Or struggle very hard, when they felt the want to. But they liked the torture. Both of them. Her and Him. They struggled because everything felt like nothing. They knew death. Absolute stillness. Complete peace. Calm in some part of every stressful minute that tore their flexible psyches apart and freed them into the rapture of the calmness again. Hallelujah. You are a good person, a kindly directed person if you feel uncomfortable when someone refers to god, and you are fine when someone refers to the spirit. And you are great when you evolve to the point where you can say "God" again and know the beauty in its ease of rolling off your tongue, dripping like a cliché into redundancy," The Father. "...I've done a lot of things. Hard things. Brave things. Mad things. But they're just things to me. I never saw myself as a hero, even though I was. It never felt like it. Besides, a hero has to have a side. When freedom is your side, you stand alone, even in the company of those that are kind of like you. Still you are your own. Every choice meaning the final philosophy."

It grabs me. shakes me. wow. blown to nothing. Will you let me have it? I want it for everything else and I can gain nothing from it. There is a great force of energy generated by holy people. I feel it. It is God. It is the message of God, anyway, a force of an intention of Love. And it overwhelms. I want to blabber. Weep. Like I feel when I lose hold the hand or the head of a dying friend. ***Why does it feel this way if there is nothing wrong with dying?*** This great bubbling of emotion. Boiling out of my face.

I believe I understand. The tears. The crying. When death is coming. When death is taking. Don't be afraid. It is because the soul is emerging. It is becoming uncovered by the human condition. And this overwhelming sensation of love and loss and eternity that one feels when facing death in front of you or inside you is the majesty of the truth of what we are. That's it. It is so emotional, so powerful, because we are being shaken by its power. Its fundamental rawness of force graces us with the dignity of a moving life.

<u>Wasted Hard Time</u>

"What a waste. What a waste this time is. What a waste for everyone here. A criminal. Alone in a cell. Most have no visitors. No hope. It was lack of hope that made them criminals in the first place. With no other options a man must become a criminal to remain free. Sometimes we get imprisoned when we rationalize in an instant that a little time is better than making another war. Maybe there is silence to be sought. Poor humans. Poor controllable beasts. Wasting their time in prison instead of taking a fine opportunity to go deeper and deeper into the silence. Even if I cannot silence my mind because it is malfunctioning. Because it is trying to tell me to die. Even if, I can still find a way to access that warmth in my guts, that breath of burning ice that leaves my nostrils cold that occurs naturally when the bellows of the spirit pump. That sense of nothing. That truth of death. The knowledge that I will be free always returns no matter what thoughts my mind may be making me have. Free. I believe it because I know it. It is proven to me. I believe who I experienced from. Although I do not know what it will completely feel like when I have it. I just know that I must try to feel nothing. And go deeper. Deeper. Damnit...deeper. Stiller," The Father, neither good nor bad. Neither. Neither man nor god, but both. Wasted himself on the silent breath that scrapes the edge of the abyss. The consumption of spirit. The scent of holiness. Alone in a cell. A man who needs no hope. Freed from need.

The cell of life. The cell of the mind. The lie. This is not who I am. This is thinking. I am not this. Why can't I stop? Reason cannot free me. It only makes more mind. More barrier between me and the truth. Strange. Perfect. I can always think through this spirit. It has no identity but the mind can identify it. Will my thoughts become kinder in time? Are they now? How can I remember?

THE USERS

"I was thinking on people I have known. Considering their reasons for doing the meaningless actions they carry out. I thought on one, with such an ugly face, I thought of how it would be to see it again... watch it approach me with a smile. They always come with a smile. I thought of how it would first speak, because it is they who want to initiate their dark game of superiority and place, affirming the glory of their strength. All so that they matter. All for their depthless importance. Sick. I can hear her words, like it was only yesterday that I loved it like it doesn't have an empty gut. It had a smart mind, but it could not understand its soul. It did not have courage to look into itself and see that it is worthless. And I interrupt, "Enough. I remember what you are. I will not let you think that something didn't happen. You cannot use me. You will not get what you want to get out of me. No happy shallow feeling you nasty lying filth." And I would walk away. Drenched in the aura of coldness. And the User will have to search into their own soul a bit, just to cover up the pain they would never face. I hate this empty disease. I will do what it takes to treat it," That Father. "Cut them deep enough so that they will have to give up and retreat to the spirit, and maybe then they will see what they have become."

"Such ugly cloths. I look the way I look as a result of my purpose. They look the way they look so that someone will think that they are of that certain purpose. We commit an act upon the user that shatters, in rapid hearts rates, hyperventilation, and tears, as they must hold the knife to someone else's throat. Watch them crumble while the auditory knife pierces them."

The Roots: From the Ground

"The first layer I see is war. That is the first thing I see when I direct my view inward. I see anger. It is hard to see it because it is so close to my immediate consciousness. It is so loud and sad. But eventually, more and more, then I get to notice it. See the rage. And I realize the work it takes to exist. I see what the fear makes in me. A filter of cold strength meant to hold out what is deeply powerful. I do not want to be affected by these emotions. I want to function in order to gain, to gain my desire, my reason. Even now. And deeper than that, when the rage is far above, so far I can barely hear it. Here in the depths, like on the bottom of the ocean, as if evolution and reincarnation moved in the opposite direction and we all become fish again. And so I see the drive of it, a profound feeling when you feel it for yourself. The worry that binds my mind. I see it. I fight, I rage towards it, to be calmer. I use my abilities and I am peaceful. Unattached to the fear I can see in it. I know that I can do what I am trying to do, but the worry holds me. I am glad She died first, so She did not have to think so long. Her mind gripped Her so. Poor Girl, Happy Hero. I worry about how others will suffer. Even when I suffer greatly I am fine. Ultimately...through misery. I will either live or die and deal well with either. As well as I dream it. Most suffering I feel is from other people, the nastiness of their egos. The sharpness. The pride. The pride. The pride. And everything that grips the mind, strongly. I love so strong, I am forced to hold it at bay, but when it flows in complete comfort...that is when I feel the best. It slows me. It drowns fear. And I float. The path of ultimate love is the right way to go. It's a different world. But first one must suffer for the great care of all around him whom are wrong. My ego is war. And my Spirit is True Love. Therefore my wars are not for gain. They are for fun, and so that I may go deeper for them, for activity as this body on this planet in its slice of time. Will anyone first see the humility of this, or will you see the ego? The ego is not really here. The ego is light on me. But your ego doubts, hates, wars, blindly and fiercely. Ironically, with my light ego, and your will so unwilling to be fearless, you, as they'all, still suffer under my existing power that is not doing anything at all to them. Fear is imaginary, proof is real. Who will know how much I loved them? Who will know me, what I really offered...and who will know the bias that glorifies them in the belief of wasted words?" Spake On. "How quickly will hope be pride again?"

The Art of Guarding the Mind for the Weak

"People do not understand what restraint is required to deal with them. People do not know how they have imprisoned others. There are few people that I can be myself with. Few. Nearly none that ask for nothing to please what they desire. Hardly any see me. Few that know how happy and free and amazing my personality is when I am free to not curb what I say. There are not many people intelligent enough to have overcome so many biases. To free themselves so that I may be free. It is rare to see those that have found such love. Holy in every way. But there are a fewer more yet that I can show sides of myself. I am often as people desire. Still me, but curved and curbed for their pleasure. I enjoy this act of secret charity. It is how I serve this world," The Father spoke and reminded me of my long but shorter life, wherein I'd been many things, and so came to tolerate the phases of others. "I have seen a dark version of this. Where one mate I had used for her advantage. She was intelligent. She was a Dark Hearted wench. I remember it the first time I saw it. She replied to someone with a phrase she would never use. A phrase he used, someone else. She used it to gain. None of these techniques can be used to gain, or manipulate in this fashion, or they lose what they are. She warped people for her amusement. Most people do not know they are dark. It causes them to not become as strong as they could. But most are ignorant to what light and dark is. But it does not change what they are. They will be my enemy. These users. These Takers hiding as Givers. They can be strong. I have been deceived. A person of the Light has conquered the insecurities of her ugly face and do not use these things as tactics, but to stop those seeking power with them."

Another Result and Consequence of the Path

As I aged and as I became more and more detached I was unable to feel the pangs of my age. I rotted, but did little to prevent it. It was not my concern. My consciousness was larger than my body by now by then by whenever. Time does not touch us at the end. We are present in the same moments as anyone. We will feel the slight fear of death, but it is only the body feeling it. The fret, the anxiousness, the waiting of Death, is calmed, and there we are. In some crappy pain, that we have no control over. And as the body grows more useless, our spirits become more encompassing. More who we are. More of what we have been throughout eternity. Constantly returning to Free you fools once more. To save the monkeys. To stop the "good" from enforcing themselves from security for more security. To stop the righteous from defying any god in its name once more. ...Hard it is to convince a man that just doesn't want to die...again.

It's ok. Be calm. I know that we do not leave ourselves behind. And time over time I feel the dead I've known come and touch my soul and I understand that all of them actually loved me. And I loved them too. Even through the tornado of thinking. And at that moment of when the finale of breaths sighs out, if I focus on that feeling that cares without gain, and is the love that keeps another alive, then I will come back around again to be surrounded by these loves once more. This feeling is beyond an emotion, this love is the force of your being, and requires the density that proves it's real.

<u>Anything You See</u>

Most people cannot see how the media, as a consensus, directs your anger. Even if they are using sensationalism for ratings, they are still manipulating. Still harming. Still building hate. The result is clear. Constant and repeating. Nothing you see that profits should be believed. It has been made to trick you. The smart ones pretend that you already know, and act smug about it. Hate, preference, reactions, and superiority sells. A product is "the best." "Everything" is rotten. Think about certain issues. Don't you see the massive amount of news that is not talked about in the Dark Society. Don't you see how the same issues are pounded and pounded, just to make you think certain ways, in simpler ways, in ways you can. Just to make you think of hate, an emotion that sticks by an issue and watches the issue and earns capital for someone else by doing so. Think of it. Doesn't everybody hate something? Don't you? Your thoughts are not your own. Stop them.

Are you sure you have to have an opinion about that? Move on, without granting salvation or damnation in the catalogue of your unstable mind.

CHARACTERS

"The Awake and Existing have deconstructed and reconstructed him/herself beyond the need to keep a persistent constant persona for an image. I care nothing for my image. People will always see me as something other than I am because their perceptions are not as advanced as one that has pursued my path. They cannot understand that I moved beyond the restrictions of having to appear to be me. What happened with Her was special. We were both able to move beyond the concept of a definition and create our own. I struck down my own daughter, it was beautiful the play of it. Some people are good at speaking to people, some are good at analyzing, others are sexually uninhibited, people develop all sorts of defenses and releases that make them advantages in situations. And people think that these defenses are who they are. But they are not. The Existing, that person dealing with the singular occurrence he or she is in, knows that he is not his personality and can use any aspects of any personality for any necessary purpose. This is the boundary our limitless ideals that mean nothing. I can be anything. Anyone. And accept everything. I cling to nothing. Nothing is permanent, especially me. My body is programmed to respond in certain functional ways on this planet. We are slaves to these responses, reigned by who we think we are...but, we must let ourselves go. We are a fleeting dream to awake from. And we can control the dream when we stop trying to own it," The Father.

HERO

A Hero is one that creates his own cause, to be owned by it instead of another human. One that does not require guidance of manipulation to act. A Hero is wise and sees the risk of his loss before he begins a hardship, and he acts. He continues regardless of the outcome, for the simple sake that he believes in what he has created as justification for his deeds. The Hero endures the agony he has chosen, he is not merely someone who suffers randomly, he suffers by his own decree. His own will to fight without fear of perpetual failure for a result. He pushes on into damnation for whatever reason. He knows his reason is only a tool to allow him to do what he wants. It is the source of his pride. And the root of his arrogance. This is the trap a True Hero must conquer. He must not need to win, and if by chance he does, he must let his reason go, so he does not make others worship it and in return create another Hero to destroy himself. This is the cycle of Heroes. And too many weak think they are Heroes through false reinforcement of value that they have learned in their worlds of false education. A Hero must be free from his own heroism. He must believe he is dirt, and he should walk barefoot upon himself. Covered in his own filth, so he does not forget. Or else, he may believe in himself, by means of his reason, and he would make an authority, and become everything he ever hated. A Hero turns from himself, the hardest thing to do for one that must be so well defined to carry out actions no other has the stomach or personal sense of glory for.

A whisper...*"Zarat..."*

"So much time...."

"Alone..."

"In the end...the hot steel burning through his skull was his treaty to the world."

"Thank him...You were likely next."

"I desire the depths of a woman's soul. It has made me love many creatures in many ways. I want to see the goodness. See the passion. Feel how it hurts them to not have absolute storybook satisfaction. I know their fantasies. I know their lust. I am the type of man women show this to, because I will allow it, their fullness. They want my strength to dominate them, but they are surprised at my gentleness and passion. What women in this Dark Society do not understand is that my power is naturally occurring it is not manifested for control like theirs is. But, if they want the ravaging enough they will detach themselves from the insecurity and fear that arouses them. And I can take them as they dream. Only the most intelligent women can let themselves become something else to experience fusion. These are the women that know they do not have to be the most intelligent. Beyond the scars of insecurity and the fears to not being independent and strong and never vulnerable there is absolute beauty and a course of ever deepening ecstasy that deconstructs a woman's limits to the point of Nirvana-like sensation. It can set a woman on the Path to Perfection. However, it is all too rare an event. This is why The Girl was so great. It is absolutely harder for a woman to achieve the absolute goal of the Supreme Freedom. They are harmed too easily by life, so easily slighted because of the conditioning and production of ideal illusions; meaning, when emotions seem more real they are harder to transcend. I am marveled by those so beautiful that they face the direction to Truth. It helps when one dies. But a man of non-controlling power and a woman with an open heart and no expectations can know the passion every woman craves. What keeps every woman, but a few, from this great feeling of love and with no need for security is the acceptance that others may be stronger than them. They are so afraid of not being as strong and as indestructible as they should be. These are the Scars of feminism. There is no phrase that a modern warped woman wants to hear more than "I love you" and there is no greater phrase that she fears. It is sad the level of fear. Disgusting for how they cling to it with avarice. Too sad to hate it. If a present woman could let go of her weak ideals she could know love. If she chose to be vulnerable and not fear pain she could know love. If a woman gave herself to risk she would grow and actually become stronger with no need for gain. But these Scars on the minds of modern woman do not change that modern men have the same scars from insecurity and will try to gain power over them.

Mutual, caring, cooperative love, without the binds of force and selfishness to become the ideal that never was, this love is Love. The real. Not the shallowness of wanting another human being to be exactly perfect for the ease of your comfort. How much freedom has been taken, how many lives have been lost, to the anger that someone is not an Ideal? See the violence in the cruelty of modern "love." When people see ease and contentment of a love with effort spilt forth for a mate, it delights a seer. But they do not understand that the mutual surrender of dominance and power is how you achieve it. So long as the ideal of control, defined cheaters, and power is the basis of relationships, Love will become more and more rare, and less and less men and woman will ever have truly moving earth shattering Experience that changes the mind and sinks us into the many paths to universal absolution. If we fear our minds, our bodies, and our vulnerability to bare them then we will never know the bliss of accepting ourselves and being able to love and be loved. I desire more purity. Thank God he comes to me and shows me his soul. Thank God there is no judgment, no restriction to his thoughts. I Love Him, the OverFeeling: Bliss. Hmph. Feminism brought shame to vulnerability. Shame to not being the winner, the strongest. Don't they see that all of the Reasons they accept and refute are from the same Darkness. They are the same promotion of dominance and superiority. No they will not see. They do not want to see what they have become. They do not care about others enough to Become something more."

Thoughts.   Thoughts.
Thoughts.
They cease to exist the moment they exist. And they propel us further into tomorrow.
And so we are changed and warped. And we have more to deconstruct. Start now.
It will only become harder to stop. Go deeper. Gain freedom. Gain your life.
Too late and you may not remember how to end it. True as truth may be.
The Existing gains and loses nothing and cannot be controlled and is always vulnerable without fear and will experience everything rooted in stillness and perfection.
The Existing is the only One that can know love and ecstasy and not lose anything in it.

"Any path you choose you will become transformed. You will become a type of person. When you follow this path you will gain the ability to understand what other's think. Most people can only comprehend what their individual mind can think and they become angered if another person that can only understand what their individual mind can think doesn't understand what his individual mind thinks. And anger grows at the fear that arises because we believe for that instant, within the sub-conscious which we can see perfectly clearly, (it is not subtle to us)...Within that instant where fear is evoked we are defending ourselves with anger, we have reverted to the old mechanisms of trying to survive when we feel the most frightening feeling a human can feel...the feeling that Control has been Lost. Suddenly we don't think that we are safe in our environments because we suddenly don't feel the hallucinatory sense of empowering stability and we fight to survive with basic instincts. It is one thing to witness this happening and document it in other creatures, including humans, it is quite another, much more factually superior thing, to be able to see the functions happening within your own body. That is a deeper consciousness, gained by the One that lives deliberately. And you make less actual war in your life because you are free to see that someone's mind merely worked out a reason... the reason was wrong...so you can tolerate them even though they are an idiot. And instead of losing a life to being a shallow unintelligent power seeker you will become wise. Calm. You'll be able to stop yourself from harming yourself through the programmed impulse of our ancient carbon forms. These are the supple fruits of this path. Do you notice the difference in taste? That _is_ simple complexity,"

ANNALS VII, VERSE LOST, THE BOOK ACCORDING TO THE NON-IMPROTANCE---to be remembered in a book without ritual. Ritual creates an image for the mind, a distraction from the soulful meaning behind any real truth and is only something to bring the habitual back to over and over. Church is for community, not for God, God is found alone in darkness when you realize you are alone and you are going to die. It's called giving up on the body. It's the sensation of Freedom. Community is found Online, therefore church is no longer needed, but we keep the spirit, and we may burn the dogma, or leave it to the shelf and the dust for a later generation to marvel at how reasons fuel impulse. And then they will come here, and know us as Friends to witness how we overcame that.

Escape ritual. Overcome tradition, but realize what feeling people were getting out of it and what, if anything, they did, while using that feeling.

"I have spoken to so many people. All manner. I can start a conversation with anyone. And people will tell you everything about themselves. I ask, "What do you do for work?" or "What do you do for fun?". An old salesman trick to keep someone's mind off the sale so that they don't defend themselves against being sold, a trick Americans hate and demand. Make them think about anything else besides the stress. And people love to think and tell people about themselves. I have had so many women. Why? Simple. When one first meets a person they want to bear their hearts, show the best of themselves. You hear the best from people in the beginning. Overtime, usually a short time, pride, insecurity, anger, hidden emotions, true selfish motivations, and hallucinations that they have faith in, reveal themselves. And Darkness seeps through the intentions they desire to have, but do not have. So many, so many different lives, men and women and children and animals, all, beautiful in their roots, but putrid overtime. Showing me all the nastiness I do not need in this world. I tolerate so very little of it. Some hearts cracked though I had been devoted to them, because I never let myself see too much of the grotesque in a human. I guess, I have a weak stomach. But given the circumstance they too would betray me for their place. But sometimes, so rarely are those that prove me wrong, and stand to show me their test of patient time. To show me that they believe more in their purity than their humanness. These hearts are most precious and always worth killing and dying and living and saving for," The Father.

There are too many voices here. A mind is polyphonic. You can't know whose they are. You may try to figure out who they are. Who they belong to. But you cannot tell. You can't, but will think you do. But there is no evidence except for that which you make-up. No clues. You are wrong. Always doubt. Always never believe so strongly in your thoughts. Learn how to loosen their grip so it relaxes your body. You think that just because you think it you are right. And you will bite and bark at anyone that does not have that same made-up thought. Pride will build the karma of your life. Thought upon thought. Coming from the same selfish place where you believe in yourself. Building your image of Greatness. Don't believe it. You know as little as everyone else, and most you know is because someone shared it within the pool of education. Your selfishness spreads the resentment against you. You made this life, karma is your choice of it. Even if you know a lot. You are nothing near that level of anger provoked by having to be right, by having to be the one that chose the right path, you cannot justify your nastiness. You are wrong. And always will be, like every voice in Her head that tries to reason and convince you that your actions are good. Forgive others that do not know these truths, they are as stupid as you once were.

This is telepathy. We can hear the thoughts people burn. More can enter us, we push nothing out. Time and life are free to flow through this receptacle. It is a result. The mind loosens a bit on the Road. The Road of Enlightening. To Awake, and Exist. And what you think will be a benefit will be more like a trial until you learn the technique of no concerns, laced by the Inner Smile, pursuing only Happiness.

NOTHING MATTERS
AND IT IS FINE THAT IT CAN

"There is only one dichotomy in man. There is the side that wants to matter. And there is the side that cannot matter. There is what survives. And that which cannot die. Man. And God. The Spirit echoing the intentions of Existence. Quiet and all encompassing white noise. How can you find an oxymoron to be truth if you do not have faith in giving up the definition that makes you deny it? How do you learn? Where will you apply your belief in this lifetime? The weight of the future lies on what you choose to believe. What path has better results? Their fear or our real no-fear. And our ability to accept all circumstance with a smile, no matter how it would destroy weaker humans, or rather less adept, differently evolved humans. But no matter what they are they fall to this Philosophy, the Universal one that analyzes its own existence from its point of secure or insecure perception. Can you accept that you mean nothing? And what does that mean? Fool, friend. Nothing, without the thought of nothing. Real nothing. All thought is audio hallucination meant to keep a dead ego alive. The hallucination is not important until you don't need to think anymore," Father. Talking. Blabbing. Saving his soul. Living in ease. Talking the reoccurring anxiety down and around that his body repeatedly triggered as it lived in a chronic and weakening state. Don't you see the perfection of his happiness? Even sadness is happy, because it is not real to him. Sadness, like himself, lives for a moment and dies, burning its expansion of energy.

<u>Babbling Rambling</u>

When will this stop?..When will I be able to stop thinking?
When will silence be all I hear?

When we think of God, we do not have to think of and defend and die for a specific being. That is not real. False. Foolish even. Listen. Calm down! Children fight back when people have different ideas. Love me. Want me to be right. Justify it. Now listen. People must notice that the god is fake but the move in emotions is practical and functional and accomplishes positive and purifying "effects," so long as the intermediate step of fear is gone. ,,,, ,,,, ,,,, ,,,, ,,,, where was I going. Just because you didn't get to hear it and judge it and approve or condemn it doesn't make it any less of a fact.

God shall be momentarily defined as that which is present in Physics and can function with a dose of theoretical animating energy, sometimes called the Secret Drop.

Will I die here? Will I be able to work through my mind enough to finally act? Surely freedom is what I desire most. Surely the one factual right that all rights stem from and is still cried for across a whole planet. Are we free? Am I? Yes, but I long to die in a field. In a stream. One that would slowly rip away my flesh and bone and guts. A deep soily, marshy stream. With pores like a black sponge. Everything decaying into fertility.

Another Nightmare

I'm awake. "Hmmhh." Interesting. I tried everything to pull myself awake. Every time I realized again and again that it was only a dream I tried

. I fought. I fought to break free. I made war to change it. And every time I tried to escape I justified it as existing. I promoted its validity with my war to stop it. I could escape and find peace if I was making war to stop it. And like all egos, my ego reacted the same way when confronted. It fought me back, it fought against me. I was offered every type of suffering I have ever allowed myself to worry about in the dream. The trailer I lived in, in the depths of the Mexican desert was rolling. My brother was too arrogant again and thought he could do something he knew nothing about and he tried to replace a power line. Even when the dream offered me sex to try and keep me in it, I quickly realized that this too was just part of the same nightmare that I was supporting. Only when I rejected the beautiful, ugly whores and allowed them to begin ripping apart my flesh with their growing teeth, leaving "my" arms bare in bone... only when I surrendered...only when Stillness came over me...then the dream ended.

There is always peace in Stillness. Always refuge in the Emptiness. We always return to Silence. If we know how. To fight avariciously for our made-up noble causes; to seek comfort and peace through politics or physical war only makes us what we never wanted to be. It only makes us believe in the oppressive illusion, and it only makes the illusion defend itself, like every abstract illusion claiming a concrete and possibly immortal identity. If we can let go of the struggle of life, the validation of our existence, then maybe we can awake from this "awake" dream too. Maybe we can truly end the course and clinging to of endless lives, even while living a single life. Peace exists when we stop fighting and no one wants to fight us anymore. We must let go of the illusions that perpetuate this slave world. There is always peace in Stillness. There is always peace for those that apply their Faith towards it. It is a Holy Path. A path that leads only to True Freedom, ready to be slaughtered by those that need constant action to distract themselves from their own impending oblivion. Peace lies in the Emptiness of that impending oblivion. Peace lies in the stillness that comes when we relax the spasms of the brain and emotions and we no longer feed the fever that makes us ache. Soon I will awake in death.

Is that smoke? hmmm. A flicker of a butter lamp?

"Do you think that these choices are easy? Do you think that it is not hard? This path is a war. A war that makes you the victim, the loser. It is the only war where you start out to lose. Knowing. Hoping. Because it means more, changes more, when it is tragic. I know pain. I loved deeply. I was in the perfect relationship. Perfect. We never fought. Always loved. And I realized why one day. Her ego. My ego. Perfectly balanced. She went my way so easily. And I so easily went hers. I knew what I would give her. She would give me everything. She used to validate her ego. I had to force her to notice and deconstruct it, and this would drive us into turmoil. She had to take from me. I made her. She went against every ounce of instinct to be kind to make her survive for what she had. She fought the ego. She could not let it go. Don't fight the ego with force, fight the ego with kindness. Release it. Every ego rebels against its government when it is oppressed. I am my ego's government. If an ego does not feel free it will fight and kill to know freedom again. And it will fight and kill to keep the freedom. But if freedom is constant there is no more rebellion. A nation must be free to be and remain stable," The Father, "The moral is...we lose some along the way...there are people we cannot free...and they suffer...and we watch them...and there is nothing we can do...but ease their want to war."

<u>Guards</u>

One of them came to look at me today. To stare at me. A guard. Contemplating his own mortality as he looks at an old man. Never able to feel my suffering, always only feeling his own. A society without real compassion. A society of prisons and politics. A society of the powerful and the hypocritical. I foresee a world without judgment. I foresee a world where righteousness is dead. And the only prison is the prison of the self. Holding us here until we rise away. A world of easing an ego, gentling it, instead of <u>e</u>nflaming it. A world of understanding instead of condemnation and control. A world without fear. This world will fall, and the rights of the people will thrive. "Your mind is a cage," The Father. The guard stared. Perhaps a thought surfaced.

"Quiet, Prisoner," Enslaver.

"Only an idiot would assume I am a prisoner," The Father.

"You're in prison," Idiot.

"You assume I have to be," Father.

"You're an old man," Child.

"I believe I have enough strength left to show you what real power is. It is the right of anything that lives to defend itself and make itself free, no matter the imprisoner or the reason. A human should escape those that believe they have the right to punish," The Father.

"You broke the law," The Programmed.

"The laws of man, of power, and security. Not the laws of nature. You broke those by thinking your judgment and your fear is greater than my Will. When the patient is deemed incurable it is proper to show him the weakness of his assumed superiority. To end his genocide of freedom, to stop his ownership," The Father.

"You'll die in here, not me," Cruelty.

An old man rises. Slowly towards the bars. The authority is content to believe he is powerful and does not flinch. The old man reaches the edge of the guard's security. The lesson is swift. Quickly the shirt is grabbed. Strongly the ignorant is pulled. His head smashing and echoing through the halls, "Metal on bone." A pleasure to destroy him. To end his vengeance on a world he knows only liars in. The old man sits back against the far wall, where he has sat for days. Other illusionists come with authority hidden in their clubs.

"What happened here," The Angry. Needing answers. Needing an idea, a justification to slaughter me. Wanting it, to prove that I am wrong.

Speaking slowly, feebly, "He began to cry. I asked him what was wrong. He told me I reminded him of his grandfather. So, I got up, I grabbed his shirt, and bashed his face against the side of the cage until he could not be sad anymore."

"You son of a bitch old bastard," the limited, "Fuck you, you couldn't do that."

"And he couldn't be capable of empathy," That Father.

He has his good days and his bad days.

To Care

"A relationship is in a state of Bliss when both people concede naturally. When surrender to the other's will is easeful. Neither person feels as if they have been taken advantage of. It becomes a pleasure just to be around the other that cares about your wellbeing so much. This is love. Where there is no winner, no controller. When the heart is light and floats easily with the mind to the tendency of the other. Sometimes there are situations where you have a strong choice, or you believe you are right, and you feel frustration and even anger, but this too, in this realm of perfect flow, is the gift that allows the masters to let it drift from their minds with the laughter of the knowledge that it does not matter. It changes nothing if either is right. Logic leads us to choices, people do not lead us. And naturally we begin to laugh at something else. Forgotten is the need to be right, to be superior, to matter, to control. Gone. Every relationship is happy when there is less take and more give. But it must be mutual and all encompassing, and not fearful and blocking. It must be real, not an image of what is real. Always give more and the other will do the same out of gratitude, by reflex, by caring, by humility, by love," The Lover; The Father.

<u>Karma</u>

"Karma is the result of your intentions. Of what people heard as truth in your words and what your actions proved. If a person uses people, if a person wants to gain something from the interaction of others; then a person's life will leave them empty. If you do not drive towards Genuine Behavior, without any agenda of gaining, people will not care genuinely for you. It will be a caring of necessity, or politeness, or dogma. Shallowness breeds shallowness. Depth can be filled with a great deal of dense Love. Genuine, naturally occurring, Affection. This is the Karma that builds in your life, it flows from the intentions of your words. However, this is as far as Karma goes, it still will not keep me from a prison cell, and the circumstance of this physical world. So, if I was alone forever, if I never had a chance to yield genuine affection again, Karma would mean nothing. Especially, since Karma can always be transcended, in an instant,---like anything that controls our fate through the accumulation of a living pattern. Even if fate were on us we could still ride calmly the waves and laugh as we try to survive. Just to keep this dead body alive," The Father.

Karma is not a revenge system. Karma cannot "catch up" to someone. Karma, if anything, is the reaction of egos upon an individual ego over the long-term as a result of human vengeance and fear. Karma is also the addiction to any feeling. Karma is habitual.

The Priest sits softly at the edge of the cell. Watching how the intention of The Father's heart to strive to what is Nameless. It would all simply overcome him. It appeared to be deep meditation. Meditation without a single definition. Just infinity. The gentleness of Nothingness. Sometimes, the Priest could see what is happening in him. He could even know. Sometimes thoughts would take him in the state; his half open eyelids suddenly closing. When the mind would begin to hallucinate again, he clearly rose back up to the base consciousness. The weight of the physical world would very clearly press back to his face. Sagging it back to the effects of his life. Meanwhile, his mind begins the constant thought process that will lead him back to the Peace once more.

"The Karma, the pattern of your life, will remain to a degree in any new life, until you can break past the frontal consciousness," The Father spoke clearly.

The Father just began to speak. The Priest could have been there, or could not have been. He smiled at the Priest. Aware of his affection but the Father did not think it. He noticed it with no mind. The Priest laughed.

"Is that all you have to say?" The Priest guffawed.
The Father nodded and turned towards the thoughts forming images in his head.

SERMON OF THE PRIEST
<u>SALVATION</u>

What people need to know is that they are Saved. Right now. It's true. And all you have to do is realize that you are. That's it. This is what is meant by accepting the word of God. This is what it means. Realizing it. Not enforcing it. No. But, the news is even better than that. You don't need to be saved. There was never a chance of you being damned in the first place. Too many people that did not have a spiritual connection have interpreted spiritual scriptures. Too many people sought stability and strength and power for their religion, and when these things are pursued it is <u>impossible</u> to see from the perspective of the Spirit, to be Spiritual. Where there is strong message, where there is organization, numbers, and publicity, there are nearly unintentional lies, misinterpretations for the "good" of something. But the good news is, is that these self-righteous, these fearful fabricators, did not mean to harm, it was merely the result of people wanting to matter, so much that they tried to do something. They are not damned, like you can't be. Seeing oneself falsely is a common insecurity that has harmed Countless. Though misfortune has befallen others because of certain people it does not mean that we should hold judgment against them, even if we must fight them. It is hard to be human. And we must be as God is and let them know there is nothing they have to seek forgiveness for. We love them. For they too, are the Holy Spirit. Our equal in every Existing way. So, if you want to be like Jesus... Turn the other cheek if you can, and focus on that quietness that's inside you. It will help you find peace. And hopefully, one day, you will not have to search for peace, because you will have Become It. Simply because you realized that inside you there is something that cannot have power, that cannot damn or judge, and that is what you really are. Everything else is just a Dream. Awake when you are ready. But you must keep trying to open your eyes, it will not be given to you. Only you can Awake from your spiritual sleep.

"Once while in deep prayer I heard the voice of a monk. I was there with him in my deeper mind. I was there. He asked me, "Why are you here?" I replied, "To go deeper." He answered my statement, "Fool. You seek power there. You are already there. You want to strive on, become stronger. This is your great trap. With all your greatness, will you know when to stop?...Truly. My prayers had become unstable as of late. My aura had been shaken by something that wished to threaten me. I did not lose, but could have. I may have lost my body and anyone near me may have been at risk. Hmm. I should not push outward in search. But still...I wonder what techniques are out there. How will we know if I do not risk my soul?" The Priest to The Father.

<u>Vanity thy Name is Audience</u>

"I once filmed a piece where I kept the face of the woman I was in the scene with blurred. I played the part seriously. I played myself. Knowing. Knowing always. What this would do to my weak audience. I knew the filter they see through, of course I did, I had passed through it. They hated the film. Felt disturbed by it. The disturbed are always the ones that are weak. Strive to not be disturbed. They saw vanity in it. And they thought, "This jerk can't even see his own vanity. He's such an asshole. He preaches about the fucking ego and look at this." This is the cruelty in their thoughts. I wanted them to notice it. The Darkness that strikes them blind to possibilities other than selfish thought. Their psyches are diseased, in constant search of a reason to damn or save or avoid. And when they read what I have written they think, "He's doing it again. Playing it off, like he knows so much." In the Darkness you cannot recognize compassion or hear truth. You hear lies and you witness hate, beneath the false veil of the Darkness. It makes you angry, like everything makes you angry. And within the Darkness you will glorify yourself to think that you are the Compassionate. The One that is Right. If you think you are right you should let go of that. Only an individual, a self, can choose to see their filter. It is so much work to hate everything for Reasons you just heard and thought you made-up. When the wall falls, it feels like I am underwater. Again. Death is inside me," The Father.

Who are you?

"My thought process is slow and methodical. I turn over a single thought again and again. Pondering it. Mixing it with other thoughts. I can see my thoughts moving. It would drive most people mad to think in this manner and have a malfunctioning brain that echoes thoughts everywhere and from nowhere. And then I must compare those thoughts. Churning in mental muck. But I am wiser than the simple man. I can accept it. I can choose not to fight it. I don't need to fight. I know what it feels like to "accept" I know. I know, so I evoke it. I make the emotion happen. It is why I could perform before the Audience. I had the ability to change how I felt about something. That's why I was great. I could silence the natural churning that makes me who I am and focus on a single thing or on nothing at all. Power is no power. We do not suffer like you do. It is never life or death. Death is always present with the knowledgeable, with the Fearless. We pursued madness, learned about what man fears, and we learned how it manifests. Through fear, we confronted the resistance to the loss of control. And we stopped using it. We knew it, so we didn't fear it. Even when we became truly mad with our malfunctioning bodies. We still held consciousness while most people are lost in their brains. We that know sit always in the stillness, known as death---the Spirit," then noticing he was thinking. Noticing he was only dancing in the mind, making more poetry for no one. Talking about the Spirit, but within the true consciousness of the Spirit you don't think about it. Thinking belongs to the body, and it dies with it. Yes. The mind speaks with us. Conversations with what knows. The mind strives to understand the soul. The mind will strive to understand anything. We learned the importance of directing our thoughts, always away from what steals people's lives.

"I met him. The Cousin. Long after. The one that drown her that day. In him was always an insecurity. A want for importance. A want to matter. I felt that this insecurity kept him from seeing the Truth of His Majesty. Since he thought with the whole of insecurity it kept him from being able to see how significant his spirit actually is. So I told him of the story. Spoke it to him in however many words. In however much time. He listened to the Story of the Simple Girl. She who strove to freedom and peace. And killed herself for it. And I think he gained such a gift as the story unfolded. As he understood the beauty of what he had taught her that day. Such a tale at such a point would have made me near cry, but hold it cool just on the surface. The Greatness of its gift. One cannot know until they touch it. Sometimes, pride, in the right amount, pointed in the right direction, can show someone the right path. Where they know for an instant that it's Right. It's factual. I know because I've touched it. It was funny and Awesome how his voice softened as he aged. Appreciatively noticing his value. Seeing further just how important and significant the spirit that is in all people truly is. When pride does not know fear, it is valuable," spoke the prophecy.

<u>Fear and Shame Darken Religion</u>

I remember growing older and older. I remember those older than I, slowly, suffering away their final days. I remember that fear was used to keep them alive. It was not used on purpose. But it was used to make them obey the Dark Path that compromised, not their pride, but their Being, their lifeforce, because they wound up serving pride, because their pride was too afraid to fight back. People that sought power in religion created hallucinations in peoples minds by suggesting the existence of Hell and Penalty. I saw no person face their death without fear, save those that did not believe in the Penalty. Those that already had seen part of death and felt dead. Those that knew truth and not suggestion. People cling to life. So afraid to let go. So, so, so afraid. They have their bodies mutilated and transformed to cling to life for only a few more weeks or months or days. It doesn't matter. So greedy for what they think they own that they would prolong their suffering. In a society of Light, death is not feared and the old allow themselves to journey into it and the young let them go, fear and greed do not drive the price of healthcare into Space.

Hell is Here and Now. You make it for other people by pursuing your pleasures. Sure. We seek pussy and we harm the cunt we keep. Once I held a love in the rapture of my being and she trapped me soothingly in her heart; this girl, not The Girl, but this one, dreamt of a woman I was about to have an affair with and she killed the girl... she had never even met the woman I was to ravage for my pleasure and her enjoyment. Though it was possible for my love to not feel slighted by the act, she had not reached such a place, not quite, so I would have created Hell for her. Pained her. Created pain for her because of my greed, my lust. Although, if I had hurt her, surely her want to be with me would have forced her to become stronger by letting the act go...for this is True Love. True Love holds nothing, so it doesn't even have to let go. It is in every action, even the actions of controlling programmed survival, like sex, or in my case, powerful sex, still everything is seen from the center of love. And Love is always considered. And reason will fall upon reason upon the point that returns us to the epicenter of love. Because she gave me the gift of Serving Love, I made sure she would not suffer. Not to say that I did not have the affair. I just made sure she would not suffer if I did. But if she did, I knew that her holy heart would keep her on the Path and she would gain from me giving her the Teacher of Pain. Because she sees from love, she would always stay on the Path, and eventually be able to absorb hardships beneath her feet. Even if her actions too were selfish or advantageous. It is not our intentions or our goals that make us holy, it is our root and our honesty of how we see ourselves and what we shall do for Universal Resolution.

"Always, I have fought to teach people the way to absolute freedom. Then the Girl spoke to me with Her soul, She wanted me to see what She burned into herself to construct Her identity. The way She thought it, the times She'd built it. And now, as time has passed, I realized that I must stop my teachings. I must give up. Freedom is for each individual to have. Within themselves. It can be granted to no one. I will fight no more. I will surrender to the knowledge in my soul. To the path of salvation, to no purpose, but Nirvana," The Father.

FAILING, BUT NEVER LOSING
FALSELY ALARMED

As I came to see him lying, his face smashed against the floor. Him unable to move. "Bad Day," I thought. It's so fucking cold in here. As I waited for the cell door to be unlocked, as I waited for that clanging of the light metal against the heavy metal, tinkling, and made all the more piercing by the cold. The cold pain I have in my hand is not on the outside. It is on the inside. I'll never know why, or what. In the blood, that he'd been drowning in, that he'd been sucking up his nose, and throwing up as it filled his belly...he was breathing heavy. This scene is hued blue and grey. And he lives on. A fable laid out for me:

The Officer and The Baker

Bringing cause you thump your hand,
and offer me a favor.
Smooth and slow you weave your curse,
your eyes glazed over.
Your soul encased in sheets of glass,
sealed from its maker.
You analyze our fingerprints,
and catalog the Baker.

signed,
Bloody Deliberate Fingerprint

I'm pretty sure he's laughing in his sleep, while his body he brought to a dormant state to rest, he may well be aware of everything around him. Never trust the scientifically probable sleeping. What did he give to be able to harness it and choke it and make inspiration pour? The Priest – *in a dusky hue*

"I have seen deeply into my subconscious as of late. I have found fear. Deeply buried, long contemplation. I have a fear of the coming Alzheimer's striking my mind in such a way that I forget how to silence it. Will the mind try to trick me into not being able to think that I can stop thinking? The mind has always fought for its survival. The body has a function and it wants to use the mind to protect itself. But the soul knows it is not important, and it wants the mind to think that. What if I can't remember how to find my spirit, I mean, become aware of it? What if my mind wouldn't shut up for me to be able to notice my essence? The body wants me to fight. To kill. To breed. To prosper. This is what the body wants. It wants to live. All religion counters this. But once humanness is present within any religion it is corrupt. Once prosperity is used for power it is...

"If my teeth hurt one more time I'll have to open my eyes," like a comment in a dream. The mind burns with insignificance.

"For the whole of His time with me he rarely deliberately meditated. He rarely silenced the mind completely purposefully. Not by thinking at it. Not intentionally. I would find him set against the wall. Or laying on the floor on his back. Staring. Breathing steadily. I often sat with him. Trying to be a reflection of the Love and Peace he was searching for. Trying to be completely there with him. It helped him. It moved him closer. He could feel me there, there with a still heart for him to be accepted by. He could not remember that he had done it. His mind wasn't there anyway. It was not being used to record. There was nothing to fear so he did not have to force his mind to remember anything. Whether he could remember it or not did not change his constant want for it. His knowing that he required it. His desire to touch what he saw as Her. It felt like She made Him feel. His will to continually try at peace would lock The Great One into bliss with no record in his mind. Every space. Every gap. Every moment we are not thinking. Every moment we are existing without forcing fear upon ourselves,

these are the moments that we notice everything. Our mind moves slow enough to see it. And we realize we are It. That which we have been searching for, and we are not afraid. That's the result of this Holy Quest. Lives flow forth, until they end. Until that second. His words stopped. His eyes starred into eternity...and like a rip cord he was beyond the limits of life. And he knew silence. Free from the duties his mind created for him. Free from the babble of philosophy. The grace of his truth engulfed him. I saw it in his eyes. An empty look only God could give to me, and only I could claim as my own. Thank you for that gift, My Friend. Thank you for the knowledge that we are all already saved. Right now. Right now. I wonder how he remembered it?"

The Inferiority Complex

"We struggled to matter. We sought peace and comfort. We did not seek supremacy, but we did seek Freedom. Freedom from those that sought power. We believed deeply in ourselves. And we fought. All of us had killed for that lust to be free. We sure did. We all had the Disease too. We just began to work on a cure for it. None of us could escape the programmings of our childhoods. We coveted our own lives so that they may end by our own hands. We fought to be able to die. We fought against those that were too afraid to die. For those that spoke with the authority of Gods. What the manipulated (by fear) don't realize is that God does not seek authority. How could a God exist that would damn Itself by condemning Its creations for acting in a way that It designed? If one seeks authority in life one does not follow God. One worships desire. And we desired to be Free. Even as we overcome the designs of this world, and learn the physical nature and spiritual nature of HumanKind, we are still very much human. Very much designed or manifested or evolved to the definition of human. Very much not a God. Very much something that must realize it is still evolving and work to do so. Maybe the next Evolution will be able to control it's spiritual body so perfectly that it will be able to choose the prime bodies, perhaps the prime bodies will be built in labs and brains will be transplanted from the wisest, or the greediest. Perhaps...this will be the nature of the another coming war," The Father.

It does not matter how people say it, how people manipulate it (like the Darkness in all sides of the News), it doesn't matter if you are remembered as a tyrant or thief or king or a god or you are completely unremembered, what matters is you're very simple existence as a function of a living moving Universe that you imagined was so vastly important. You, like me, will burn and fade away so that something more may come, each generation the superior of the last that will try to hold it down and fearfully parent it. We can make-up any reason for living, we can believe that we made it up like everyone else does, but it does not change our simple function. This we can see without the illusion makers and without our hallucinations that make us function.

"All I am doing now is reasoning away my guilt...just another psychological defense mechanism to ease the function of a living life as this particular human," The Father Spakes On, "The work it takes to keep my confidence to continue my cause is great. When my way gets shaky, when I fear that what I say might hurt someone because they will take it personally and greedily and darkly, I must accept what I am. I shut the confidence off. I stop wanting it. This is the path of mastery. An enlightenment we will try for you, to sacrifice ourselves to...It is possible to be Free. After the resting of my ego the confidence is easier to induce. The mindset easier to hold without insecurity making it. It is a condition not induced by neuroses. This is far different from the way of Darkness, the opposite of it, in fact. The paths and their results are far different."

Compassion can be real, and it dissolves inferiority, and you can gain all the benefits naturally on this caring path, or you crave power and will fake it for your chance to manipulate a group, this is the Dark Path that is defined and practiced in many groups, but the primary in the West is freemasonry. Our True and attained Power is Over the power of those that would seek it, because we do not suffer to maintain a phony, adulterous, and coward's illusion.

I Am a Sacrificial Pyre

My personal progress has slowed greatly. The only way I can form a thought is to think through this mind of the Spirit. My brain cannot function much anymore. He used it all up. The problem with thinking through the Spirit Mind is that it stimulates the Mental Mind. The thoughts he made for me access this route too easily. Sometimes I want. I want to not have to record this journey anymore. Then I could go deeper. One day I hope to not feel compelled to help people find these Truths through these thoughts. I hope that my Mind will stop Warring for peace and that my soul will be able to go that smidge deeper where the mind no longer needs the brain. The battle for Freedom enslaves many lives to tasks like writing, and failing, but the victory of the hardships I have faced have given me a silence, an eternity, a pitch of reality that I could not have found without the suffering of my slavery. The path, the happenstance does not seem to matter. It seems we are mostly thrust into life's dilemmas by our own difficult to control whims of Reason and those of others. The trick is to have an innocent soul and an innocent mind, forgive yourself instantly and journey on. Innocence is warped by shame. So let shame go. And I will stay deeper on the path. The power of purity of an intention, an intention that seeks to gain nothing, this power brings Freedom. I have more of His thoughts than of my own left. My life was worth something because I sought nothing for it. My duty was to testify for the Glory of the simple beliefs made masterful by the unwanted, fearless, souls that truly trusted in their unbeneficial, equal eternity.

1 amongst 1000's of Notes:
I am left only with stories as my body has no more ability to live.
Death is close by. How much longer must I wait?

Wait.

"There were always so many amazing, wonderful breathtaking things
to do in life. The hardest part of life is choosing the few great things.
Choosing an experience...
What will I know today?
Happiness, Sadness, Suffering, Love.
Life will use me, waste me, and destroy today.
I will love to wait, and waste, and see."

Time is moving.

And tomorrow, like every morrow, I will be reborn again.
As unaffected as before.

THE REBEL PROPULSION

"In my life I have always loved adventure. It has always made my life more difficult. If I wasn't committing a crime, or starting a war, then I would have an affair. The addiction came naturally to me. My thoughts with all of their good intentions would make me these situations. My mind would justify, and Reason, myself to these points, into these circumstances. People always complain that life doesn't go their way. People can't understand it. This is because people cannot separate themselves into the deeper consciousness that allows us to see the mind. Our lives are inventions of our minds. Our scheming minds, always using its tools to defend us. Always controlling us, propelling us into the next hard course, through a system of thought. Functioning as a human, in a specific, observable way. We are an amalgamated pawn of the reacting audience. Your world is an invention of your mind. The greatest knowledge on Earth is the Way of stopping it. The chance to see it. To see how it has lead us into everyone's opinion of us, none of which are perfect. This is overcoming the ego. This is true power, that yields no power. Things will change, but stay the same. When I see my mind running on I think of all the madness of all the sadness of all the joy of all the fate drawn out by this mind. I think of what it thought, that made me do or not do, that made me live. And I am at peace to know that it will stop when I am dead. I am also at peace to know that it is fine whatever it makes for me on this planet. I thank Existence and Emptiness that I have had a chance to go Deeper and see my mind controlling me. I am Grateful that I know the Peace of stopping it from deep levels, and that I know what Heaven is," The Father, "Thank you for sitting. Thank you for listening. Thank you for echoing back the stillness I was trying to find."

"There are no words that I could speak that could stop the hallucinations of the mind that makes anyone. It is best to reflect back the beauty that they want to reach, even if they can't see it through what the mind makes the eyes see," The Priest.

"I am awaking from the Dream of Life. It feels like a I am gaining control over the propulsion of a dream. Like I am underwater. Always like I am underwater. Always like there is nothing to fight or defend, but a present and Existing Universe to be buoyant within," The Father.

THE SOLUTION
Harmony

"The solution was simple because everyone had the same problem. The goal is absolute peace within every class of the populace. Everyone, in every class, in every situation, just wanted to feel more safe. More calm. On a societal spectrum it was easy, but no one could stop thinking of satisfaction long enough to think about anyone else's stability (it is not their fault, but it is their fault if they know about it and don't try to fix it by not pursuing training). (Anyway,) It was possible to let everyone be as sustained as they wanted to be, if people were willing to fix the dysfunction of anger and non-trust that breeds in most (misdirected) people after failures. Both sides could help, the socialists and the independent and collective fascists of the ruling government, the remnants of the fading Dark Society, thumping quieter and quieter like a waning child's pride. If a bedrock of money; money is the blossom of all goodness; was made available for the very poor and education followed suit by informing the simple function of the capitalistic system it would work. Capitalism depends on invention, something that makes something easier or increases its value. Innovation comes from those that must and have the heights to dream to, and not from those that have, and think they hand it down; those that have used funds to mark the pride of their imaginary place. Pride is why money never trickles down, money stands as evidence of the right to not be terrified and to be full and warm. All the while capitalism nearing its meltdown as it runs out of poor populations to enslave, and the youth build their rights for the coming youth. It is solution time. So as we travel up the imaginary ladder of too many broken rungs, always sell something that you can at least triple your profit on. A society without a real and true foundation of reoccurring capital struggles with innovation and our evolution is slower than it can be. Inflation moves quickly. Protect yourself. Find a way that the people that want to encounter you will feel calm and open when they see you. Small town markets, bazaars, see the positive faces that receive your rent. Grow with it. Let me see all People provided with a revolving fund with a fixed principle that accrues a healthy amount of interest, large enough so that the funds increase quick enough to support and allow for another income and opportunity in time for the life of an individual, never randomly ending in abuse, suicide, or a mass shooting, or ever in the sense that existence is nothing, or that anyone had been a "nobody."   A person that pays is treated differently, so we must all be able to pay, servitude optional, with training paid. Imagine an entire nation without recession, without risk of collapse or the possibility of sales from the fear of it; and families without abused members; imagine practical fearlessness. People will keep working because they have <u>hope</u> that they can try again, because we Dream Big non-stop. There is an old and dying belief that people need to be shamed or tricked or threatened with death to enter into work agreements with other people, but the urgency of the youth is massively programed, like our will to care for each other without prejudice, and our success is craved on every side with little solutions for it, but we dream upward because there is so far to dream even as we're mocked for having nothing. Enforcing the will to dream, and removing the perpetual ability for it, is cruelty, and a consequence to the darkness that is waking up to the light that makes it easy to trust within. The funds must be provided without condition, shame, or manipulation. A continuous charity, ran by banks, funded by the taxing government, propelled by the populace, and educated by those that have succeeded in a system that gave everybody a chance. Funds trickling up to those that control the commodities, because their parents once dreamed and loved big and cultivated them. Everyone wins and no pride is hurt, no one even loses power, everyone gains, an enabled mass in large numbers increasing the opportunity for innovation. The wealthy will feel safe when the poor are stable. Uncertainty yields desperation, desperation yields fear, and fear yields cruelty and violence and self-destruction, which is crime, as a natural response within the body to stop the discomfort or the uncertainty in a person's sense of survival. Peace is still probable. Recognize what causes people to suffer. Violence is a response that occurs when equality is preached but power is coveted for its sense of comfort, and imbalance is left unaddressed because they are the grievances of distant voices viewed as non-threatening, like your children. Everybody wants a chance, and when or if that chance fails, everybody wants another chance. Life is simple. We must treat it that way," The Solution.

There are too many shameful views to institute the <u>single</u> fund through a government with a democracy. Shame and police would be brought in to maintain and deter abuse of the fund by its members. Therefore, this Utopian ideal cannot be performed through the government, but The Solution may come from the noble private charities, often of great past Presidents. Epiphany strikes: Congress has the power to enact the Perpetual American Opportunity Tax Credit and put dreaming back into the system, and remove the

<u>For the Living</u>

I know that you will seek wisdom from my final words.
I know that if you see me dying
that you will want me to say something most true.
I may not be able to.
I may not have my mind.
Stillness may come too quick.
Do not try to find importance in my passing.
Let it pass.

I want to die so well for you.
So that just before you see my eyes lose focus,
you see gentleness. Or just before I breathe my last, I breathe
calmly.
So that you know it is alright to live.
And when you die...
I will try to stay with you.
Be with you. Let you know that somehow you are still loved,
and focus on that solid feeling.
I would try, regardless of whether or not I might burn some for it.
These wishes make me try so hard to overcome this cycle.
My absolute compassion for your love for me...
I would bend time for it.
Want drives me strongly for the sake of non-attachment,
so that I might let go of my own path
and serve you in whatever way I could.
This is the raw power of a grateful heart.
For you who tried.
Who loved me so much that you fought yourself
You changed yourself
Because you did not have the ego, or fake confidence,
to blind you to your own suffering.
You, holy Beloved, that loved so deep
that your faith drove you to prove that I was right.

Sit with the pain of my passing. Try to feel it.
Do not run from it. Do not think on it. See if the feeling can lead
you somewhere.
If all you can feel is the ache, please let your heart remember the
calm feeling of love,
and the steadiness of my spirit beside you.   Dense.

"I have known many wars...I have killed. I have stolen, ravaged, and conquered. I have lived well. These are the deeds that people fear happening to them. These are the acts that The Frightened will use to murder, imprison, and steal freedom from The Fearless. They fear the deeds themselves because they are ignorant, and are certain they can commit them and are certain other people are like them. They have spent their whole lives thinking of power and place and institutions. They missed out on Wisdom because of their choices. They chose the other side. So what. What they miss is what I have served with my deeds. The Reason I chose. My Reason was not chosen by fear, for security or stability. I served those that Loved. Those that had the capacity to make love a conscious reality by vowing themselves to serve it. To be devoted to a single person. To sacrifice for their happiness. It is a Great thing to give your life to another. To find someone that deserves it. That can resolve to the prosperity of the partnership. To gain without desires. To Love regardless of the war...for the sake of the Love," The Father.

"The techniques to find the love we are vulnerable for are simple and soft. This type of love is the only valuable thing on this entire planet. It is the awe we know when we stare into another person's very soul, and we see ourselves looking back. That is what I love to have access to. The personal, the person, without an image or act. I see it, feel it, am all encompassed with it from you. You show it to me, and I crave it. It is beautiful how there is no give and take between us because we offer everything. The Fearless know Honesty and from Honesty comes Love. But people miss it all because in Capitalism only materials have value, how can they see it? Even love is only a tool to them..."
The Priest.

"There was one I loved best. One that I served. One that would lose everything for Love. For No Reason. The purity, the non-selfishness,

the living for the Hell of it, for the adventures that warped Her. For the Girl, whom did not need a name...She beyond the illusion of what will die when we die...She laughed in it because she knew it wasn't serious. For Her I made a war and offered Her my mind, and with no doubt, She used them and left me and scarred me with the mark of it forever. She gave me the greatest gift I have ever known. She taught me how to cling to nothing, to be controlled by nothing, definitely not by Her. Absolute Freedom,"
The Father.

"I still see Her in you. Not just in your soul. But as you, in this life... She changed the person you are. A man becomes a better man when he cares for something. I mean better for himself, of course. He can see more of what he truly is. More of his absoluteness," The Priest.

"My great gift to women is that I made them see how a man could treat them without a vie for control over them, and I'd save them by not standing it from them. So long as they gave themselves to me and let me use them willingly, they would have me at their disposal as well. To gain nothing in the physical world but sex and survival while baring their souls for adoration. It is not much to ask," The Father..."They were used well and with kindness."

The Muse

When you see her you know that you would kill men for her.
You are certain that you would die for her.
This is the power of the Muse.
She holds you. Captivates you. Admires you.
...Loves you...
And you are Aware.
You'd give yourself to her,
for her pleasure,
by your risk.
She creates for you. She eases your task.
Inspires your dreams and quells your nightmares.
The Muse. Holy Beauty. Gleaming from your soul.
I see in her the dawn of thought.
I am careful to keep them calm,
careful to care gently for them,
each must feel like your love for them is absolute.
It is all that they ask. All that they want.
Serve them as they serve you.
The Power of the Muse.
The energy of its sex. The penetrating of the mind.

Yet...what you must know about the Muse...
most of them will reveal themselves to you...
and fade from you...
knowing that the artist has too great a power on them.
Fearing the actuality of the fruition of their ideals.
Like a day, they begin and end.
They will always know that your love for them is half-diluted by your brilliance,
trapped in your dancing mind.
But there may be one...One, maybe Three, that serve It and you absolutely.
Those that choose your game for themselves. Precious, like
Death.

If you give them love in exchange for the glimpse into their soul,
then most, though away, will love you for your lifetime.
This is the type of love that gives a man strength when he must press
forward, again, while he's beaten.
A Muse comes in countless forms. Any form. And the movements
are sweet.
Like drops of bliss into your Being. Finding the way to get it out.

Sermon of The Priest
Criticizers

Criticism is the chatter of the Darkness. The background noise for all the holy that notice it and must, unfortunately, tolerate it. And a holy person must see it for the truth of doubt and insecurity in the words of the critiquers. The holiest person can see it all so well because that person has been through it. The holy person sees himself as this Darkness and wants badly enough to be something different. He changes himself. Turns from the negative. Stops the glorification of his ego. Chooses everyone else over himself. Everyone has criticized me for something. I have displeased everyone. It is easy to displease the Dark and demanding criticizer.

He speaks of "Him". Of "He". Of "Man". For factual reasons. "He" is more prominent in spiritual life. It is easier to see through the man's illusions. However, women know holiness vastly and deeply and truthfully when they reach their goal. <u>Because</u> it is harder. But deeply rare. Plus, it is a trick. A trick to the woman that can see, to the holy, if there happens to be any in the audience, which is not likely. A tool, a lesson, for that woman to see through the "He," to feel no inferiority. To get the irrelevancy of meaning in this context of truth. To hear it through the same voice that is speaking it. A voice of love. A voice that believes in love and so thinks through it. If you did not see it and set yourself free...if you felt insecurity...meaning if you formed an opinion of an intangible word, if you made your mind work to justify it or defy it...then you are not the holy....you are not smart. You are not...that is all. If you want to be, you have a long, long way to go. You must manifest the Hero's Soul, and want no control out of it. That is the problem with all of the "minorities," they do not seek equality and peace, they seek control and power and vengeance as a false cure for resentment. They seek justification. <u>You</u> are in the Darkness. Accept this. You have to see it to overcome it. Stop thinking about yourself, *stop being so concerned with staying alive and endlessly climbing to nowhere, but business class...And maybe you will see something new. To behold something without fear.*

"Once I kept the emotional burden of many lovers...while I was living with the best of them. I never saw the others...I would only make words for them. Each of them allowed me something. Something deep and caring. Something powerful. They allowed me to have an intimate friendship with them. Not sexual, although there was some of that. But...You see...you see it, my Friend," The Father said to the smiling Priest, "My mind is very strong. Very smart. My gift and my curse. I fell in love with my imagination. It is easy to think about a million philosophies rationalizing the mind and using the mind to un-rationalize the mind. But to be beyond the mind in the instant of discovery where you see the mind worshiping itself. Almost feeding itself. When you realize how the momentum is making you fantasize about someone that isn't there when someone that is present is giving you exactly what you fantasize about. My God, or anyone's, or No God. My mind will keep me from everything good, simple, and beautiful that is all around me at this exact second. My God. The mutation of the babbling mind took God away from HumanKind. We cannot find God again unless we stop it. We must be very still to see the subtlety of existence and function in everything we seem designed to destroy."

"The adventure is a Great One. To have a Revolution that returns us back to the point before revolution. There must be a revolution where wealth cannot be redistributed and where no power is taken," The Priest.

"What are you talking about? Were you even listening to me?" The Father.

"No, I started to, but then I started to think of something, and my mind ran away with me," and so simply they began to laugh together. Enjoying their similarities and revel in the pointlessness of their thinking. Bathing in the Joke of their life's work. Loving that they have nothing to fear. The mind is the root of all contradiction.

"The mind creates an image so strong with want and desires...it always dreams in ideals too...always creating hope to dupe people into their next action....like getting people into relationships with people they can't even see are bastards," The Priest.

"I knew you heard me," The Father.

"No. The mind just likes to masturbate. Eventually the tone of the conversation would make me spew forth exactly what you spewed," The Priest. "Seems as if we have slipped in it and lost the conversation."

They laughed, because they can't lose this kind of conversation.

<u>Reality</u>

As he awoke he realized that he had been controlling the dreams. Many dreams. Over and over they poured out from the hallucinating mind. And within every scenario he could do as he pleased. He himself, within the dream, was not a hallucination being made to do as the dream world wished. "I possessed consciousness. Between the raping and the killing, all the natural things we want to do, that are programmed into us, but repressed by a functioning society...I could tell the truth. The truth is that everything, every doubt, every hope, every pain, every pleasure, all of it, is a functional hallucination within the world. Everything programmed as a response guided by our personality. Of course it is. Because in reality we are a spirit. A being that knows no fear. A being that is at peace. The base as seen through the soul of the Holy Girl. When we know it, we know no fear, we are at peace. And most greatly, for myself, I know now completely, that I must be entering into meditation by shear force of will to want to reach the pinnacle of consciousness. When my hallucinating mind is gone... When I focus on waking up, not just from myself, but from everything that is an illusion, made to mask the truth for functionality of the creation...my Heaven...even though I am trapped in a fake world I can imagine, I am Free, and will know greater freedom when I can die. I will be able to reach it. I will push onward. I will even be able to break free from the illusion that I am the spirit, and what makes it believe in itself, which clearly means I, in a spirit's consciousness can break free from the cycle of having to occupy a body. Freedom from a given identity, any identity. The absolute defying and absolute acceptance of everything that exists to the very level of human reality. It is good that no one is here. No one could understand the majesty of what we are, of what we can know, of where I will go...It is a great and isolated Revolution," The Father sees through eyes unclouded by purpose, "I am not good or evil, but I am human and functioning. Never follow the authority of the hallucinations of other fake minds. The path and its reality begins and ends in death."

<u>Corpse</u>

When we found him: The weight of his head slammed downwards into the edge of the writing desk, catching him before he slammed face first into the bars of the cage. Geez, what that would have looked like. His mouth was hanging forcibly open, probably thrown off its hinges. He must have been yelling, speaking. Yet his open eyes, seemed to be calm. Like he was looking far out across an ocean of spirits. Like there was no Sun in his eyes. And not even a single risk of his assassination. He must have been speaking to The Calmed. Their Utopia expanding before him.
Perhaps his body lunged forward to be held up in the arms of the young Girl, whom he fought and died for; a final kiss to begin again and an ending lift, that rang with the metallic clang of a Legend's face into the writing desk's edge, tearing open his forehead, that forced his reflex and head back and over, slamming him dead into the cold steel bars. I swear to God, the Man died standing up.

In the end every cell around him had been emptied. He always wanted to die Alone
--with no one wanting anything from him.

I, so conscious of my presence, whispered close to his listening ear, "Leave this place. Look at no one. If you see that daze of ignorant malice staring back into you their fear will take your heart again and fill you with rage. Go from this place and leave all society behind. Leave with love in your heart. Go deep into the woods. And never return.." Just then, The Father's nose poured blood, and the hair on the top of his scalp went bald...and it smelled like rain, like there'd just been a rainbow there. He wrote to leave the body rest for three days. We laid him on the cot, covered him with a grey wool blanket. Decay began...just, nearly immediately. Enormous flies gathered by the hundreds. For him, I slaughtered them all. Brother of war and peace.

It was day 365, an anniversary in our relationship that came with a gift from me to him; I was the one whom found him. It's when it starts to get mathematical that the track of fate seems to tick you into it. The Universe stamping impact on an event straight into you. I didn't see him every day, but a lot of them during that good year.

The Death of Friendship

Heavy on the voice. Sad. Cracking in phlegm, but held together by the subtle pride that a Holy Man has for another, "...I don't know how much you remember now. I don't know if you met me early enough to record me in your failing long-term mind, but still my mind lusts in still Bliss at the thought of you recalling any of this. Will you even know what was achieved? Are these words written somewhere on your soul as a sensation in a place that one day, in one life, you may remember? I shall remember you in this way: As a sensation that I can recall. A presence that let me feel what stillness is. Too simple. What seeing is. What realizing is. I can find the thought and have the hand, warm but lifeless, in my hand again. Will you remember my chosen efforts for your comfort? But you fade away now like every Hero forgotten and compromised for weaker reasons and illusions of mattering. Only because people do not want to make the effort to remember the sensation of goodness they first held in that moment that they knew it was all going to be alright. Failures of the sinful selfish mind, blinded by pride itself, unable to see what it is.   You haven't spoken for some time, two days. Are you still thinking? Or are you finally still...completely. If people could realize that in the end they don't really know anything, they fail...one by one. Designed to die, somehow, somehow designed, even if it was randomness or the propulsion of mathematics as a moving force, somehow designed. It has functioning parts meant to fail...Every thought wasted so that we can be constantly reminded that it all means nothing, unless we give our good meaning to it, using the mind for something better. Meanings are lies to trick minds, some of them unintentional tricks brought forth by protection mechanisms. And if it is unintentional it displays the mind's slavery and lack of control. Stillness in madness. All people need do is realize they are mad, and stop it. With any mind we can make reasons towards it. Holy...holy my brother, was the journey to walking away from power, realizing that no one is fit for it, as you lived for Enablement. The answers do not lie in reasons. The soul exists, an unowned spirit. It does not need reasons. Reasons are for living and dying. Do not trust your memory now. Your concept of reality is gone, it is likely wrong at the end of this life. Remember the dense stillness and don't let the Universe move you.

I shall do for you, My Brother, The Father, like you did for Her. I vow to compile the heart and mind that you have infused into me as a grand collection of your torrent of soulful passion, so that people will know that you are real, and can be known as I can know a Friend."

<u>We Live On after The Last Thought</u>

What was that hiccup? I'm dead. I knew it. Soft. Will I lose my mind? It is gone. I broke free from it. I have reasoned for too long. My thoughts can go. I will still be myself. Oh. Yes. I will keep Her though. The one that sent me this Way. I will thank Her. Wait
.   Beautiful.
I didn't think anyone would come for me.
  Thank you.

I felt it. I felt the twitch. He did it. Not in his body. He loved his mind too much. He reasoned too deeply. But there in the Bardo, the moment after. He awoke from the Dream. And he broke forth into Freedom. Free to live or die to be without fear to be the breath of a mountain to be the sound of water to explode into life to know that he is Free. Free enough to be able to reach Her, just beyond the grip of gods, and just within the next concept of eternity.   To know that he is not alive. To have that gift that will gives a fighter of the self. To be that sensation described best by Man as Love. It's what we are when we are Fearless. It is a fact that you will eventually realize you are.

It is here and now. At the end of my days. At the requiem of my mind. Now I must put to test the techniques I have manifested from my soul, this independent spirit. I turn to the void and smile across it. I will return to the wilderness. Alone. Unnamed. And I will ready myself to leave this world. Now I am in the state of perfect rediness. I have finished his Great Book. And I do not need to remember my own life to help him. I will leave my mind here. Take with me my nothingness. And finish what They started. My heart absorbs in Love. I will look at no face. See no eyes of pain and fear. I do not want to see people not trying. Not changing for the sake of hope. .. .. Were those thoughts? Where are they coming from? Why can't they complete themselves anymore? I seek the creatures beyond thought, free from it. They will teach me the final words to forget. Where there is no power, only life, only death. The stream will remember my true name and tell me. And without a thought I will go from here. Why is man's only thought to overcome the system? Science, Religion, Politics, Business, everyone is only trying to overcome the system. Break it. Do we have the strength for the true Revolution. The Revolution to break the destructive system of ourselves. Nothing else takes HumanKind to what it truly wants.

THE NATURE OF THE MAN JESUS, THE CHRIST

The message of Jesus Christ is that you should always be willing to die for the belief in humility, compassion, and hope of human beings being able to make themselves that which he had the courage to be. Will you die for the sake of Love? Would you not matter for it? Will you let yourself be crucified in front of your mother because you believe in a simple truth that allows you to feel calmness? Are you willing to make your mother weep the tears of True Love? Do you love Humanity this much? Would you make that hell for someone to live through?...You must choose not to follow any power, any opinion, any that have formed an institution. This is why the Jews, the Romans, any organization, throughout any time, would have slaughtered Jesus to preserve their own power. Power, all of it, authority...Is Darkness. Darkness; Meaning...an absence of God, an absence of the warmth of Love, as cold is the absence of heat. Jesus' final message to us came as he lay on the cross, with his last breaths, through the pain and weight of his body, pushing slowly down on his lungs over the course of several days, while gravity stretches him ...He spake: "God, why have you forsaken me?" Telling us that we must choose the path, the path of sacrifice, the path of willingness to die for the hardest cause. The cause where at the end there is no reward and no salvation. You do it, because you know it is the most holy," with flair and a wave of his hand, "And fuck anyone that criticizes it, that defies it, they will find a reason to kill it, fuck them. You disapprove, you disapprove, you tisk, you judge, you crucify, because your heart chose the Darkness. You are the lineage that crucified Jesus Christ. Sacrificed him to have a little for yourself. To belong, to stay, to feel like someone will do something for you because you met their qualifying and Dark religious terms. A piece of a Kingdom of Dirt. Judgers. Murderers. You send people to die for the betterment of the world. Jesus failed you, but triumphed for himself. Just as you can triumph, by choosing no power, no security, just like Jesus The Christ you can choose the path of pain and acceptance of this pain. Pain comes when you defy the ruling class of your Existing environment (your parents, your education, the police, and laws). When you defy the ruling class and refuse to be a part of it, you will finally be acting like Jesus. Finally breaking Free. Refuse to rule. Yet, churches beg for the dime you scrape together so that they might worship idolatry and keep you coming back for fictional rituals. Churches are corrupt, anyone of them that takes money and promotes and threatens you with a Hell that you choose? Leave this church, and its hell, and never return. All of you in your shiny suits and fancy dresses, all of you that came expecting "Sal-a-vation!" to be given to you because you deserve it, you brothers and sisters, it was your power that killed Christ and it is your precious power, and the fear of losing a feeling of it, that will kill the next messengers to come. Expect it. Power is the sin on the hearts of all within the Darkness. Pride is the anchor of your soul. Vengeance and justice are you acting upon pride, making something to rebel against and make war at. To be like Jesus you must be willing to die while suffering and gain nothing. If you hang on to your life with fierceness because fear grips you than you will be too easily bought off by what the Devil really is," The Priest.

Only by giving up on salvation can you know it. This is the path. It has a pretty funny punch line.

<u>Remarks at the Funeral of
The Father</u>

"When he reached out to me in where I thought that I was alone, I was less afraid..."
unknown

"You could be anything around him, except someone taking someone else's Freedom. He chose his values. And for someone unwise like myself, who did not have the ability to see the best way for those with our tendencies, he guided me to keep my life calmer. He spoke, and he taught you. He even knew when you would rebel against him and he would let Pride calm, and he would chip away at you. Helping you see what he knew. He was our Father. He made meaning for us whom had none, and just wanted a little, just faith in something we all had."
Unknown

" I love you."
unspoken

"I loved him."
almost thought.

"He would not want me to question what I have become? How can I drive through the emotions, what am I not willing to give up? What am I hanging on to? In death. Myself."
Paulson, R.

"Over the years his voice grew deeper. And towards the end, I heard, he couldn't talk. When someone cares they talk low, because it is a slow steady pull from the depths of the soul to bring out what people can tell is mystifying, struck by it the normal person must fight through their fears and their doubts, but rarely came those that knew what it was and had to hone it, for confident reasons they had no reason to doubt. The Naturals. The OverMen that let us use them, gently, and kindly." A Reformed Prison Guard

"Maybe, he was healthier than he made out. I think he chose to die, but definitely chose his prison, because he didn't want to be afraid again, like he'd felt when being hunted by man. The undertone of wars left behind in him...he braved through it, of course he did, Heroes do. But he eventually just didn't keep the Will to hold it off. He needed to go, no matter what. He had to get away from it. He knew it too well. Though no one that knew him would think so," The Priest remarked.

"If the road leads to nothing... If what you have no one can take... If you are already where you need to be... If you know the soul is complete, then Freedom awaits. You are the image of no image. You are what does not need to be pushed. Seek the stillness of a Mountain Lake."
His reasons for no one but himself. Unanswering to your calls.

"An Actor goes part mad because they can come to feel views that aren't true. Like, an Actor can resent themselves because they are playing better people than they are. But that's just a presentation, a performance of effort. A mood. A feeling to be Entertained specifically...He told me that. He saved my life by saving my perception," an Actor spoke about a man un-seperated from him, but uninvolved, but life-changing.

"He'd make you look directly into your Humanity. He'd reach inside you, through your doubts and beyond your soul and pull something out of you and as you looked at it you felt your mind shift and felt strength and pull, and just as I was becoming afraid he told me I was already there, and the pull toward The Edge subsided. And I felt calm, as everything I worried about I was no longer afraid of."
The Echoes of Epic Parrots that Begin to Remember the Same Things

"He was the first man to convince another man to pick up a shovel and the first man to convince the last man to set the shovel down." A Farmer/A Sodomite/A Lawyer/A good sensation without a name.

The Father's body sank into the depths.

A plaque was manifested beside the sea that read:

IN THIS OCEAN:

THE FATHER

AN AMERICAN
LIVING AS HE DREAMED.
THE STORY CAME AFTER.

There is a great war about to come from nowhere, and it will seem that there will appear to be many sides. But there are only two. Neither good, nor evil, just opposing. Naturally designed to eventually clash their own clearly designed construction. On one side there is a group that feels pride. Great pride. Those that believe in Heaven and Hell, believing in their own moral superiority. The Darkness. Most of the sides will belong to this category. Those that fear having no power. ... ...

The second side is made up of the <u>holy</u>. Those that know there is no Heaven and no Hell to fight and crusade for. There is Love. There is stillness. There is death. The Light. Unmoving, they work for its destruction. Listening to its impending cries. Knowing suffering waits and they will ease it when it comes. Be friends with these people. Deny all others until the time comes to care for these weak. The Light calms the heart of fury that draws us closer to obliteration.

Every choice, since the first choice, has been leading to these precious moments to come. Don't you see??? It is not the Great War that is coming. This war is happening. Now. How are you choosing? Can you stop yourself from leading to war, again and again? Can you pull yourself away from destruction? Can our spiritual Technology save you from the failure of your life? From the choosing of Pride. Can you win the war within yourself that leads to war, and meaninglessness without meaning? Can you allow yourself to be unimportant? Are you willing to let your programmed identity die, so that it will slightly loosen its grip on you so that you can control it?

Page Lost

Page Lost

My brothers and my sisters do you not see? Life is hard. Journeys are sad.
Have mercy on each other!

Our duty is to serve It, in Life. For the course of all Existence. Serve well in it. Serve softly in it. So that you might let go of it. And return to a higher place you've been trying to find all this time.

Your rapture is now, though requiems are happening. Can you ask for forgiveness with no selfishness in your heart?
Can you break free?

In the state of Rapture my mind feels cool. Cold even. It is very emotional. I burst out crying so often when I hear the voice of truth in such a way that I am struck dumb and all knowing, trembling in my becoming. My sinuses are wide open and the air is crisp and chills my upper lip. This is as I have recognized the path. Do not turn from it once you've felt it, or you will have to find it again. But don't worry, it will be okay. :)

<u>PROLOGUE AT END OF THE EPIC II</u>

And after so many pages...Am I at peace? Have I said what I needed to? Did I tell as many people as would listen? Was I able to rest? Yes.

And I found that the results that I have found battling against my own Reasons is a noble path that can dismantle Pride and it leads to Freedom. So long as I have just a little more money than I need to survive, maybe a few months ahead, then I am fine. The war remains peaceful, unless circumstance and slavery force me to survive, and gain the stigma of crime. Crime would stop if there wasn't a group of people trying to keep a slave class in this country. The military must be converted, gradually, into a force of HealthCare workers and professional, non-moralistic Mediators void of the vengeance that damns. HealthCare is the path out of a war-ridden, starved world. If it is not so hard to survive, then the rebellious spirit is less likely to find something to rebel against.

<u>Before Birth</u>

I could be a snail. Happy to be slimy, slow, and protected by a conspicuous spinning spiral shell, not knowing that I am waiting for a man to throw me under a shed to be left still and alone. I can find peace in anything. Enjoying its limitations and advantages on my environment. To be what I am and not be tortured by it, to not let it torture those I love, to not hate what I am...anything...To direct my mind with its natural forces. Do I want to be Free? Want it. You will want anyway. Direct your want. Use your reflexes to be what we all want to be. Free. Zen. Existing. Our Masters find the way to be at peace as anyone because they faced the loss of everything in many states and many forms.

Already, his caring, and his free imagination is pulling him back to physical form.

<u>What of the Dark Society?</u>

The Dark Society fell like any society. The military rises, revolts from terrorists with ignored grievances occur, the interior society not having any individual survival skills thanks to specialization witnesses starvation in peril, small genocides followed from shooters, mass murderers, and serial killers blindly trying to prove nothing is real and death is present, while trying to convince their made-up enemy that they are exactly like them, while never becoming what they wanted others to be. Prisons seemed to stay intact somehow...

Yet, generation followed generation and each new and evolving group of youths came closer, to waking up from the prides and prejudices of history, and bore witness to their growing Choice. Mysticism and damnation falling away while we took our awakened consciousness forward, finding a familiarity in all living things, far beyond Earth and the old beliefs of irrelevant religions, and We stayed blessed steadily with the renewing electrical light of Science as we learned to make the world where we found ourselves Existing.

On the Third Day following The Father's death, Zarat's letter arrived.

Knowing that Zarat was unaware that the Father had died, the Priest took the knowledge and The Father's influence that was still held over his Being from of his fallen Friend and replied to the middle-aged Zarat:

Great Zarat,

Rise up unburdened by the life passed. Take these works enclosed and give them to this Land. Give them the thoughts of the Free. We are unashamed of our flowing Humanity. We see ourselves in all that exists.

Whatever events built in you that brought you to your oblivion beside the Lake, whatever her inertia made you choose, you are one whom must remain Free. Your calmness your reward as the wars of common humans mean nothing of your battles in life and death.

Cordially,
Father

PS: She came.

To Escape the Large Mind
Fame isn't Real

Stand Still.

Fame is not natural humanness, but it exists in nature. Fame is unnatural because a person will not stare at another person for hours, even looking into their eyes, while thinking anything that cannot be met with retaliation or the want to be liked. The Famous, face pure judgement without fear, from an audience that damns at an instant. Stepping into Fame is best done when the pursuer has disposed of all image in their psyche by implementing Calmness. Only the brave, the definers, will seek to be singled out.

When you go forth and stand in front of people, and you choose public Fame. It takes an exposed heart to do it, but when everyone is looking, and you feel the many unseen eyes of conflicting friends, relatives, and strangers, and you even look at your own feigned confidence and realize what it does, and what it holds for those that don't think only on their own, that need to hear to know, it can make your Ego a resounding beast in defense against feelings when the body is safe and should be naturally calm.

Once The Famed amaze you, you have lost your ability to become them, this image of a human in that situation. Embrace equality, and the goal, and enter directly with handshakes to make millions of people happy, deeper, and closer to calmness and inspiration.

When some people talk to you, does it bother you that they demand a positive sensation back in the expectation of their smiles? They seek to ease the loneliness of the doubt that leaves them knowing that they fell short of the answer, and so they must Exist, and in the hope they beg from you to match the energy they want with a bright story...give to them some compassion, but make real the tale, because they want to know that they have not lost reality, that it was alright that they were all the feelings they are now asking you to shine on them. Give them the truth, in a beautiful form, and this will soothe them most. Be Genuine to all who seek pleasure from you.

Do you believe this tree sways? Only to the wind.
No voice sways me, but I hear them.

The trap of the Big Mind, the Fame Mind...other people thinking things about what you're doing, and your job depends on what they think...It can pull you away from yourself...IF you believe Fame is something great that you are.. When it isn't. We are not our Fame. It is something great that, and anyone, can do, if they have confidence in it, which gains the huge and rare advantage of being able to talk in front of an audience of people. Believe other people can do it, and avoid arrogance, assholed-ness degrading, bitchness vying for fictional place, and whatever someone else detachedly comments about, because they too are in the Big Mind, their Societal Mind when they see you, the Famed. Compassion for their mind and their suffering can remind you how you'd see yourself through a detached screen. They are only saying what they think about society, and not what they think about a person; what they say in front of the painting they'd never say personally to the painter, but it helps them define themselves. Let it be OK. Be Present. We are not the Big Mind. Each person is only like a single thought in it, and this thought is not unique. It is available to Feel and Experience for ANYTHING with a Spirit. All things have something. An Essence. A sensation that we can perceive through the Majesty of our Big Mind. Our Public Mind is the Mind we must now balance. Our Bigger Mind. We seek peace inside and out amongst the minds we should collaborate with.

Everyone knows the one whom stands up and speaks. A "good" human does not sit down and let "bad" things happen.

<u>Know Your Author</u>

The Author, Stephan Pacheco, possesses more than 50 credits as an Actor, Writer, Director, and Producer of Film, Television, Stage, and Literature. He began acting at age 11, and began to develop significant works in the Humanities at age 14 with contributions to poetics and sociology, with an overall theme that continually addresses the insecurity that is the fear of death, while still entertaining his reading and listening guests toward an equalized Freedom.

Mr. Pacheco maintains that the 3 books of the <u>Manifest Utopia</u> series are a vast metaphor for his youth which signifies the struggle, suffering, and emotional options and revelations for the randomly impoverished and vulnerable in a nation and State that is still dependent on the reoccurring enslavement of its unfortunate children, while security yields a false sense of detached supremacy.

The Author wrote these books for the reoccurring youth audience, and especially for the balancing rebel ones, and during the age at which the young characters lived, as a means to present Friendship to his reader and a motivation to rise out of exactly what the Author was experiencing at the time, instead of hypocritically parenting to an unequal situation, that he would be detached from.

His current literary projects include film and television developments, and a "secret" 4th book in the <u>Manifest Utopia</u> series where Zarat faces his middle-aged years, his angst, and an intriguing encounter with a new and enlightened character, The Benevolent Officer.

Liberty Core